A CLEVERLY (UN)CONTRIVED COMPROMISE

A PRIDE & PREJUDICE VARIATION

JENNIFER JOY

A Cleverly (Un)contrived Compromise: A Pride & Prejudice
Variation
Love's Little Helpers, Book 3

This is a work of fiction. The characters, locations, and events
portrayed in this book are fictitious or are used fictitiously. Any
similarity to real persons, living or dead, is purely coincidental and
not intended by the author.

Published by Jennifer Joy

Edited by Debbie Brown

CONTENTS

FREE BOOK

Want a free novelette?
Join Jennifer Joy's Newsletter!

CHAPTER 1

SEPTEMBER 1811, PEMBERLEY

Fitzwilliam Darcy leaned against the limestone column in his mother's rose garden and breathed deeper than he had in the last three months.

His little sister was safe. Only months ago, Georgiana had sworn her heart was forever broken, but now she was tilting her chin and smiling. She looked so much like their mother, it made Darcy's chest ache. She was a young lady now. When had that happened?

He crossed his arms and pressed his lips together. He knew how to keep a boy occupied and out of mischief, but a girl…even worse, an heiress on the edge of adulthood with a considerable fortune and a disposition to please?

After five years without their father's protection,

Darcy had perfected his skills of intimidation. One look—posture rigid, marked scowl, arms tight over his chest, eyes conveying anything from boredom to disdain—effectively discouraged scheming men from preying upon his fifteen-year-old sister. Unfortunately, the young man to whom Georgiana now directed her smile was too well-acquainted with Darcy to take his threatening looks seriously.

"Darcy, must you stand over us like an angry sentinel? Your glower is wasted on me." Charles Bingley moved over to make room on the bench he shared with Georgiana.

She looked up from her sketchpad, her charcoal poised over the page, to regard Bingley with a tenderness that had stolen nights of Darcy's sleep lately.

Bingley waved Darcy over, apparently impervious to her fluttering eyelashes and blushing cheeks. "Thrill your palate with these delicious strawberries before Louisa eats all of them." He cast a pointed look towards his eldest sister, who ignored him as she dipped a piece of fruit deeply into a bowl of clotted cream and popped it into her mouth. Her husband napped on the blanket beside her, which explained why the supply of strawberries had not been exhausted; Mr. Hurst had an appetite worthy of his girth.

Darcy might believe Georgiana's heart to be safe with Bingley, but he would not encourage her daydreams of love and marriage until she reached a more appropriate age.

Like thirty.

He flipped up his coattails and sat between Bingley and Georgiana. His sister was too shy to protest or even hint at her displeasure, unlike the object of her portrait, who sat across from her on a blanket before a colorful rose bush.

"A bee! Squish it!" Miss Caroline Bingley interrupted her preens and poses to flail her arms. She was surrounded by the last of summer's second flush of roses, the full blooms hovering over her hair like a prickly halo.

"Take care of the thorns," Darcy said for at least the third time.

Miss Bingley inclined her head, ignoring sense in favor of affectation. Did she think she conjured images of Aphrodite growing roses from her tears? One false move would soon dispel Miss Bingley of that sentiment. "I am perfectly aware of where I am, Mr. Darcy, but I thank you for your concern."

Darcy clenched his jaw and held his tongue. His concern was for the flowers.

Miss Bingley heedlessly arched her back and then lifted her arm over her head, making a show of elongating her neck as she shifted a curl to drape over her shoulder. "It is so very warm," she purred, directing her avaricious eyes towards Darcy.

"Gracious, Caro, are you quite well? You appear to be suffering from a spasm." Bingley's concern received only a glare from his younger sister in response.

Darcy feigned a cough and looked away. *Good boy,*

Bingley. Unlike his sisters, he held no ambitions of grandeur. A point in his favor.

Mrs. Hurst commented on cue, "Where is your parasol, dear? I would hate for you to ruin your lovely alabaster skin. Do you not agree, Mr. Darcy?"

He did not agree. Pale complexions looked sickly and bespoke an unseemly disregard for nature, but this he could not say. "Perhaps Miss Bingley would be more comfortable indoors."

She fluttered her hand over her throat. "I would not dream of altering everyone's plans." Again she raised her arm over her head, leaning perilously close to the bush. Darcy rather wished she would return indoors. Between the thorns and the bees feeding off the blooms, there was very little chance of Miss Bingley remaining unscathed. While the lady deserved such a lesson, Darcy had tired of her complaints.

"Halloo!" shouted a deep voice.

Darcy's heart jumped into his throat in the split second before his brain registered the source of the startling call. Georgiana squealed and leaped to her feet, dropping her portfolio on the bench and jumping into her cousin's open arms. "Richard! This is a lovely surprise! William did not say you were coming!"

"I knew nothing of it." Usually Richard's calls were a source of great pleasure, but his sudden appearance after months of duty worried Darcy. Had something happened?

Richard's gaze met Darcy's over Georgiana's head, conveying curiosity and wonder...but mostly relief.

Darcy relaxed a bit. Explanations would come later. Georgiana was happy again, and that was all that mattered. Richard spun her in a celebratory circle and gently set her down. As he looked up, his eyes widened and the corner of his lips twitched.

Darcy heard the shriek before he looked over his shoulder. He had completely forgotten about Miss Bingley. She was stuck, the bush's thorns snagging and pulling at her gown with her hair frizzed in the shrubbery.

Definitely not Aphrodite.

"Calm yourself, Caro. You are making it worse—Ouch!" Mrs. Hurst sucked on an injured finger.

Several servants came running to assist, having heard Richard's boisterous entry, Miss Bingley's increasingly loud protests, and their party's noisy pleas for her to calm herself.

Nodding at the gardener, who stood nearby with a pair of shears and a woeful expression at the sight of his abused bushes, Darcy motioned for the man to cut the offending blooms. Five snips later, Miss Bingley rose to her feet and staggered forward, thorny stems poking out at odd angles around her wild coiffure.

As the servants scurried away, Darcy noted hands covering mouths and eyes brimming with amusement.

Mrs. Hurst attempted to free a dangling bloom, but Miss Bingley's withering scowl made the lady recoil.

Richard was the first to recover. Mischief in his eye, he swooped an elegant bow. "Miss Bingley! The epitome of fashion, as always. You will soon have the ladies of the *ton* wearing rose clippings in their hair."

Miss Bingley lifted her chin, but she was too aware of social standing to glare at the son of an earl, even if he was only the second son.

Richard's smile widened.

Darcy called to the nearest footman. "Please ask Mrs. Reynolds to send some of her ointment from the distillery to Miss Bingley's room."

The corners of her lips turned upward, but Miss Bingley's expression was too pinched to deem it a smile. "Thank you, Mr. Darcy. Shall I join you in the music room once my maid sees to my hair?" Clearly, she had had enough of nature.

"And waste this glorious day indoors?" Bingley replied. "I had hoped to ask Miss Darcy if she might sketch my likeness." He propped his foot on the bench and looked off into the distance. "Is this dignified enough?"

Georgiana giggled. "Very dignified."

"You will have to stand still, Charles," Mrs. Hurst chided as she settled onto her blanket. Her husband, whose sleep had been disturbed by the recent excitement, looked about him as though he had quite forgotten where he was and with whom.

As Miss Bingley walked stiffly toward the house, she glanced over her shoulder to hiss at her sister, who was too distracted with fruit tarts and cream now to pay her any heed.

Richard elbowed Darcy. Nodding toward Georgiana and speaking as low as he was capable of doing, he asked, "What is this?"

"Nothing I shall speak of here."

"It is just as well. My visit is not without a purpose. A word in your study? And perhaps a glass of your smuggled brandy? I am parched."

They made their way to Darcy's inner sanctum. It overlooked the rose garden, and Georgiana's laughter could be heard through the open window.

Richard helped himself to the contents of the sideboard and settled into a chair with a view of the garden. "I had expected to see Georgie still in the doldrums. Am I to understand that we have Bingley to thank for this welcome change?"

Darcy raised his glass and took a sip.

"What do you plan to do about it?"

For too many nights, Darcy had tossed and turned pondering this very question. "I had thought I might encourage Bingley to let an estate of his own."

Richard raised his eyebrows. "You take a keen interest in his life."

"He is a trustworthy young man with a fortune of his own."

"Meaning?"

"He is not after Georgiana's dowry."

"I doubt Bingley is after Georgiana at all! He is as agreeable to a countess as he is to a scullery maid."

"Precisely. It makes him a safe choice."

Richard swirled the amber liquor in his glass. "Are you certain she is in love, and so soon after Wickham?

Could she not merely be acting as most fifteen-year-old females her age do?"

Darcy scoffed. "Georgiana is a Darcy through and through. She feels deeply, sincerely."

"Just because Bingley is a saint in comparison to Wickham does not make him a suitable match for Georgiana. You cannot be serious, Darcy. Bingley falls in and out of love quicker than I change my waistcoat. He has been wanting to purchase an estate since his father's death, but he is too fickle to settle on any one place. He is capricious, wholly manipulated by his pernicious sisters, and too reliant on others' guidance." Richard's tone was grave.

All traits Darcy had considered.

"He is young, but what better experience than estate managing to help him gain the resolve he lacks? You must own that he displays an admirable strength of character to be so unaffected by his critical, grasping sisters."

Richard continued swirling his drink, clearly unconvinced.

"As for guidance, he only requires good direction until he is able to make his own choices."

"And you are the best one to give such direction? As if you do not already have enough to manage, you must take on Bingley and his entire household? He is a man, for goodness' sake, not a property!"

Reasonable arguments, but they were all nullified with one, simple, undeniable fact. "He makes Georgiana happy."

"And what Georgiana wants, she gets? You are coddling her, Darcy."

Darcy felt the accusation like an undeserved slap in the face. What did Richard know of the past four months? His cousin lived his life by the orders of others—be it his commanding officer or his mother. He had not been in Ramsgate. He had not dealt with Wickham or seen Georgiana's heart break before his very eyes. He had not been forced to conceal what, if discovered, would ruin her prospects. Clasping his trembling hands together, Darcy commanded his voice to steady. "She wept for weeks, refusing to eat, and keeping to her rooms. I tempted her with instruments, music, paints, books… all her favorite things, but the only creature she allowed to console her was Serafina."

"Why, then, do you not give her another cat instead of Bingley? Georgiana might only like him because she senses your approval. You do not need a new project; you need a wife! You are soon to be twenty-eight."

"Is that your purpose in coming here, Rich? You might have spared yourself the journey and saved your breath, for I cannot rightfully see to my own happiness until I am convinced that Georgiana is safe and content."

"And you think Bingley is the answer? You do not know how to help Georgie any more than I do. She needs a sister. You need a wife!"

"How could I neglect her for another woman just when she is recovering from her heartsickness? You cannot expect me to be so cruel."

"She seemed to be perfectly fine to me minutes ago."

Darcy gestured wildly. "Thanks to Bingley." Clasping his hands again, Darcy calmed his breath. "I am well aware that he is full young, but so were we once."

"Can you remember that far back?"

Darcy ignored the comment. An eternity had passed since he had been able to live with only his own future in mind. But his experience had taught him that a great deal could be learned in a short period of time, and this gave him hope for Bingley. "A few years managing his own affairs, having others dependent on his care, will grant him the maturity and steadiness he lacks."

Richard looked at him askance. "He is a puppy! A lovable puppy, but time consuming and far too amiable for his own good."

"I shall not actively encourage the match. In fact, my aim is to encourage Bingley to let an estate some distance from Pemberley. There is a serviceable property in Hertfordshire, only half a day's ride from London. It has been empty for several years and will need more of Bingley's attention than the other options my secretary found."

"Keep *you* occupied, you mean. What if Bingley falls in love with some country squire's daughter? What will you tell Georgiana then?"

"He will be too busy for flirtations."

Richard barked a laugh. "Bingley? Too busy for a pretty face? This is high-handed, even for you!"

A floorboard creaked outside the door, putting a quick end to their conversation. Georgiana's beloved pet wandered inside, pushing the door wider as she passed, the bell around her neck jingling with every step.

Richard leaned down to pet her. "Was that you that made the floor squeak? You should tell Cook not to feed her extra scraps. Or is this the doing of the mouser in the kitchen?"

Serafina left Richard to hop onto Darcy's lap, displaying her superior taste. "She is too grand a lady to pay the tomcat any mind." He rubbed under her chin. "Besides, with the servants trained to listen for her bell and Georgiana's constant doting, such an unseemly union is unlikely." She leaned against his chest, rubbing her head against his jaw and purring loudly.

"Cats are not as fastidious as you are. Come, Darce, I have had to delay romance until I could afford to wed without being mercenary in my selection, but you—"

Darcy did not care for the direction of this conversation. "How are your investments performing?"

Richard frowned, but he allowed for the shift in topic. "Thanks to my early investments in the colonies, I have had sufficient capital to invest in other industries. Had you not advised me against Trevithick's steam locomotive, I would be even better positioned."

"His ideas are sound, but his engine is too heavy. In my opinion, Matthew Murray and George Stephenson will do more to advance the locomotive."

Richard grinned. "While you and the gentlemen in your clubs argue over who to back, I shall continue to invest in the steel used to make the iron behemoths."

Darcy was glad Richard had used his strategic mind to benefit himself outside his military profession. He could not remain in the army forever, nor was he the kind of gentleman to be content living off the charity of others.

"That was a nice aside, Darcy, but I shall carry out my mission. Every year you delay marriage gives Aunt Catherine more reason to believe you intend to marry Anne."

"Aunt Catherine is delusional," Darcy grumbled. He would rather talk about trains.

"Yes, and also vociferous and insistent. Seriously, Darce, Mother wants me to have a word with you... as if I or anyone else can convince you to do anything you have not already resolved to do. God help the woman you decide to marry. She will have no choice at all in the matter."

Darcy felt his color rise, heard his pulse thrum in his ears. "Aunt Helen expects me to take her counsel when she was the one who insisted I allow Georgiana more freedom? That I set up her own residence in Ramsgate? Need I remind you how Mrs. Younge came to be in my employ?" Serafina hopped down from his lap and left the room. Darcy wished he could follow her and leave Richard to his mother's interfering orders.

"Mother regrets Mrs. Younge, but she came so

highly recommended by her friends, really, you cannot blame her."

Darcy could, and he did, and he resented Richard for suggesting otherwise. Nobody else took Georgiana's protection as seriously as Darcy did.

Richard sighed. "I see you are determined. But, Darcy, love blooms where it will, and it will thumb its nose at you for interfering where you are not wanted."

He was one to talk. "I assure you, I only have Georgiana's best interests in mind. And Bingley's."

Richard filled his glass. "Let us pray the young ladies in Hertfordshire are not so handsome, plentiful, or charming as Bingley finds the young ladies to be in London."

Darcy was not ignorant of the challenges before him, but he knew estate management and young men like Bingley much better than he did the confounding mind and tumultuous emotions of his own sister. He raised his glass and drank deeply.

CHAPTER 2

*E*lizabeth Bennet scraped her boots, untied her bonnet, and shook out her damp skirts. Checking her reflection in the mirror placed in Longbourn's entrance hall, she smoothed her fingers over her untamable hair and prayed that the high color in her cheeks was due to exercise and not too much exposure to the sun. Not that Elizabeth minded. A sunkissed complexion was the mark of a hale constitution and a healthy regard for nature, but her mother would not be convinced of its merits.

Outside the walls of her childhood home, over the sprawling fields, Elizabeth was at liberty to roam and dream. It was her only time alone, free from the constant reminders of everything she was powerless to change about Longbourn and its residents. Today must be perfect, and Elizabeth had devised a plan.

First, she found Jane, the eldest of the five Bennet sisters and Elizabeth's dearest friend. Jane was often praised for her beauty, but Elizabeth found her graceful character, sweet nature, and calm strength far more admirable. Her sister sat by the window in the drawing room with a basketful of lace, ribbon, and trimmings on one side and a pile of muslin gowns on the other.

At the other end of the room, Mary, the third eldest of the Bennet sisters, was playing a grim tune. Poor Mary. If only Papa would allow her to study with a master. But unless a miracle moved their father to do something to improve his daughters' unfavorable prospects, Elizabeth's subtle hints would have to suffice. "Mary, dear, perhaps a livelier song would suit the occasion best."

"But I only know the one, and it has no singing to accompany the melody."

Perfect. "Why draw attention away from your technique with song?" Elizabeth turned to Jane before Mary replied, hoping the seed she had planted would take root and lead to a more agreeable performance at the ball that evening.

Mary began a piece over which she had labored and now played to perfection: Bach's Minuet in G Major. An uncomplicated air. No lyrics and therefore no moral message or notes beyond the comfortable reach of Mary's limited vocal range.

Plucking a wad of knotted ribbons from the basket, Elizabeth sat in the chair opposite Jane and began untangling. "Are Kitty and Lydia still asleep?" If the two youngest sisters begged Jane to alter their gowns, they should be helping. More likely, they were lingering in their bedchambers to avoid Mr. Collins. As Papa's heir apparent, he would inherit Longbourn, and he had already threatened that he intended to marry one of them.

"They have departed for Meryton," Jane replied.

Of all the ungrateful, selfish... Elizabeth pinched her lips together. Saying her thoughts aloud would only upset Jane, but if those two did anything foolish to spoil Jane's night, Elizabeth was tempted to lock them in their rooms and bury the key or lace their afternoon tea with some of Mama's sleeping tonic. There was only one reason Kitty and Lydia would venture into Meryton so early in the day. It wore a red coat and shiny, black boots.

Mary stopped playing. "They told Mama they would purchase shoe roses for our gowns, but they shall waste their money on sweetmeats and flirt shamelessly with the officers."

"Who accompanied them?" Surely not Mr. Collins. Elizabeth cast a wary glance about. Where was he? She would give him no opportunity to importune her with an unwanted offer of marriage.

"Sarah."

Elizabeth sighed. The first thing Kitty and Lydia would have done is ditch the maid.

Mary added, "Mama sent her to the apothecary to fetch more nerve tonic."

Good. At least there would be a sufficient supply if it came to that. "How long ago did they leave?"

"Not a quarter of an hour ago." Mary turned to the instrument and resumed practicing. She might not mind receiving Mr. Collins' attentions, but Elizabeth could not wish such a match for any of her sisters.

She would concern herself with the annoying man later. Right now, she needed to prevent her family from ruining Jane's chances again. She stopped chewing on her lip. "We shall not overtake them, but we can ensure they do not get into too much mischief before we arrive."

Jane pinned the needle into the bodice of the gown on which she worked. "I do not know how I shall finish these gowns in time without a walk into Meryton, much less with one."

"They can do without new lace," Mary called over her shoulder without losing her rhythm.

Elizabeth felt little sympathy for her youngest sisters. "I saw to mine days ago. Besides, more hands make for light work. They should help stitch their own gowns."

Mama's voice drifted into the room before she rounded the corner. "Has Lizzy returned yet? So much to be done and the ungrateful child dashes off to Lord-knows-where! She has no respect for my nerves. Just like her father." Her caps fluttered around her face. "Oh, there you are. Just in time to help Jane. My girls must look their best for Mr. Bingley's ball. I am convinced he will announce your engagement tonight, Jane."

"Mama, he—" Jane tried, but their mother was like

17

those heavy steam engines Elizabeth had read about: impossible to stop once she got going on her favorite topic.

"A ball to celebrate my Jane's recovery!" Mama clapped her hands under her chin and swayed. "I knew you could not be so beautiful for nothing."

As though Jane's chief accomplishment was no more than the pleasing features with which she had been born—features which their mother was quick to point out were similar to her own in her youth. Next, Mama would lament their precarious position without a male son to inherit Longbourn, and then she would bemoan Mr. Bennet's imminent death, proclaiming they would all be cast into the hedgerows when Mr. Collins took possession of their home. She would not-so-subtly imply that it was Elizabeth's duty to marry that oaf, and then she would repeat the one thing that never failed to make Jane cry herself to sleep at night: "If only my beautiful Jane was married already."

Elizabeth grabbed Jane's hand and tugged her toward the door. "It is for that reason we shall see that Kitty and Lydia return with our shoe roses. Jane cannot manage alone, and if we all help, she will have sufficient time to rest before the ball." And now the clincher. "You do wish for Jane to look her best tonight, do you not, Mama?"

"Oh, I had not considered that, but of course she ought to look her best if Mr. Bingley is to propose. How clever you are, Lizzy! Let me ask Mr. Collins to accompany you and you may be on your way."

After several frustrating lost minutes, during which Mr. Collins kept them waiting in the hall, Mr. Hill finally approached, hands clasped in front of him, face downcast. "I regret to inform you that Mr. Collins' boots are nowhere to be found."

"Nowhere to be found? How can that be?" Mama fanned her face, a sure sign of her increasing agitation.

Elizabeth reached for her coat. "'Tis no matter. We shall not be long."

Mrs. Hill helped her and Jane into their warm clothing, and Elizabeth saw Mr. Hill share a look with his wife as he crossed the hall to open the door. What was the pair up to? A subtle wink from the faithful manservant confirmed that he knew more about the disappearance of Mr. Collins' boots than he let on. Elizabeth would have kissed him on the cheek, but her mother was watching.

Neither the chill in the air nor the mud squishing under the soles of her half-boots dimmed Elizabeth's resplendent humor. Thanks to the efforts of the Hills, she had successfully evaded Mr. Collins, Mary was practicing a pleasant tune she would perform to advantage, and they would snatch Kitty and Lydia away from Meryton before any harm could be done. It was a beautiful, perfect day. "I think I shall buy the Hills a sugar plum before we return," she told Jane.

"That is thoughtful of you, Lizzy. They shall enjoy a well-deserved free evening, though I daresay they will have Sarah stay up to receive us."

Elizabeth looped her arm around Jane's. "What of

you, dearest? To have Mr. Bingley host a ball in your honor...?"

Jane blushed. "You would have me believe he arranged it for me when it is no such thing."

"Is it not?" Elizabeth peeked at her askance.

"I dare not flatter myself so much."

"But do you not wish for such a marked display of his favor?"

Jane collected her thoughts, then replied slowly, deliberately. "Of course, I do. Mr. Bingley is a kind gentleman and an attentive host."

"Then what is the problem?"

"It is so painful to have one's expectations dashed. I would rather not have any. You heard him say that he is just as happy here as he would be anywhere else, and his sisters are accomplished in ways I shall never be—"

Elizabeth hugged her arm tighter. "And their money comes from trade! Do not convince yourself that you are undeserving of his attention, Jane. By birth, you are his superior; in temperament, his equal; in the heart, his perfect match. You must believe me. You are worth a hundred Miss Bingleys."

Jane looked down. She was too modest to admit what Elizabeth knew in her bones to be true, and it made her angry that anyone should make Jane doubt her worth. Had she not suffered enough superior airs during their week-long stay at Netherfield Park to last a lifetime? From that, Mr. Bingley must, of course, be excused. He was the perfect gentleman and an exceptional host. But his sisters' airs and condescension offended all convention.

And then there was Mr. Darcy. That such intelligence should be granted to such a proud, disagreeable man was a grave infraction of justice. Every opinion Elizabeth gave, he challenged. Every conversation, he turned into a debate. Every time their eyes met, he frowned and crossed his arms. The pompous, insufferable...

"Ouch, Lizzy, you are pinching me." Jane tugged her arm.

Elizabeth loosened her hold. "Sorry, dearest. My thoughts took a sour turn." She would not waste another moment on Mr. Darcy. He was not Mr. Bingley's guardian for his opinion to be of any consequence. Smiling at Jane, she shared one of the conclusions she had pondered during her morning ramble. "In truth, love is a great equalizer. It cares not for station, fortune, or connections. Its only requirement to thrive is to be returned in equal measure. Mr. Bingley loves you, Jane. Of that, I am certain."

The uncertainty in Jane's eyes made Elizabeth more determined to prove her point.

Unfortunately, that was the same moment the confectionery came into view, and who should be blocking passage into the shop but Lydia? And that was not the worst of it. Not by the least. Mr. Wickham held something out of her reach, and Lydia shamelessly leaned over him, hopping, squealing, and draping herself all over him to fetch whatever the source of her desire was.

He, at least, attempted to pull her off, though Elizabeth feared that his forbearing smile only encouraged Lydia rather than conveying embarrassment.

Kitty was too busy batting her eyelashes at Mr. Denny to be of any assistance.

Glancing about to see who of their neighbors witnessed the mannerless display, Elizabeth's lungs seized when she saw Mrs. Hurst and Miss Bingley riding through Meryton atop their fine mounts, sporting their fashionable riding habits, and looking down their noses at Elizabeth's sisters.

Drat!

Before Jane's dreams burst into flames, leaving nothing but charred hopes and despairing ashes, Elizabeth crossed the street to pry her shameless sister off the poor man. "Quick, Lydia, you are expected at Longbourn."

"Not until he gives me my sweetmeat! It is mine!" Lydia lunged for the treat.

Elizabeth clenched her jaw. All this trouble over a sweet?

"You said you did not want it," Mr. Wickham replied, graciously handing the wrapped treat to her petulant sister.

Giggling, Lydia allowed Elizabeth to lead her away, calling over her shoulder and waving wildly. "I shall save my first set for you at the ball, Wickie!"

Wickie? As though throwing herself at the

gentleman were not enough, Lydia called him by a pet name on the high street? With Mr. Bingley's sisters watching? Oh, the shame!

Elizabeth tugged her forward, keeping her eyes level and her chin up as they passed the impatient horses and their gloating riders. She could practically feel the ladies' sneers, and Elizabeth hated how her face burned despite her best effort to keep a placid expression.

"Lizzy, slow down! You walk too fast!" Lydia complained.

Only once they had reached the edge of the village and were out of earshot of the gossips did Elizabeth slow her pace. "Have you no sense? Did you not think that your blatant flirtations with the officers would be noticed by others?"

Lydia shrugged and pulled the brown paper off the sweetmeat. "Sugar plum." She twisted her face and stuck out her tongue before handing it to Elizabeth. "Here, have a sweetmeat. You are just jealous Mr. Wickham was flirting with me instead of you."

That it had not even occurred to Elizabeth to be jealous struck her. She had believed that she favored Mr. Wickham, but here was undeniable proof that she thought no more of him than the sugar plum Lydia was so eager to cast off.

The hoof-beats behind them grew louder. Elizabeth prayed that the pernicious pair would ride past them without so much as a by-your-leave, but the wind had shifted to the east, taking the last of Elizabeth's good fortune along with it.

Jane and Kitty curtsied.

Miss Bingley towered over them, the ostrich feathers in her hat billowing in the unfavorable wind. "A glorious day, is it not? So much to see."

Mrs. Hurst smirked beside her.

Elizabeth dropped a token curtsy. "Good day, ladies."

"Shall we see you at the ball?" Miss Bingley asked.

Lydia beamed. "We would not miss it for the world!"

Not if Elizabeth could help it. She watched the messengers of doom ride away, her forced smile pinching her cheeks, and she planned her checkmate. She must be persuasive if she was to convince Papa to forbid Lydia and Kitty from attending the Netherfield Ball.

CHAPTER 3

*W*riting letters usually came naturally to Darcy, but not this one. He suffered as much as Bingley, who sat at the other end of the table in the morning room attending to his correspondence with increased affliction if his frequent expostulations were a fair indicator.

Since settling Georgiana in Darcy House at Berkeley Square with her companion, Mrs. Annesley, Darcy had written to his sister every day. Richard was currently stationed with his battalion at Windsor, so if she needed either of her guardians, they were both within a convenient distance to attend to her.

Georgiana seemed content. Between her lessons in music, language, and art, her frequent trips to the bookshops, and Serafina's kittens (Richard had been right about the mouser in Pemberley's kitchens), she was advantageously occupied and entertained.

Darcy asked what she learned, whose artwork,

music, and literature she presently enjoyed, and inquired after the antics of the four kittens. Her letters were a joy to read. But when it came time for Darcy to relay some of his news to her, his pen ran dry, his mind as blank as the page in front of him.

What was he supposed to tell her? That Bingley had met "his angel" at the first assembly he had attended? That since their arrival six weeks before, Bingley had sought out every opportunity to be in Miss Bennet's company? That, busy as Darcy had kept Bingley with rides over the property, meetings with the bailiff, improvements to the house and property, and repairs to the tenants' cottages, he had underestimated his friend's desire to win his new neighbors' approval? Darcy was exhausted and in ill humor while Bingley had an endless supply of energy and charm.

Tonight, to further cement his favored standing in the community, Bingley had arranged for a ball—an extravagant affair with hired musicians, hothouse flowers, champagne, and food brought in crates from London. Of course, a great deal of foodstuffs were also to be procured locally. Bingley could not ride into Meryton without being hailed as if he were a hero by shopkeepers and landowners alike. Darcy dreaded the evening to come.

He folded his letter, intending to return to it once he was capable of writing a sentence without grumbling. He looked out the window, enjoying the pleasant quiet in the parlor while Bingley's sisters were away. The fallow fields looked softer here, spotted with beechwood groves running along springs. He half-expected to see Miss Elizabeth Bennet walking there, her bonnet in one hand and a handful of herbs and wildflowers in the other.

Leaning back in his chair, Darcy chastised himself for allowing the vivacious imp to cross his mind. He had never met a more confounding lady. She was clever, confident, and impertinent.

While Darcy admired her pluck every time he witnessed Miss Bingley's inability to provoke or humiliate her, Miss Elizabeth was the chief source of his woes. She had her eye on Bingley for her eldest sister. She was his rival, an obstacle to his own sister's happiness.

Unfolding his letter, he took a deep breath and refocused his attention, determined to finish it, but he was prevented from writing another word by the return of Bingley's sisters.

Miss Bingley strode across the parquet floor with affected dignity. She settled into the chair nearest Darcy, angling her chin just so, smoothing her skirts and preening like a puffed-up bird.

He could not rise from his chair now without being abominably rude. Tempting...

She tapped his arm as though they were the most intimate of friends. He pulled away, but if she noticed, she hid it well. Her entire demeanor bubbled forth with delighted mirth. Darcy wondered at whose expense Miss Bingley had found so much pleasure.

"You will never guess whom we saw creating a

scene in Meryton." She tittered under her hand. Her self-importance fed itself off the shortcomings of others; Darcy took no pleasure in it.

Misunderstanding his stony silence as an inducement to continue, Miss Bingley lifted her chin higher as she spoke through a widening grin. "Miss Lydia Bennet was shamelessly flirting with Mr. Wickham on the high street."

Darcy shivered. The mere mention of that profligate ne'er-do-well made his stomach churn. The libertine had won over finer ladies, including his own sister. Darcy could only imagine how easily an unrefined girl without restraint or sense like Miss Lydia would fall under Wickham's spell.

Miss Bingley cackled, her gaze probing his, looking confident of his approval as she leaned closer. "It took both of her sisters to pry her off of the poor man."

"I have never seen Miss Elizabeth's face so unbecomingly red!" Mrs. Hurst chirped.

Darcy's ears rang. He folded his letter once again and collected his writing implements into their case.

Bingley's countenance darkened. "How fortunate that Miss Lydia has sisters willing to protect her and neighbors willing to overlook her youthful exuberance."

Mrs. Hurst huffed. "She shall be a plague on the reputation of her family until they are rid of her."

"If they can convince anyone to take her!" Miss Bingley added with a haughty look at her brother,

"Anyone so unfortunate as to attach themselves to the Bennets will suffer from the connection."

Mrs. Hurst nodded. "It is a miracle she has not ruined them already! No gentleman of quality could consider marrying into that abominable family. The risk to his own name and position is too great."

While Darcy agreed with the Bingley sisters' views on the subject, he could not approve of the cruel manner in which they delivered their criticisms. To encourage them was wrong, but to defend the Bennets was unthinkable.

To his credit, Bingley did not back down from his sisters' attacks. His agitation was apparent in his furrowed brow and heightened complexion. "Perhaps an attachment to a family with higher standards of conduct is precisely what the Bennets require."

No! Darcy bit his tongue.

"And what fool would take on such a challenge?!"

Miss Bingley's forceful rebuttal received Mrs. Hurst's zealous support.

Bingley looked down, visibly defeated. That he had not defended his own actions or Miss Bennet's family more thoroughly added to Darcy's conviction that Bingley's affection for the lady did not surpass the superficial. A man in love would not bend at the first hint of trouble or allow anyone to challenge the depth of his devotion. Although this knowledge suited Darcy's purpose, he would have liked to see his friend stand up against his sisters and take charge of his own life… just not at the expense of Georgiana's tender heart.

Having finished chastising her brother, Miss Bingley turned again to Darcy. "Mr. Wickham would be a waste on Miss Lydia. I believe Miss Eliza would make a finer match for a penniless soldier. Do you not agree?"

Another shiver. Another twist in the gut. "No," he groaned, not fully realizing he had done so aloud until Miss Bingley gasped and tittered again.

"Are Miss Eliza's eyes too fine for the likes of a common soldier? Do you think she aspires for a loftier prize?" Miss Bingley batted her eyelashes. She must think herself clever for using Darcy's words against him, but he felt attacked.

He crossed his arms over his pounding chest and assumed his most indifferent expression. "I hardly know why you think I should have an opinion."

That was not a complete truth. He knew precisely why Miss Bingley would tease him about Miss Elizabeth's fine eyes. Irritated beyond the limit of his patience, he had once defended her, praising her intelligence and appearance with the sole aim of silencing Miss Bingley. Would that he had held his peace! She had tormented him about it ever since.

He looked again at his unfinished letter. Six weeks of torture and discomfort, and for what? Bingley was no surer of himself now than he was before he let Netherfield Park. This venture had been a disaster from the start.

As much as Darcy hated to admit it, Richard had been right. Darcy would do well to encourage Bingley to pack up his house and return to London directly. Bingley would forget Miss Bennet within a week. The Bennets seemed to be a resilient bunch. They would find another unmarried gentleman of fortune to sink their claws into. So long as Darcy had a say in the matter, he would not allow them to catch Bingley.

Now he just had to help Bingley make it through the night without doing anything he would regret.

CHAPTER 4

*C*harles Bingley wished he could be more like Darcy. To have his caliber of self-assurance. To meet Caroline's taunts with cool indifference. Maybe then she would respect him more.

She rose from her chair, pretending a casual air when everything about Caroline was calculated. "I should make certain the servants are managing my plans for the ball to the best effect. There is so much to be done, and all without the advantages of living in town." She accented her complaint with an arched brow at Bingley. As if he himself had not arranged for the music, the decorations, and some of the food to be brought from London! What else would she have him send for—the entire town?

"We shall not detain you then." Darcy said the perfect thing to encourage her to quit the room and promptly returned to a letter he had been composing. Darcy was always writing letters. Letters to Miss

Darcy, letters to Colonel Fitzwilliam, letters to his steward and housekeeper and secretary. So many letters. Bingley despised correspondence. His thoughts came too quickly and changed too frequently for his hand to pen them down.

He imagined that Jane Bennet had lovely handwriting. Everything Miss Bennet did was graceful and refined. She calmed everyone around her. Even Caroline and Louisa behaved nicer when she was near.

Bingley settled into his chair, content to contemplate Miss Bennet's fine qualities. She was beautiful—an angel with golden hair, porcelain complexion, and sapphire blue eyes. She was genuinely kind. Even when she had fallen ill at Netherfield, she had been the most delightful patient. Bingley had not heard one complaint cross her lips, though she must have been miserable. It had been a pleasure for him to see to her comfort—send for the apothecary, ensure the maids plumped her pillows several times a day, and consult his housekeeper and cook about remedies—anything to ensure Miss Bennet felt welcome and properly cared for.

Even in illness, she was steady and composed. Precisely what Bingley was not and wished he could be.

Being a romantic at heart, he had often imagined his ideal wife. Jane Bennet exceeded his every hope. It hardly seemed fair to offer for a lady who surpassed his best imaginings when he did not feel so certain about where he stood in her estimation. Was he the husband of her dreams? He would very much like to be, but as he was in everything, uncertainty plagued him.

With a sigh, he came out of his dreamlike cloud and turned to Darcy. His friend would know what to do. "Do you think Miss Bennet would accept me if I made her an offer?"

The tip of Darcy's quill broke, and he swore under his breath.

Bingley did not understand his friend's reaction, which distressed him as much as every other conflict did. He quickly changed the subject. "How is Miss Darcy?"

"Very well. She speaks of little more than Serafina and her kittens."

"I love kittens. And puppies. Baby animals in general. How old are they?"

"Nearly six weeks."

How could he forget? Miss Darcy had written to Darcy about their birth shortly after they had arrived at Netherfield Park. Truth be told, Bingley had forgotten all about them until now. "I always wanted to have a cat as a pet, but Caroline does not approve. She says that their hair ruins her gowns."

Darcy's brow furrowed. "You seem more suited to dogs."

Bingley supposed he was. He certainly had the temperament of a dog: friendly disposition, eager to please, enthusiastic to greet friends and meet new people. Not an unpleasant image, certainly, but not very flattering for a man. He would never think to compare Darcy to a dog.

No—Bingley knew he grinned, but he could not prevent it—Darcy's disposition was more comparable to that of a cat. He did not need or even desire the approval of others and only granted his notice to a select few. He sulked in corners at public assemblies and glared at anyone who dared approach him. Definitely a cat.

Darcy broke the silence, startling Bingley from his diverting musings. "Are you certain you wish to marry now?"

"I have a house, I am of age, and I would like the company. Why should I not marry now?"

Bingley did not know what was wrong with his reply for Darcy to inhale so deeply. He did that when his patience was being tried. "Speak plainly, Darcy. I cannot read your mind."

Another deep breath. "Are you confident that Miss Bennet's attachment is as strong as you claim yours to be?"

"Yes." Bingley's certainty wavered. "No." But that was not the answer he wanted at all. "Maybe? Oh, if only I knew, I would not have to ask you."

"Until you know your own mind, how can you know what qualities you most admire, what traits you seek in a lifelong companion?"

"I shall be whatever she wishes me to be."

"And you expect her to be as yielding as you? Who

would run your household? Who would make decisions?"

Bingley understood Darcy's point, but Miss Bennet was much stronger than his friend gave her credit for. "Miss Bennet is soft-spoken, but she knows her mind. Only, she is modest—"

"Or is she *indifferent?*" The way Darcy emphasized the vile word gave Bingley pause.

He sank back into his chair, feeling limp and numb. "I—I do not know. Is that what you believe?"

"You possess a trusting nature and see only the best in everyone. As a result, you are more easily swayed than you ought to be."

That was nothing new to Bingley. "So long as I surround myself with good friends who are smarter than me, then I hardly see the deficiency. I have learned a great deal in the past weeks—thanks to you."

"Estates can be bought and sold or let for a short period of time, but marriage is forever. As such, it is not something I should advise you on. It is *your* choice to make. *You* will be the one to live with the consequences, good or bad."

Bingley grimaced. What Darcy said was absolutely right, though Bingley did not like hearing it. He really was a dog. Even now, he wanted Darcy to tell him what to do, ever desirous of a pat on the head and a word of praise once he carried out his command.

Bingley had to do better than that if he wanted Jane to marry him. Or she would be better off with a puppy as a companion than with him as a husband.

"To rush into a union is the height of foolishness, and you, Bingley, are more intelligent than you give yourself credit for. You only lack the confidence to carry out your own decisions."

"And how do I gain this confidence?"

"Through practice. Trial and error. Above all…time."

Bingley frowned. He did not like that "error" bit. Or the "time." He knew he was not stupid, but how could other men be so certain? "Do you never doubt yourself?"

The blank expression covering Darcy's face was reply enough. He clearly had no idea what insecurity felt like.

After a long pause, he spoke. "Do you doubt your feelings for Miss Bennet?"

"No," Bingley replied firmly. Then again, he had been in love many times, and every time he had been convinced of the sincerity and absoluteness of his affections. What made him believe this time was any different? He did not like the idea of loving a lady who did not return his affections. "But you have made me doubt the depth of hers. What should I do?"

Darcy shook his head. "That is not for me to decide."

Bingley regretted asking the question, which had sprung off his tongue too quickly. Darcy was right. If he wanted to be the sort of man Miss Bennet could admire and respect, he must start making his own decisions.

"Only promise me you will not do anything in haste," Darcy continued. "You would do better to quit Hertfordshire and return to London than to rush into an unequal match before you know your own mind or can discern hers."

But Bingley's attention had been diverted, and he absently nodded without fully hearing his trusted friend's counsel. He suddenly recalled an adage his father had often uttered:

He who never undertook anything never achieved anything.

It had been many years since Bingley had thought of it, but it popped into his mind as clearly as if his father stood before him saying it now. Had this been what his father meant?

If Bingley was certain about Miss Bennet's inclinations, then he would do his best to be the husband she deserved. He only needed to know the extent of her regard.

Nothing ventured, nothing gained. He could do this. Being more impulsive than deliberate, Bingley would find out that same night. He had decided, and he would do what he must to stick to his decision.

CHAPTER 5

*N*either the two-mile march to Longbourn nor Elizabeth's appeals to reason were sufficient to stir her youngest sister's conscience. Lydia refused to see how her actions might affect Jane or anyone else.

"Mr. Bingley will be glad to have a lively sister when his are so stodgy. Did you see their pinched faces? Lord, what a laugh!"

It was not so much the stodgy sisters whom Elizabeth worried about. It was Mr. Darcy. Mr. Bingley relied heavily on his guidance in estate matters, and who was to say whether he would not also trust his opinion in matters of the heart?

Elizabeth could practically see Mr. Darcy's disapproving stare. Gentlemen of his circles were all propriety and appearances. She had to own, this was not without good reason, but it was maddeningly frustrating when her own family did their level best to make themselves scandalous.

Elizabeth glanced over her shoulder. Jane and Kitty followed shortly behind, their breath puffing clouds in the crisp air. At least Kitty appeared contrite with her downcast eyes and solemn silence.

Hill opened the door, and Elizabeth slipped him the sugar plum while Lydia dallied removing her bonnet.

"Did you get the shoe roses?" their mother called from the drawing room.

Elizabeth pinched the bridge of her nose. She had completely forgotten.

Jane whispered, "I will see to Mama."

"I shall join you." Kitty slipped away from Elizabeth before she could be dragged along with Lydia into Papa's study.

Lydia tugged against Elizabeth. "Oy, you know Papa does not like me to go inside his book room. I'm too noisy."

Elizabeth tightened her grip around Lydia's arm and knocked on the door once, then twice.

Lydia began to look smug. "Serves you right for dragging me here. He's not even in."

Tapping the door again, this time Elizabeth pushed it in. "Papa?"

He looked up from the papers spread over his desk. Papa had many interests: botany, bees, language, and literature. Nothing practical or advantageous to the estate or his wife and daughters. Despite that, Elizabeth loved her father dearly. He was a clever conversationalist, witty, and insightful in many things except that which was most useful. His staunch refusal to address reality when he preferred to live in a sheltered bubble of knowledge had contributed to Lydia's poor behavior, and if she was not checked, she would ruin them all. When Mr. Collins inherited Longbourn—an unjust but eventual reality—Mama's worst fear would come to fruition. They would be dependent on the charity of their relatives—Aunt Philips, who did not want them, or Uncle Gardiner, who did not have room enough for them.

Elizabeth pulled Lydia forward with her, closing the door firmly behind them. "I had to pry Lydia off Mr. Wickham on the high street."

Papa's eyebrows shot up, a suitable reaction at first. Until he chuckled and said, "Is that all?"

Elizabeth leaned forward against his desk. "Is that all? How far will you allow her behavior to decline before you take notice? Mr. Bingley's sisters were there, and you can rely on them to give a full report to their household."

He waved her concern away. "People will talk no matter what we do."

"But must we give them so much fodder? They may very well conclude that an attachment with such a shockingly improper family would reflect poorly on them."

Lydia plopped her bottom down on the nearest chair with a huff. "Lizzy is overreacting. I was merely reaching for a sweetmeat Mr. Wickham offered me."

Elizabeth clenched her hands to keep from shaking her sister. "You were reaching over his person in what can only be described as a garish display of bodily contact." She appealed to her father. "If you do not check her, she will ruin us!"

Papa clucked his tongue and shuffled the papers on his desk. She was losing his attention. If she did not press her case now, they might as well wave goodbye to Mr. Bingley. "It is my firm belief that until Lydia and Kitty can show that they have matured enough to behave properly, they ought not to be allowed out in society."

The door opened, and Kitty appeared. "But I didn't do anything!"

Papa sighed. "Shut the door, Kitty."

Closing the door and taking her place behind Lydia's chair, Kitty repeated, "I didn't do anything."

Elizabeth would not back down now. "You should have stopped Lydia, but you did not. You always follow her lead."

"I do not!"

Lydia twisted to look up at Kitty. "Yes, you do! You're too much of a ninny to think for yourself."

Kitty crossed her arms and pouted.

"And you"—Lydia turned to look at Elizabeth—"you are jealous that I steal all of the attention away from you and shall marry before all of my sisters."

"Only a fool would take a silly girl for a wife." Papa held up a paper, perusing over its contents. "Surely, gentlemen of quality recognize Lydia's youthful exuberance. It is harmless."

Elizabeth's heart sank. He would do nothing. She offered him proof and a simple solution. Still, he would do nothing. Still, she tried.

Clenching her hands, Elizabeth said firmly, "But it is not harmless. Not if it costs Jane Mr. Bingley and the rest of us our reputations."

He set down the paper and rubbed his fingers over his whiskers.

Encouraged, Elizabeth pressed, "Their behavior will not improve until they experience the consequences of their actions."

"And what is it you suggest?"

Glory be, there was hope yet! She looked at her sisters. Kitty stared at the floor, her chin quivering. She only lacked the confidence to come out from under Lydia's shadow. But unless she strengthened her own character, she would always be susceptible to others' influence, especially Lydia's, who watched their father with a smugness that fed Elizabeth's courage. Taking a deep breath, Elizabeth answered, "They should not be allowed to attend the ball this evening."

Lydia rose to her feet with a shriek. In a performance worthy of Covent Garden, she fell at Papa's feet, her voice choking with tears until she secured his handkerchief. "You could not be so cruel, Papa! I shall behave! I shall behave better than Lizzy. Only let me prove how well I can behave when I put my mind to it."

Papa patted her on the head. "There, there. Do not cry."

Elizabeth's hope cracked and her stomach churned as she saw where this was so clearly going.

"Is this the punishment you sought? You see how sorry Lydia is, and how she has promised to improve."

"If I were convinced she knew how to behave, perhaps I might believe her." Elizabeth spoke through clenched teeth. What had Lydia ever done to deserve such leniency?

Papa chuckled and patted Lydia's head again. "You hear that? Lizzy doubts your sincerity, but I am not so stingy in my credulity. I expect you to do as you say, but I also see how you will never improve unless given the opportunity to expose yourself, and you cannot very well do that from here."

Elizabeth groaned. That her father had used her own words against her smarted almost as much as his negligence.

Lydia blinked, her eyes lighting up as she began to understand the meaning of his words. Springing to her feet, she planted a kiss on his cheek. "Thank you, Papa." Her pretty smile turned to an ugly smirk as she passed Elizabeth.

"She should not be allowed to go," Elizabeth appealed once again.

"Oh, Mr. Collins! Whatever are you doing standing at Papa's door?" Lydia exclaimed.

Mr. Collins' flushed complexion told Elizabeth that

he had heard enough of their conversation to merit a sermon on the importance of maidenly virtue.

With an evil arch of her brow, Lydia added, "If you were looking for Lizzy, there she is. And if you have found your boots, I am certain she would appreciate you walking her into Meryton to buy our shoe roses."

Elizabeth was not given to a violent temperament, but she could have killed her sister right there.

"Close the door on your way out, Lizzy." Papa dismissed her and shut out Mr. Collins in one fell swoop.

The hallway was too cramped, and Mr. Collins seemed content with the close proximity. He smelled of perspiration, and since he was wearing his slippers, Elizabeth surmised he had not yet recovered his missing boots. At least she would not have the burden of his company for the walk to Meryton and back.

He followed her line of vision to his feet. Clearing his throat, he said, "Mr. Hill found my boots after you had left for Meryton. I apologize for not being present. A lady of your sensibility ought not to carry the burden of correcting her younger sister's misconduct. Her Ladyship, Lady Catherine de Bourgh, would praise your modesty and—"

Did the fool not realize how his compliment confirmed that he had been eavesdropping? The nerve!

Elizabeth raised her hand to stop him. His nearness and flattery gave her a headache. "I am sorry, Mr. Collins, but this morning's exertions have given me a headache."

He bowed. "Of course. I shall ask Mrs. Hill to send you some tonic. I saw she keeps a well-provisioned still room. Not like the one at Rosings, but ample enough to suit…"

If Elizabeth did not depart, he would continue elevating the residence of his esteemed patroness at the expense of her home. "Pardon me, sir. I really must retire to my room."

He bowed again. She was at the stairs before he peeked up to see if she had observed the elegance of his gesture.

Lydia met her at the top of the landing, her eyes gleaming with her recent triumph.

Elizabeth tensed. "I will be watching over you tonight. Any hint of impropriety, and I will personally see you returned to Longbourn."

"You tried to prevent me from attending," Lydia hissed, her victory taking a harsh turn. "I will return the favor, Lizzy. You may count on that."

"You wish for me to stay in from the ball? I would volunteer rather than be forced to watch over you."

"You will be sorry for trying to spoil my fun. You will see, Lizzy, I shall get even."

Elizabeth's head genuinely hurt now and standing in the hallway listening to her sister's empty threats did nothing to lessen the ache throbbing at her temples. "Do as you wish, Lydia, as you always do. I only hope the rest of us are not forced to pay the price for it." She continued down the hall to her bedchamber. It was going to be a long, arduous night.

As tempting as it was to wallow in despair at the exhausting uphill battle ahead of her, Elizabeth did not dwell too long on the obstacles, instead turning them into challenges. She refused to allow the events of this day to dampen her excitement for the Netherfield Ball.

Lydia's flagrantly public flirtation with Mr. Wickham? Elizabeth would stick to her youngest sister like ink on a writer's fingers through the night.

Their father's selfish indifference? Elizabeth had a long history of managing that deficit, providing the valuable experience she would require that evening.

Mama's presumptuous proclamations of Jane's engagement to Mr. Bingley? Well, nobody really took her claims seriously, did they? Elizabeth would do her best to keep her mother away from those who would think the worst of her. So long as the Netherfield party did not hear her boasts, she could not embarrass Jane too badly.

Mr. Collins' request for Elizabeth's first dance? Yes, that was profoundly disappointing. If she was not careful, he would make good on Mama's threats and make Elizabeth an offer of marriage. She held out hope that his slippers might disappear as his boots had earlier.

The greater the obstacles to Elizabeth's merriment became, the more determined she was to prove herself victorious over her less-than-ideal circumstances. Tonight was for Jane.

Elizabeth would be vigilant, ready to check her sisters without being too obvious lest she draw more attention to their unbecoming behavior by provoking their ire and making herself noticeable to those who had nothing better to do than to refuse to dance.

Not even the prospect of Mr. Darcy's disapproving stares could stifle Elizabeth's hopes for Jane. She anticipated his criticism, and many happy hours passed that afternoon while she imagined her witty retorts.

CHAPTER 6

*I*n the weeks since their arrival, Bingley had impressed Darcy with the timeliness and efficiency with which he saw to Darcy's suggestions. Already, Bingley had made several improvements to Netherfield.

Perhaps he was a bit too hasty in some cases: his eagerness to have the exterior of the house painted before the ball at the height of the rainy season meant that all the windows in the upper floors were sealed shut. But Bingley had been making decisions and acting on them, just as Darcy had encouraged him to do.

However, it had not occurred to Darcy that Bingley might exercise his newfound assertiveness in the selection of his first dance partner to open his ball. To give a lady from such a family the distinction of preference was the last straw. To London they must return. In haste!

Mrs. Hurst and Miss Bingley, equally discontented with their brother's selection, proved attentive that Bingley end the evening unengaged and free to return to town. While Darcy cringed to have those two waspish women as allies, he was grateful for their assistance. It evened the odds against the Bennets somewhat.

Since the opening dance, Darcy had stuck to Bingley's side like cat fur on black trousers. He steered his friend away from the grasping clutches of the Bennets, encouraging him to dance with any lady who was not of that accursed family.

Miss Elizabeth proved to be a thorn in Darcy's side. Her indefatigable efforts to check her younger sisters and occupy her mother, all while laughing and conversing as she flitted from one grouping to the next, occupied her in a constant rotation from one Bennet to the next.

It was cleverly done. Anyone who was not observing her actions closely would assume she had no objective but to enjoy herself. One minute, she encouraged Sir William Lucas' sons to dance a reel with her youngest sisters, and then she returned to the music room, where Miss Mary reached the final chorus of a piece unbefitting a merry assembly. Her finale was met with polite applause from her sparse audience, who was no doubt grateful her performance had come to an end. Darcy was. Bingley's sisters hovered nearby, giggling behind their gloved hands.

Darcy looked to his side to make certain Bingley

was still engaged in conversation with Mr. Collins. He would be stuck with the clergyman for a while. Bingley was too kind. He would not know how to extract himself from the long-winded, pompous boor without being rude. And Bingley was never rude.

Knowing his friend was safe in Mr. Collins' repelling presence, Darcy returned his attention to Miss Elizabeth. He saw her shoulders tense upward as her sister mistook the applause for encouragement to continue.

To his ears' relief, Miss Mary began Bach's Minuet in G Major. It was a piece Georgiana had mastered in her first year of lessons, years ago. Its simplicity would provide ample fodder for Bingley's sisters' mockery, but Miss Elizabeth's posture had relaxed. An easy smile touched her lips. Clearly, she would take whatever wins she could, no matter how small.

Miss Elizabeth was tireless, imperturbable, and relentlessly cheerful in her efforts to keep her family under regulation. Had her purpose not run so contrary to Darcy's, he would have admired her intrepidity.

As it was, Darcy understood her motive all too clearly. With every glance between her eldest sister and Bingley, she confirmed her outlandish hope. Miss Elizabeth was a formidable opponent, but she was in deep waters and well over her head.

As she left the music room, Darcy glanced back to his friend's position. He was dismayed to realize that Mr. Collins now had ensnared Bingley's sisters in conversation and Bingley was nowhere in sight.

Ignoring Miss Bingley's obvious plea for assistance, Darcy followed Miss Elizabeth back to the ballroom. She tapped her sister on the shoulder and continued in a direct line to the refreshment table, where he now spotted Bingley standing.

Not on your life, Miss Elizabeth. Taking advantage of his superior height and longer legs, Darcy cut through the crush, reaching Bingley at the same time as the lady.

They locked eyes, each sizing the other up as two opponents did in a boxing match. She was charming and attractive, clever and engaging. Behind those warm brown eyes was a woman in possession of a keen intellect and nimble humor. She would pierce Darcy's sails the moment he let down his guard. Thus, her danger.

Bingley, gentleman that he was, acknowledged her presence immediately. "Miss Elizabeth, allow me to fetch you a glass of punch." Darcy felt his friend look at him, but he would not back down. He was not susceptible to her siren-like charms.

How long they stood staring at each other, Darcy could not say, but Miss Elizabeth only looked away when Bingley returned with a glass. "Thank you, Mr. Bingley. How kind of you to offer a parched lady a drink." With one eyebrow arched, she returned her gaze to Darcy and took a sip.

Darcy sensed that she intended her comment to slight him. He narrowed his eyes. She dared to criticize him when her own family offended at every turn?

"Five thousand a year! My Jane shall want for nothing!" Mrs. Bennet's voice echoed over the crowd. Darcy raised a brow in turn. The vociferous matron's voice faded. In his peripheral vision, he saw Miss Bennet lead her mother away. At least, he thought it was Miss Bennet. He hoped it was. He dared not look away from Miss Elizabeth. She had already caused him to lose Bingley once. He would not allow it to happen again.

"Are you enjoying the evening, Mr. Darcy?" Miss Elizabeth's voice had a hint of tightness, and her cheeks flamed in high color.

Very much now, Darcy thought. "Well enough. And you, Miss Elizabeth?"

"Immensely. Those of us who enjoy dancing are often happiest at a ball. Do you frown at that, Mr. Darcy? Perhaps you would smile more if you danced."

Bingley laughed and then drank deeply from his glass of punch.

It irked Darcy to be the butt of a jest. That the impertinent minx pretended to understand his character when she had danced no more than he had that evening heated his blood. "For one who claims to love dancing, you are doing precious little of it this evening."

He bit his tongue as soon as the words came out. Now she would expect him to ask her to dance, and he did not have the time or attention to waste.

He waited for her snappy retort, resigning himself to accept the consequences of his blunder. Perhaps there was a young lady nearby with whom Bingley had not yet danced, for Darcy refused to leave his friend unattended and vulnerable to a Bennet attack. No doubt that was Miss Elizabeth's plan. Darcy looked about, trying to find a face to whom he could put a name.

Miss Elizabeth laughed. "Have no fear, Mr. Darcy. It is not my intention to entice you to dance with anyone, least of all with me. We have nothing to talk about, and I am sure we both can think of more diverting ways of spending our time than in each other's company."

Darcy grumbled. Did she think him dull? Her dismissive manner irritated him. He was tempted to ask her for a set merely to prove his point, but his ill humor kept his senses in check. *Insufferable female.*

She leaned closer, and he caught a whiff of sweet orange blossom and spicy cloves. Fresh and light with a heady kick. How appropriate. A grin curled from her lips up to her eyes. "I would much rather Mr. Bingley ask my sister to dance again."

Darcy jerked to his full height, looking over her to see Bingley talking with none other than Miss Bennet and her atrocious mother. A heady kick, all right! How had Darcy allowed Bingley to escape unnoticed?

With a brief glare at the distracting sprite gloating at him, Darcy dismissed himself and hastened to station himself at Bingley's side.

Miss Elizabeth joined them, her smile bright.

If Darcy did not do something quickly, Bingley would ask Miss Bennet to dance with him again. Drat it all! Desperate not to cede another victory to Miss Elizabeth, Darcy turned to Miss Bennet. With a grand bow, he held out his hand. "Might I have the honor of your next dance, Miss Bennet?"

Miss Bennet, of course, accepted graciously. Bingley's brow furrowed and his lips twisted. Mrs. Bennet was delighted.

Darcy pretended not to notice Miss Elizabeth as he whisked her sister away from Bingley on his arm. It was ungentlemanly to gloat.

Then, like a flea that plagued him, there she stood beside her sister. She grinned at her partner—at Bingley, who looked with cow eyes at Miss Bennet.

Darcy attempted to engage Miss Bennet in conversation, but she had eyes only for Bingley. Bingley's partner did nothing at all to distract him from his open admiration of Miss Bennet. She pranced and spun, looking entirely too pleased with herself.

Well played, Miss Elizabeth. Well played. This was no longer a battle of contrary wills. This was a full-on war.

CHAPTER 7

*E*lizabeth's triumph did not come without cost. So distracted had she been with Mr. Darcy —*insufferable man!*—she had forgotten to check her younger sisters. Of course, the girls had lost no time in finding a pack of officers and had placed themselves at the center. They laughed so loud that Elizabeth wondered how they did not lose their voices. Would that they did!

Even after Elizabeth retrieved them, whining and pouting, from the bevy of soldiers, Kitty and especially Lydia were indecorously boisterous. Elizabeth felt Mr. Darcy's disdain everywhere she went. Being taller than most, he was easy to spot in the crush. Always, his gaze followed her, criticizing and vexingly superior.

To make matters worse, Mr. Bingley had only danced once with Jane. Granted, it was the opening dance, but if Jane's hopes were not to be crushed that evening, she needed more assurance. If only Mr. Darcy did not intimidate anyone brave enough to approach Mr. Bingley. It would serve that surly gentleman right if Elizabeth dragged Kitty and Lydia over to him. She would love to see how he managed *that*!

But allowing Mr. Bingley to see the flaws of her family so closely would only hurt Jane's chances, so Elizabeth kept at a distance and tried to ignore the heat that crawled up her neck into her cheeks every time her eyes met Mr. Darcy's.

Hours passed, supper was served, and she looked longingly at her calm friend, Charlotte, who sat with her family. Elizabeth maneuvered Kitty to join her. Charlotte was steady, and Kitty's behavior always improved without Lydia's influence.

Elizabeth wished she could join them. Pretending to enjoy herself while subduing Lydia and quieting her mother began to wear Elizabeth thin. She nearly cried when it was time to return to the cacophony of the ballroom. Plastering a smile on her face, Elizabeth readied herself to dance on aching feet. She had already lined up several suitable and mannerly gentlemen from among their neighbors to keep her sisters entertained.

"Lizzy." Kitty tugged on her arm before they passed the archway leading back to the ballroom. "I have a message from Charlotte for you, but I only have a moment before Mr. Denny claims me for the next set."

"Mr. Denny?" He was not one of their neighbors, but he seemed like a decent sort. "Who is dancing with Lydia?"

Kitty rolled her eyes. "Charlotte wished to speak to you, but you left the dining room too soon."

Elizabeth would not be distracted this late in the evening. "Kitty, I asked with whom Lydia is going to dance."

"Charlotte has some news to relay to you regarding Mr. Bingley," Kitty said, still not answering her question. She must have noticed Elizabeth's impatience. With another roll of her eyes, Kitty gestured to where Lydia stood with Mr. Chamberlayne. "See? Mr. Chamberlayne has claimed Lydia's next set. Surely you cannot disapprove of him. Come, Lizzy, Charlotte said she has useful intelligence."

Lydia waved at Kitty to join them. Mr. Denny was there, too, adding credibility to Kitty's claims.

"Charlotte said she has useful intelligence?" Although Elizabeth was still suspicious, this *was* the sort of phrase Charlotte might use. It would hardly have originated with Kitty. Charlotte knew that Jane's heart had been touched by Mr. Bingley; she had seen it for herself at the Meryton assembly. Had she learned something new?

"Yes, she begged for you to meet her in Mr. Bingley's book room."

"In his library?" If Charlotte wished to say anything she did not wish others to overhear, the room tired fathers went to nap in relative quiet was not a good choice.

Lydia's gestures got wilder. Kitty shuffled her feet.

"No, not the library. His study. The one farthest away and quieter."

That was even stranger. "That is a private room. Why would she wish to meet me there?"

Kitty shrugged. "It will not be occupied, and like I said, it will be quiet. You know where it is, do you not?"

"Yes, but does Charlotte?"

Another shrug. "She must if she suggested it."

"Then she would also know the room is certain to be locked. Mr. Bingley's study is in the residence wing."

This time, a shrug and an eye roll. "I am only repeating to you what she told me."

Just then, a group of ladies disbanded and Charlotte came into view. Perfect. "There she is. I shall go to her now."

Kitty's eyes widened. "But—but then you would never get away!" Indeed, Kitty was right. None other than Mr. Collins formed a part of Charlotte's group. "I heard him tell Mama that he meant to ask you for another dance."

Elizabeth shivered. One dance with Mr. Collins was bad enough, but she could not allow him to single her out in his attentions by requesting another.

Still, Elizabeth's suspicions were not easily appeased. Was this one of Lydia's tricks? She had been emphatic in stating that she would make Elizabeth pay for attempting to spoil her fun. Kitty would lie for Lydia—but Charlotte? Of all the places to have a private conversation, why choose Mr. Bingley's study? It was sure to be locked.

Then again, what would it hurt to have a look? If the door was locked, Elizabeth would hurry downstairs well before the dance ended. No harm would be done. If it was open, she would wait for a few minutes. Enjoy the reprieve. Rest her feet. "Very well. I shall go as Charlotte says if you will signal to her that I am waiting. I cannot be away for too long"—she gave Kitty a pointed look—"as you well know."

"Yes, yes, only hurry or I shall miss my set with Mr. Denny." Kitty scampered across the room to take her place among her waiting party.

Several couples rushed to take their places in the cotillion, forming clusters of eight.

Elizabeth hesitated. Something was not quite right.

The crowd parted, and she saw Mr. Darcy walking in her direction, his dark eyes unmistakably fixed on her. He looked no happier to seek her out than she did in being sought.

Why was he approaching her? Surely he did not mean to ask her to dance. Elizabeth's stomach flip flopped. Mr. Darcy's every word and action was calculated. If he approached her, he had a purpose, and Elizabeth did not presently feel up to the challenge of crossing swords with the gentleman. She needed ammunition. She needed Charlotte's "useful intelligence."

Taking advantage of the crowd, Elizabeth made herself small and, spinning around, she weaved toward the stairs through gesturing gentlemen and ladies waving fans. The hall at the top of the landing was dark, so she was doubly surprised when she reached the door of Mr. Bingley's study and found it open. Still cautious, Elizabeth peeked inside, allowing her vision to adjust to the darkness. "Is anyone here?"

Nothing but quiet. She entered, crossing the floor to pull the curtains aside and allow what little of the moon's glimmer through as the fogged glass permitted.

Closing her eyes, Elizabeth listened to the dimmed laughter and music drifting up from below. The tension in her shoulders eased. She would stay just a few minutes.

Taking a seat by the fireplace in the darkest corner of the room, Elizabeth settled into the soft cushions of a chair, propping her sore feet on a cushioned footstool. She prayed that Mr. Collins would not keep her friend longer than the twenty-five minutes or so Elizabeth could afford to wait before returning to her vigil. She prayed even harder that Charlotte bore good news.

CHAPTER 8

*B*ingley rarely felt irritation, but Darcy was testing his patience. Had he not acted on Darcy's every suggestion over the past weeks? He had taken a dusty, neglected estate and transformed it into a sparkling jewel worthy of his neighbors' glowing praise.

Well, the servants had done that, but had Bingley himself not overseen every detail? Had he not been the one to order the work done, send to London for supplies, and ensure the laborers were paid... once they had done the work properly, an oversight on his part and an inconvenient lesson the sealed windows in the upper floors had taught him. It was not a mistake he would soon make again.

All this, and did Darcy impart even one "well done" or "hear hear"? No. He hovered over Bingley's shoulder, a scowling chaperone, keeping Bingley from doing the one thing he most wanted to do: dance again with Jane Bennet.

She was an angel. Bingley's heart fluttered every time her blue eyes met his and her rosebud lips smiled at him. She smiled at everything he said. She made him feel like the most intelligent man in the room. A king's ransom for another dance! How else was he supposed to discern the depth of her feeling?

What would Darcy do in this situation? Bingley considered.

Darcy would never be in this situation to begin with. He was quick to decide; quick to act. And so must Bingley be. He drew himself to his full height, lifting his chin and widening his stance. Had he not been acting decisively for weeks? Now was not the time to back down. He must act confidently. He wanted to dance with Jane, to prove to Darcy that she was not indifferent, and nothing would change Bingley's mind about it. How was that for decisive?

But how? Bingley had given Darcy several hints to favor his guests with his company, and yet, when they were not dancing, his friend stood at his side, limiting his conversation. He dared not approach the Bennets, though that was precisely what he must do if he were to settle his heart on Miss Bennet.

If only he were as clever as Miss Elizabeth. She would find a way to lure Darcy away. Few could match his friend's quick wit, but she had managed splendidly during her short stay at Netherfield. Where others reacted with awe, she poked fun. Where others adjusted their views to suit Darcy's, she boldly defended hers. She debated with Darcy fearlessly, though in all honesty, Bingley could not tell for certain if she took any particular enjoyment from their debates. Bingley suspected that Darcy did, though he could not countenance why.

That was how it struck him. Who better to distract Darcy than Miss Elizabeth?

Bingley saw her standing under the archway and, heart hammering in his chest, he pointed her out to Darcy. With hardly any coercion at all, his friend set off across the room, and a delighted Bingley floated on the wings of his success to Miss Bennet… just in time to see her take the arm of another gentleman to join the cotillion.

Drat! He had been so close! So close and a moment too late. Now he would have to wait until the end of the set. Darcy would resume his post by then and unless Bingley could think of a way to distract him again, he despaired of exchanging more than a word with Miss Bennet for the rest of the evening. He needed a plan.

Contrary to his custom, Bingley backed up against the wall to ponder. He must have managed several minutes, but he grew quite restless. How did Darcy do it? Bingley could not stand still for so long, and he felt guilty contemplating in silence when he had guests to entertain.

Out of the corner of his eye, Bingley saw Caroline grin at Louisa while she clutched a key behind her fan.

Both of them stood on their toes, necks stretched, feathers waving over the heads of their guests, searching for something, or more likely, someone. It could not be Darcy. He was too easy to spot in a crowd.

Too cross to ask another lady to dance and too defeated to immediately formulate another plan, Bingley joined his sisters. "What have you there?" He nodded at the key.

Caroline clutched the key tighter, hiding it in the folds of her skirt. "Nothing of any note."

"Then why are you hiding it?"

No reply.

"Where is the key to?" Bingley pressed.

Louisa snapped, "Really, Charles, have you nothing better to do than ask stupid questions?" She did not stick her tongue out, but it was implied. Marriage had not softened Louisa. If anything, her tongue had become sharper. No wonder Hurst pretended to sleep all the time.

"You have not seen Miss Eliza recently, have you?" Caro's tone was sweet in contrast. She batted her eyelashes, a gesture wasted on him.

"Do you have something in your eye, Caro?"

"Of course not, I was merely inquiring after Miss Eliza." Her smile tightened, much like her voice.

Bingley's suspicions grew. While his sisters fawned over Miss Bennet, he had not noticed any particular regard toward Miss Elizabeth from them. "Why?" he asked.

"'Tis no matter." Caroline fluttered her fan, the key gone.

"No reason at all," Louisa added.

His unease grew the more they hemmed and hawed. Bingley watched the dancers weaving and spinning. He saw Miss Bennet's white dress and pink ribbons in a cluster, but he did not see Miss Elizabeth... nor could he remember what color ribbon she wore that evening. Blue? Yellow? Green?

Come to think of it, he did not see Darcy either. Maybe she had refused to dance with him. Again. Bingley knew it was wicked of him, but the thought brought him cheer.

He could not care less about the key, but his humor had taken a devilish turn, so he asked again, "What is the key for?"

Caroline batted her eyelashes quicker, a sure sign she was up to something she did not want to admit to. "Oh, nothing."

Knowing better than to accept her vague reply, Bingley pressed, "It is not nothing when I very clearly saw something."

She huffed. "Only the key to your study."

"My study?" It was not a room he used often yet, though he had great plans for it. He had ordered several volumes to be sent from Hatchards as well as a newly commissioned leather chair to complement the large mahogany desk. But that was neither here nor there. Caroline had not answered his question. He repeated, "What are you doing with the housekeeper's key?"

Caroline scrunched her nose. "Mr. Collins already trapped me once in conversation and would have done so again had I not encouraged him to look over your books for recommendations."

"So you sent him to my study? Why not the library?"

"You keep books in your study too." She pouted and fiddled with her fan. What was she not telling him? A key she should not have, a room he rarely used, a gentleman she wished to avoid...

Bingley narrowed his eyes at her. "You did not lock Mr. Collins inside, did you?"

She gasped. "Of course not! I only unlocked the door so that he might enter."

Louisa tittered behind her hand. "You can count on Mr. Collins to extol the virtues expounded upon in Fordyce's Sermons. You will be presumed upon to secure a copy, Charles."

Caroline chuckled. "What would Mr. Darcy say?"

Darcy would not allow his sister to play manipulative games on his guests. Neither would Bingley.

He held out his hand expectantly. "I shall see that the key gets returned to Mrs. Nichols. After I see to Mr. Collins." He still did not trust that Caroline had not locked the clergyman inside the room. With the window painted shut and no connecting door, the poor man would be trapped inside until Mrs. Nichols unlocked the room the following morning.

"No harm has been done." With a scowl, Caroline dropped the key in his palm. Tugging on Louisa's arm, she said, "Come, let us find another amusement. Perhaps Miss Mary is tormenting our guests in the music room."

"I do not know which is worse: the assault on my ears or staying here and risking another dance with a local," Louisa said.

When had his sisters become so high and mighty?

Tucking the key inside his pocket, Bingley noticed Darcy returning his way. Alone. Oh, drat! No Miss Elizabeth. No freedom for Bingley to talk to Miss Bennet or secure her next dance.

Not having experienced irritation to this degree before, Bingley hardly knew what to do with it, but he would burst if he did not do something! If only he could dispatch his friend as easily as Caroline had rid herself of Mr. Collins.

Bingley stilled. A crazy idea had popped into his mind—a harmless plan which would give him just enough time to secure Jane's next dance if he acted quickly. He nodded at Darcy. "You decided not to dance?"

Darcy grunted in reply. He had done his best to give an impression of an aloof, taciturn, proud man since that first night at the Meryton assembly. This disagreeable behavior began to grate Bingley's nerves, especially when he knew his friend to be more gentlemanly than that. It would serve him right to be set down a peg or two. "Caroline told me something interesting about my study..." Bingley began only to stop himself. If he told Darcy that Mr. Collins was in his study, he would never get Darcy to go to that room. He grabbed another name, the first one that crossed his mind. "... and Mr. Wickham."

The effect was instantaneous. Darcy's shoulders stiffened and his demeanor hardened. "Wickham would not dare to show his face here."

Bingley hated to distress his friend. What a poor choice he had made. Attempting to soothe the feathers he had ruffled, he said, "I cannot help but think that some great misunderstanding is at the root of your breach. If only you would speak openly with each other, perhaps you could clear up the matter and resume your friendship."

Bingley did not know what had transpired, but he hated all forms of conflict. It pained him to know the two childhood friends had cast aside their good opinions of each other to become enemies.

Darcy's eyes hardened. "Is he here? In your study?"

Bingley felt his eyes widen and his head shake, but he stopped himself before his tongue revealed the truth. This was the opportunity he had been looking for, and he had come so near to wasting it. The dance must be close to ending.

He did not need to lie outright to get Darcy to go to his study. A vague reply would suffice. No harm would come of it. Really, it was an innocent plan. While he did not hope that Darcy would tarry long in Mr. Collins' company, it might just give Bingley enough time to secure Jane's next dance.

His decision made, Bingley shrugged his shoulders and allowed Darcy to believe what he would.

Darcy's reaction was as perfect as Bingley had prayed it might be. Speaking through gritted teeth, he said, "I shall rid us of him." Without another word, he left.

Bingley gasped at his easy success. Just as quickly, he groaned in guilt. Lies of omission were still lies. He had manipulated his closest friend—something Bingley never did!—and the wretchedness consuming him did not allow him to celebrate his success. He had to tell him the truth.

He chased after Darcy, gaining the bottom of the stairwell just as his friend disappeared down the hall at the top of the landing. Foot on the first step, ready to run to gain Darcy, Bingley heard his name being called.

Stopping with a groan, he looked over to see Mrs. Nichols twisting her hands in her apron. "Mr. Bingley! I do not suppose you have seen Miss Bingley?"

The key! Bingley pulled it out of his pocket and handed it to his housekeeper.

"What a relief! One must never leave the private rooms open during a ball, and I regret to inform you that one of the maids admitted to leaving Miss Bingley's bedchamber door unlocked. Now I may secure your study and her room."

Bingley looked at the top of the landing. Darcy was gone. He was likely inside the study by now.

Then Bingley imagined a bevy of gentlemen standing at the edge of the dance floor waiting to snatch Miss Bennet away from him. He could not blame them. She was the handsomest lady present. But he would have his dance!

Eager to place himself at the greatest advantage, he returned to the ballroom, his mind and heart too full of Jane Bennet to yield space to the consequences of what he had just done.

CHAPTER 9

Darcy ground his teeth and clenched his fists, his surroundings a blur as he stomped down the hall. How dare Wickham appear at Bingley's ball? Had the man no sense? What did he hope to gain? If he attempted to exploit Darcy or any of his friends again, the only prize he would get would be a busted nose. Darcy had been patient and charitable for Georgiana's sake, but Georgiana was not here, and Wickham had no claim on Darcy's lenience. Not anymore.

Shoving the study door open, he closed it behind him with a firm click. He did not want their conversation overheard by anyone.

A feminine squeak and a shuffle by the cold fireplace made Darcy's blood boil. Dear Lord, not only was Wickham here, but he had already lured a lady into a compromising position. "Wickham!" he demanded.

"Mr. Darcy?"

Darcy froze, chilled to the bone. He did not need a candle to recognize that voice.

"What are you doing here?" Miss Elizabeth behaved as though *he* were the intruder.

Darcy could hardly breathe, could hardly think straight. Wickham had a particular talent for winning people over with his easy manners and false charm, but that he might have succeeded in winning over Miss Elizabeth… It had to be a trick. Miss Elizabeth would not be the first to mistake Wickham's character, but she was not so foolish to allow such a man to ruin her. He blinked hard several times, wishing his vision to adjust so that he might haul Wickham out of the study by the collars. "Where is he?"

"Where is Wickham? You think he is here? With me?"

Darcy heard the offense in her speech, and he felt the faultiness of his thinking. Miss Elizabeth's character was too strong to yield to vice. He ought to know better. But Wickham was crafty. He had so nearly ruined Georgiana. Darcy had to be certain. "Wickham is not here?"

She stood close enough to him now for his skin to tingle. Cloves and orange blossoms. He braced himself for the kick. "You think me capable of being alone in a dark room with an unmarried man?"

Darcy could have pointed out that that was precisely what was happening, but he knew better than to provoke her further than he already had. "No."

"Then why persist in this questioning? If I am above

fault in your opinion, you would have accepted my word immediately and departed."

He bowed his head. "I apologize for causing offense. You have never given me reason to doubt the strength of your character or the integrity of your virtue."

"And yet you accuse me of being ensconced in this study with Mr. Wickham? You have a strange way of displaying your confidence, Mr. Darcy." She sucked in a breath. "Perhaps that explains your behavior toward Mr. Bingley. You must trust him a great deal, or else you might make the mistake of allowing him to dance and speak with whom he pleases at his own ball."

Bingley. A small voice in Darcy's mind wondered why Bingley had sent him on a fool's errand when Wickham was not present.

The louder voices demanded justice. He had apologized. Instead of gracefully extending him forgiveness, Miss Elizabeth used it as a weapon against him. Such impudence was not to be borne. He leaned closer to her. "You would criticize me? From the moment you arrived, you have done little but watch over your mother and sisters. Would you have me believe you do so out of *trust?*"

At first, her silence gratified Darcy. But victory soon ceded to uncertainty. Darcy could be certain of nothing in Miss Elizabeth's presence.

He heard her take in a deep breath, felt her exhale against his cheek. "I admit the injustice of my accusation when I am guilty of the same. I have my reasons, as I am certain you have yours. However, here we both are, neglecting our duty to the ones we wish to protect."

Darcy's heart skipped a beat. That she ascribed proper motive to him in protecting Bingley should have appeased his palpitating pulse. Had her family not been the very ones from whom Darcy wished to protect Bingley, had she been ignorant of his aim, he might have returned the compliment. Instead, her insightfulness proved her to be an even stronger foe than he had imagined. As paradoxical as their predicament was, he had to admire her.

She continued, "I would not be alone in the dark in this part of the house without a reason. I have been sitting here for about twenty minutes waiting for my friend, Miss Lucas, who was supposed to meet me. Then you barged inside shouting Mr. Wickham's name."

"I did not shout," Darcy whispered. He could see her now. Her skin glowed in the moonlight, her lips a dark contrast. He knew he should look away. As God was his witness, he tried.

"I beg to differ, sir." Had they spoken louder, perhaps he might have achieved some distance, but her whisper pulled him closer. His gaze snagged on her curvy lips as she spoke, "Now, while I appreciate the irony of this moment given the subject of our argument, I beg you to open the door. It is inappropriate for us to be alone together. I would rather wait for Charlotte in the hall."

She was right. Of course she was right. What foolishness had come over him? Rubbing his hand over his face and through his hair, trying to get rid of the lingering smell of cloves, Darcy said, "No, I should be the one to leave. My apologies." Turning to the door, he saw it shut and heard the lock turn.

He blinked hard and shook his head, disbelieving what he had clearly seen and heard. He distinctly recalled closing the door himself, and yet, someone must have opened it only to shut it again. This bode ill. In the next instant, he ran to the door, rattling the knob. Panic rose in Darcy's throat. He raised his hand to bang against the barrier.

Miss Elizabeth was at his side, her hand cradling his fist. "What are you doing?" she hissed. "Do you want whoever locked us in here to know we are trapped together?"

Darcy knew he must pound against the door if they had any hope of escape, but her touch sent shivers through him.

Her hands were soft, warm. Where were her gloves? The fire had burned out long ago in Bingley's study; she might catch a chill. He turned his wrist and slowly opened his fist, her fingers gliding over his palm. He would have clasped her hands in his to keep them warm had she not snatched them away.

He gritted his teeth. What devilry was coming over him? Crossing his arms over his chest, he stared at the door.

Miss Elizabeth cleared her throat. "There is a

perfectly good window behind us. You can lower me from it."

He knew what he would find at the window, but he tried anyway. Gripping the casing, he thrust his weight upward with a mighty shove. The paint did not even crack. Not one to give up easily, Darcy tried again. And again.

He considered breaking the window. He imagined tossing one of Miss Bingley's painted tables through the glass, but then what? Miss Elizabeth would have to scramble over sharp shards through the opening. She was certain to be injured. The height was too great for either of them to leap from, and there was no convenient trellis or ledge to climb down.

He already knew the layout of the room. He had seen the drawings and inspected every room with Bingley and his agent. There were no other doors, no secret passageways.

The only way in or out of the study was through the locked door made of sturdy English oak.

They were trapped together.

Mr. Darcy turned away from the unopened window. The look on his face filled Elizabeth with horror. "We are trapped?" Her words sounded too small for the enormity of their problem.

Turning to the door, she began pounding. This

could not be happening. How had this happened? Why had Charlotte not come before? If she was the one to discover them, Elizabeth knew she could count on her dear friend's discretion.

But what if Charlotte did not come? What if she had never intended to meet Elizabeth in the study? She kicked the door, her toes no match for the unmovable barrier. Had Kitty lied? Had there even *been* a message? Or was this part of Lydia's plan to get even? Elizabeth kicked the door again, her breath heaving, her palms sore, and her toes throbbing.

Strong hands pulled her away from the door. Had they not belonged to Mr. Darcy, Elizabeth would have been more tempted to melt into them. The depth of her distress left her feeling weak.

Lydia had won. Oh, she had won. Elizabeth imagined her sister prancing and giggling and making a spectacle of herself while their mother proudly bragged of Jane's success. She imagined Jane, cheeks flushed with mortification, watching helplessly as the shameful behavior of her own family stamped out her hopes.

Elizabeth seethed. "I am going to kill Lydia." *If I ever get out of Mr. Bingley's study.*

Lydia was silly and selfish, but Elizabeth had never thought her so malicious to compromise her with a gentleman she knew Elizabeth did not like, and who despised her in turn. This was the height of cruelty! As soon as Elizabeth gained her freedom, she would march downstairs and drag Lydia back to Longbourn by the hair if she must. She would lock her in the nursery and toss the key in the outdoor privy where not even Kitty had the stomach to search.

Elizabeth was tempted to continue plotting her revenge, but first she must escape. She pulled against Mr. Darcy's hands. "We could break the glass! There are several sturdy tables we could use—"

The look he gave her silenced her.

"Have you heard nothing I said?" he asked.

She stopped tugging. He must think her mad, which at least explained why he still held her shoulders. Truth was, she had not heard Mr. Darcy say a word, which meant that her agitation was too great to think clearly. She must calm down or she would be completely useless.

Taking a few steadying breaths, she said, "What did you say?" She raised her chin and looked him steadily in the eyes to better convey her sanity.

She must have been convincing, for he dropped his hands and gestured at the window. "The glass is too problematic."

"We would be careful—"

"I cannot allow you to injure yourself any further."

She opened her mouth to argue, but her hands were bruised where she had beaten the door. As were her toes.

Softly, he said, "I swear on my honor I shall do you no harm. You are safe with me. Pray do nothing more to cause yourself injury, I beg you."

Maybe she had not been entirely convincing. He

spoke as though he still thought her mad. He held his palms up for her to see how harmless he was. Such a tall, strong man with such a gentle expression. Truth be told, Elizabeth had not once felt herself in danger from Mr. Darcy. Until he mentioned it, the thought had not entered her mind. "I am not afraid of you, Mr. Darcy."

Still, he held his hands up, moving her to add, "You have never given me cause to fear. We have had our differences, but I trust that you will not take advantage of this situation." She said the words and, to her amazement, she realized how much she meant them.

"Do I have your word that you will not do anything which might harm your person? I cannot allow it." He swallowed hard, his hands slowly dropping. It occurred to Elizabeth that Mr. Darcy must often find himself in the role of protector. Mr. Bingley, his younger sister, no doubt, his tenants and household staff... and now her.

While Elizabeth appreciated his gallantry on her behalf, it frustrated her logic. Her freedom was worth a few cuts, scrapes, and bruises. But his tone brooked no argument, and she knew from previous debates that she would be wasting her breath to attempt to convince him otherwise. "I promise. Are there any other doors?" She squinted at the bookshelves, trying to see a door frame or a latch.

"No."

"Any secret passageways?"

"No."

The air around them grew heavier and harder to breathe. She closed her eyes and composed herself. She must think logically, rationally. She always found a way; this was no different.

Opening her eyes, she glared at the barrier separating her from independence. She had promised she would not cause herself any harm, so she could not very well attempt to knock the door down. There had to be another way. The keyhole. The lock did not look new, which meant she might be able to pick it open.

With a silent apology to Sarah, who had spent the better part of an hour coaxing Elizabeth's curls into submission, Elizabeth pulled out a hairpin. A curl tumbled down her back. Oh bother! A weight-bearing pin. She had hoped to avoid one of those.

"What are you doing?" Mr. Darcy grumbled beside her.

"I am going to pick the lock." She spoke with as much confidence as she could muster.

"Do you have experience picking locks?"

"Not especially. Do you?"

"No, but I fear how your hair will look when we are finally discovered."

As if she had not considered that! Of all the pompous, know-it-all... A quick reminder of Mr. Darcy's kinder qualities curtailed her irritation and bolstered her forbearance. Good heavens, the man tried her patience! "You would have me cross my arms and wait for someone to discover us? How long might that take? Does Mr. Bingley even use this room?" She had appreciated the comfortable seating area around the fireplace, but she had not failed to notice the lack of glowing embers as well as the desk's lack of a chair.

"I only mean that it is to our advantage not to appear disheveled when we are finally found."

She turned to face him directly, one hand holding her pin, the other fisted on her hip. That he was right only irritated her more. "Do you have a better idea?"

"I am thinking."

"Excellent. While you think, I shall attempt to pick this lock." Returning to the door, she twisted her pin with too much enthusiasm. The pin bent and snapped. *Confound it!* Defiantly reaching for another, she pulled one free. No hair tumbling. She smirked at Mr. Darcy. He could think all he wanted. She preferred to act. "I would rather escape before anyone notices our predicament. My hair can be fixed more easily than my reputation."

Snap!

"Blast and botheration!" she mumbled, reaching for yet another pin. She refused to look at Mr. Darcy. Oh, how she hated to admit he was right! Too stubborn to admit her error, too determined to stand by doing nothing, she pulled the pin out of her hair.

Another curl tumbled down. She gestured heavenward, wondering what she had done to deserve this. She was the Bennet who got her sisters out of scrapes, who exerted herself the most to compensate for their faults, and yet, unless a miracle happened, she would be their ruin.

She raised her eyes to the heavens. Did God still do miracles? She prayed for one, but the door did not burst open. She prayed again and tried the handle. It was still locked. Evidently faith the size of a mustard grain could move mountains, but it did not open study doors.

The ridiculousness of their situation tickled Elizabeth's humor, but now was not the proper occasion to laugh.

"Pray, allow me." Mr. Darcy sounded so calm. Did nothing catch him off guard?

Her first thought was to assure him that she had, indeed, been praying. Most fervently. But he made his meaning clearer when he held out his hand.

She dropped the pin in his palm, his gravity threatening her light humor, which she could not allow. If she did not laugh, she feared she might cry. "We would make terrible thieves," she teased.

He did not laugh. Not so much as a crinkle of the eyes or a twitch of the lips. Did Mr. Darcy feel anything at all? Was his impassive composure the result of years of repression—heaven forbid a highborn gentleman show any feeling!

Or did he believe himself above obligation? She did not want to think it of him, but had not Mr. Wickham's history with the man suggested that Mr. Darcy was capable of dealing as selfishly with her as he had with his childhood friend? She could never be happy attached to such a dishonorable man.

A promising click sounded inside the lock, and Elizabeth held her breath with every scratch and tap she thought she heard. To think that her entire future depended so fully on the strength of a hairpin...

CHAPTER 10

*S*nap! Darcy swallowed an expletive.

Without a word, Elizabeth withdrew another pin from her hair.

He took it. "Thank you." He waited for her humorous banter, but she had grown more pensive over the last few minutes. If she was contemplating the advantages a union with him would bring to her and her family, she gave no indication of it. Rather, standing beside him with her arms crossed and her lips pinched, she looked peevish, though he dared not look too long. Half of her hair was down, and the sight of her wild curls tumbling down to her waist captivated him.

She ignored him, which only added to her appeal. The undivided focus with which she attempted to gain their freedom impressed him, though his pride wilted a bit at the ferocity of her determination to get away from *him,* as was evidenced in her bruised hands and feet and her willingness to impale herself on the window glass.

Miss Bingley would have sold her own sister for the opportunity to be trapped here with him. Not Elizabeth. Darcy doubted her capable of indifference or indolence. She was decisive, sure in herself and her opinions, passionate in her behavior.

Catching himself before he smiled, Darcy rubbed his hand over his face and assumed an expression more fitting to the occasion. What was wrong with him?

If Elizabeth could see his stupid grin in the dark, she would think him mad. He *was* mad! Here he was admiring the lady for her industrious determination, and what was he doing? Jabbing a flimsy hairpin in a rusty lock.

He ought to be doing something more useful to escape rather than waste time admiring the lady stuck with him—a lady very eager to depart from his company. Much more eager than he was to leave hers.

Stepping away from the door, he held the pin out to her. "Perhaps you will have better success." She plucked it from his hand and turned to the lock with nary a reply. Now he was convinced she was vexed. Never before had he observed her forfeit so many opportunities to jest. She was similar to Richard that way. Always poking fun, always quick with a witty remark.

Widening his stance, he examined the lock and tried not to notice how Elizabeth bit her bottom lip as she twisted and turned the pin in her long fingers. Instead, he studied the door itself. It opened inward, which eliminated the possibility of barging it down. He would sooner shatter his shoulder than budge the barrier.

Another pin snapped, and Elizabeth muttered, "Blast and botheration!" under her breath. Balling her fists at her waist, a picture of stubborn intention, she took a deep breath and doggedly reached for another pin.

If she kept this up, she would not have enough pins remaining to make any repairs to her coiffure.

Before her hand reached her tresses, before he thought better, Darcy reached out and grabbed her wrist. He realized his mistake the moment his hand met hers. A wiser man would have learned his lesson the first time her touch had jolted him out of his senses, but apparently Darcy was determined to act the fool that night, for he held her hand and struggled to remember what it was he had meant to say.

If he had any sense at all, he would stand at the other end of the room. Far away from Elizabeth Bennet.

"May I have my hand back, Mr. Darcy?" she said stiffly.

Face flaming, he let go, feeling powerless over his own body. Never before had his instincts rebelled so disfavorably against him.

Eager to right the appalling liberty he had taken, he steeled himself and took several steps away. "You had better stand back," he suggested, stiffening his shoulder and preparing himself for impact. This would hurt, but better that than this stupid stupor which had overtaken him.

Leaning forward, using the fullness of his height to thrust his weight forward to advantage, Darcy angled his torso to the side and charged. He hit the door so hard, he saw flashes of light. Backing up, frustrated failure fueling his strength, he rammed against the door again. And again. *Blasted English oak.*

His shoulder ached. He rubbed it, needles of pain traveling down to his fingertips, the sleeve of his coat flapping loose where it had ripped open. Yet, again, he stepped away, resuming his charging stance for another attempt.

She stepped in front of him, her hands pressing against his heaving chest. "Stop before you hurt yourself further." Her cry warbled.

Darcy stopped. The last time anyone had cried for him had been his mother the night before she died. The realization that Elizabeth cared, even just a little, made his breath more uneven.

She snatched her hands away and covered her mouth. And that was when Darcy realized how mistaken he was. Her reaction had nothing to do with maidenly affection but with a desire to conceal her laughter. The warble in her voice had not been concern but humor. Was she laughing at him? What he had craved moments ago now vexed his pride. "What is so funny?"

"Pardon me, Mr. Darcy. I do not laugh at you but in appreciation of the irony." She gestured at the door, as solid now as it was a half-dozen hits ago. "That door is more resolute than either of us. While Mr. Bingley would be happy to know his residence is so well built, I fear our position is less stable." She dabbed the corners of her eyes, and Darcy realized that Elizabeth's humor was not intended as a jab but as an attempt at bravery.

Darcy's agitation instantly calmed. If she could make the best of their situation, then so would he.

She shook her head, and while he did not hear her sigh, he sensed it. "I have spent the last seven years protecting Jane's prospects. I refuse to be the one to cast doubt on my sisters' reputations."

He stiffened. Why would anyone doubt them? Did she not know he would do what any gentleman in this position would do and make an offer for her?

Her brittle chuckle threw him off balance again. "Come, Mr. Darcy, you can hardly believe I expect you to make an offer to me—a lady you consider 'barely tolerable'—or to attach yourself to a family in every way beneath you... save in one aspect." She stood taller and spoke more firmly. "Like you, I am the offspring of a gentleman. In that, we are equal."

The accusation kicked Darcy in the stomach, mostly because she was right to think so poorly of his behavior. He had been angry and resolved to dislike Hertfordshire.

He had hoped that some time and distance away from Bingley would soften Georgiana's juvenile attachment to his friend, but the letter he had received from her the same day of the Meryton assembly had made plain how little he understood his sister's heart. And that dreadful assembly had proven how little control he had over Bingley's. How could Darcy be anything but miserable knowing how Georgiana would expect him to promote the match when Bingley's eye was too easily turned by a handsome face?

Darcy had been in a dark mood that wretched evening, and Elizabeth had suffered for it. His comment had been cruel and undeserved. Not to mention an outright lie. Elizabeth *did* tempt him. Hers was the sort of beauty which improved on further acquaintance, the dangerous kind that captivated the heart and engaged the mind. He really ought to stand at the other side of the room. But first, he must make amends. "I regret what I said."

"Do you?" She arched an eyebrow and looked up at him pertly.

"I would not apologize otherwise."

"Oh, yes, I have learned that you would rather not speak at all than say anything you do not mean. While such honesty is to be praised, it also condemns you, for we both know that you meant what you said."

Her terrifying logic made him weigh his next words more carefully. Nothing got by Elizabeth. "I had my reasons at the time, but they do not excuse my poor behavior, nor will they influence what we both know must happen when we are found."

There, he had said it. They had been alone together too long to escape consequences. It was time to face their fate. If they were intelligent about it, they might avoid scandal.

Her fists now balled at her hips, and Darcy got the distinct impression he had said something wrong.

"What *must* happen? I would rather have my freedom than be forced into a union neither of us want. While there is still the possibility of escape, no matter how small, I shall not give up. You are under no obligation to me, Mr. Darcy. I would rather choose ruin."

She refused him?! Of all the women with whom he could be trapped, was this the one lady who would rather face ruin than marry him? One look at her disheveled hair and his torn coat would be more than enough for even the most liberal of libertines to condemn them. But she would fight until the very end. How could anyone be both so maddening and charming, so stubborn and admirable?

CHAPTER 11

*E*lizabeth bit her tongue. She had refused him! Why on earth had she done that? Elizabeth was not mercenary, but neither was she so foolish to think she or her sisters could survive this scandal unscathed. Her only hope was that one extraordinarily discreet person came to their rescue, or at least someone bribable. But now Elizabeth's sharp tongue had put paid to that.

If only she had more options, more choices! Apparently, Mr. Darcy had already made his choice, and like the men of his station accustomed to always getting his way, he expected her to acquiesce. Well, while there was still hope that a lenient, accommodating person would free them from this wretched room, Elizabeth would not yield without a fight. She could never be happy with haughty, selfish, disdainful Fitzwilliam Darcy.

"I did not phrase that right," he said. "I wished to

assure you that I shall do what must be done to protect your honor. I could do no less."

His explanation was unexpected—and Elizabeth had to admit, kind—but she did not trust him. She hardly knew him! "Do you always place such a high value on honor?"

"Yes!"

She had offended him. Given all the times he had offended her, her neighbors, and her family, her conscience did not suffer much. Had he been more gentlemanly, she would have extended him more mercy.

But she must also remember he had been kind to her. Although Elizabeth did not want to marry him, if she had no choice, she would do well to understand Mr. Darcy better. "I have heard reports to the contrary which puzzle me."

He took a deep breath, the kind her father often took when he had had his fill of nonsense. "You question my character?"

Elizabeth would love nothing more but to unleash the profoundness of her discontent on Mr. Darcy, to spar with him until he felt the blow as intensely as she did. But she must think beyond this moment if Mr. Darcy was to be her future.

She knew she was perhaps the only person to question Mr. Darcy's character... to his face, that is. But she truly did not know what to make of him. One minute, he charged into a room breathing threats, and the next, he cradled her hands so tenderly, her stomach fluttered.

Before she could reply, he whispered, "What reports?"

He sounded so downcast, she almost regretted the question. Almost. She must have some answers or believe herself to be shackled to a contemptuous nob. Lifting her chin, Elizabeth met his gaze squarely. "Did you deny Mr. Wickham the living your father promised him in his will?"

Crossing his arms over his wide chest, the fabric covering his arms straining, he spat, "Wickham." His eyes hardened, his eyebrows lowered into a deep V, and his lip curled.

Elizabeth's curiosity rooted her in place. She was not afraid of Mr. Darcy. As little as she liked him, she knew he would not raise a hand against her. Mr. Wickham, on the other hand... Well, he might be the trained soldier, but Elizabeth would wager every penny she had saved that Mr. Darcy could easily best him in a fight.

As barbaric as her thoughts had become, the image of Mr. Darcy looming over Mr. Wickham in a boxing ring thrilled her. Which could only mean that she had been reading too many novels. There was nothing thrilling about boorish Mr. Darcy.

And then, in the next breath, he loosened his arms, at first letting them dangle at his side as though he did not know what to do with them. Then he raised one to rake his fingers through his hair, a gesture he had done repeat-edly in the time they had been trapped together. Drop-ping his hand, looking almost humble, he finally responded to her question. "My father loved Wickham. He regarded him as dearly as the second son he had always wanted." His voice wavered. "At one time, Wickham was my closest friend." He paused and ran his hand through his hair again. "My father gave him many advantages, among them a gentleman's education and a guaranteed living at the parish church. That much is true."

Elizabeth had wanted answers so badly, but seeing how uncomfortable Mr. Darcy was, how hesitant he was to speak in his own defense when Mr. Wickham had been so quick to throw accusations against him... it made Elizabeth feel wretched for bringing up the subject.

Why had it never occurred to her to doubt Mr. Wickham until now? Had she pressed him for details, he gladly would have supplied them, his speech oily-smooth and practiced.

Unlike Mr. Darcy, whose raw speech proclaimed his honesty. She would hear no more. "Please, Mr. Darcy, you do not owe me an explanation."

He continued as though he had not heard her. "I honored my father's wishes. Wickham was granted his living, but he had no interest in the living or my father's wishes. He sold it for the sum of three thou-sand pounds."

Elizabeth sucked in a breath. She nodded, seeing

with no great difficulty how Mr. Wickham could be the kind of man Mr. Darcy described.

Far from boastful, Mr. Darcy sounded sad. "I agreed with Wickham that he was ill-suited to the church, and I gladly paid the sum." He shoved his hand through his hair again. "There is more—much more—but I beg you to be patient."

She nodded again, stunned. He did not owe her an explanation, and yet he gave her one, offering her more if she would but wait.

Elizabeth knew what that meant, and the realization made her stomach sink. Mr. Darcy would not feel compelled to reveal anything more to her unless he felt himself under obligation. To her.

Elizabeth wanted nothing more than to insist on her freedom, but how could she be so doggedly stubborn when her family would pay for her decision? But neither could she accept her circumstance without struggle or pretend she did not care what would become of her.

She imagined living like her own father—without any interest besides his intellectual pursuits because nothing he could do now could ever undo the past. He had agreed to the entailment, confident in his ability to produce an heir. That confidence had eroded with every daughter borne to him. He had not always been so indolent and sarcastic, though it was difficult for Elizabeth to remember so far back. But she cherished those memories and hoped that the kind, attentive father who had taught her and Jane, and whom she had loved so dearly, was still there somewhere. She could not live as he did without becoming bitter and tetchy, just as he had become.

Mr. Darcy cleared his throat, reminding Elizabeth of the precariousness of their predicament and her deepest desire to be free of it. He said, "Disguise of every sort is abhorrent to me, but in this circumstance, I believe it might be our only salvation."

Elizabeth looked at him in surprise, although she supposed that she ought not be. He had said that he was thinking of a solution, and he must have meant it. She could have embraced him for the sliver of hope he offered, but she restrained herself.

He continued, "The room is dark and the curtains behind Bingley's desk reach the floor. Someone is certain to look for one of us, and when they eventually search here, they will find you, alone. I shall simply hide behind the curtains quietly until you leave."

As much as Elizabeth wanted the plan to work, she had to point out the flaws. "We could still be here for hours! What if they are searching for you? They will ask me about you."

He hesitated to reply, and she sensed his struggle. There would be nothing more to do but lie and say she had not seen him or some other misleading statement.

"You are clever and will think of something appropriate."

The last thing she had expected from Mr. Darcy was a compliment. "Thank you," she replied, although between the two of them, he was the first to think of a solution which might actually work. "You are clever, too."

Mr. Darcy laughed. "I do not feel clever right now, I assure you."

She smiled. They were not out of danger yet, but hope (and Mr. Darcy's humor) lent her cheer. "Nor do I." She twirled a curl around her finger, her neck warm under the curtain of hair. Her hair. As quickly as Elizabeth had relaxed, she panicked. Reaching up to pat what remained of her coiffure, confirming that the damage was just as bad as she suspected, she exclaimed, "I am a mess! What will they think when I am found?"

"That you were motivated to gain your freedom and use your hairpins to pick the lock."

She shook her head vehemently. "If I were truly alone, I would have merely sat in one of the chairs, perhaps fallen asleep to pass the time, and waited once it became clear that I could not escape otherwise."

"Can you not claim a fear of the dark or of confined spaces?

"I do not fear the dark or small spaces, Mr. Darcy, but I fear for my sisters' reputations and the bleak future that would cast upon us. My family and closest friends, of whom most are present this evening, all know this about me." And now, Mr. Darcy did too. She grabbed a lock of hair, twisted it, and tried to stuff it into place, but her rebellious waves refused to comply. "I never would have attempted to pick the lock and ruin my hair unless—"

"Unless you were trapped here with someone. With me."

"Do not flatter yourself, Mr. Darcy. I would have reacted the same way had I been trapped with anyone else."

He chuckled, as she had hoped he would. "I suppose that is some consolation." Rubbing his hands together, he looked toward the window. "If you stand closer to the light, I shall be able to see better how I might help."

Elizabeth felt her eyebrows raise. Was Mr. Darcy offering to arrange her hair? He did not appear to be teasing.

He must have sensed her skepticism. For the briefest moment, he looked down at the floor. Then, as though to defy his vulnerability, he straightened himself to his full height. But she had seen a new side to him, brief as it was, and it loosened what had been tight in her chest. "One of the few things that soothed my mother during her illness was to have her hair brushed. Her maid had so much to do to see to her care, I often took over the task." His defensive tone softened as he spoke. "When she passed away, I missed her so much, I offered to brush my sister's hair." He shrugged, as though the tender image he had shared was not the most endearing story Elizabeth had heard in a long while.

"I fear that what I require is much more than an expert brusher," she teased, appreciating his offer all the more for his embarrassment.

He folded his arms over his chest and grumbled,

"When Georgiana's hair grew long enough, I had the nurse teach me how to braid it. I braided it every night until her maid took over the task. I am qualified for the task."

Elizabeth pressed her hands against her heart. As much as she wanted to tease him about his expertise, she could not add to his discomfort. She imagined Mr. Darcy's thick fingers trying to smooth and twist his little sister's hair without snagging or tugging. It challenged every assumption Elizabeth had formed about Mr. Darcy. Did she know him at all? "Your sister must have appreciated the special attention from her older brother. That was kind of you."

"I am a poor replacement for our mother."

Elizabeth's lungs seized in sympathy. "Does Miss Darcy remember her?" she murmured. Oh, she hoped so. As troublesome as Elizabeth's own mother was, Elizabeth could not imagine her life without her mother's affection and concern. Perhaps Mama cared a great deal too much about her daughters' prospects and futures, but the fact remained that she cared.

"Our mother died when Georgiana was only a year old. My sister became the apple of our father's eye. She felt his loss intensely when he passed away five years ago."

Mr. Darcy's snub from the assembly lost some of its sting in that moment, and Elizabeth found it easier to overlook his proud, taciturn manners. She was not ready to forgive him completely, but Elizabeth felt the quickness and harshness of her own premature opinions. Although Mr. Darcy was still the proudest man she had ever met, he might not be as arrogant as she had believed him to be.

At that moment, Mr. Darcy was not the enemy. He was her partner.

Moving closer to the window, she turned so that her back faced Mr. Darcy and lifted her hair off her neck. "Is it very bad?"

It seemed like an eternity passed before he joined her at the window. His breath tickled the back of her neck, and she shivered even as heat spread over her skin.

CHAPTER 12

*D*arcy stood behind Elizabeth, the moonlight glowing off her exposed neck. Orange blossoms and cloves swirled around him, and the impulse to bury his face in her silken hair made him tremble.

He swallowed hard, reaching for a chestnut lock, his hand near her shoulder, when he saw her shiver and wrap her arms around her waist.

Darcy had not noticed the cold before, but he did now. Elizabeth had been in the study much longer than he had. She must be chilled to the bone.

Contorting himself to remove his torn coat, he wrapped it around her shoulders.

"Oh!" she exclaimed, then proceeded to burrow into his warmth in a way that made Darcy's arms itch to wrap themselves around her too. "I know I should not accept your coat, but it is deliciously warm. Thank you, Mr. Darcy."

"My pleasure," he choked, his voice low and gravelly, his body burning. His pleasure? A simple "you are welcome" would have been more appropriate. How had he thought that helping Elizabeth arrange her hair into something more decent was a good idea? Nothing about this situation was proper.

Shaking his head, willing the icy draft seeping through the sealed window to cool him, Darcy took a step back and focused on the task before him—the task for which he had foolishly and impulsively volunteered.

He cleared his throat. "No problem is without solution." His voice sounded strained and unconvincing in his own ears. He was exceptionally good at solving problems, so why was this so difficult? This was just like braiding Georgie's hair or brushing his mother's. He closed his eyes, pretending it was one of them standing before him. But Elizabeth's dark hair did not miraculously lighten to flaxen blonde, nor did she gain in height.

Stretching his arms out, careful to keep as much distance between them as he could, Darcy assessed the damage to her coiffure. Half was up; half was down. The remaining pins would have to make up for the loss of the others. If he braided some of the loose hair, he could wrap them in such a way as to support the rest. It was a simple matter of weight distribution.

Feeling more confident with his plan, Darcy wrapped the first curly lock around his fingers. It was softer than he had imagined. Gently, he divided the strand into three equal sections, combing his fingers through and pretending there was no intimacy in his action. It needed to be done; nothing more. But dash it all, her hair smelled good!

Gritting his teeth, Darcy proceeded.

Elizabeth's hair resisted his placations, seemingly mocking his efforts. He mumbled under his breath.

"You sound like Sarah. She claims that my hair makes her feel incompetent."

"I can sympathize." Georgiana's hair was smooth and fine and easy to plait, but Elizabeth's hair was unabashedly rebellious—not unlike the lady herself who defied society's expectations and, if he were being fair, *his* expectations.

Pinching the braid's end, hoping it would hold until he secured it into place, he twisted it around another loose lock and clamped it under the same pin, holding his breath all the while. "Does that feel secure?" His voice cracked.

She shook her head and hopped in place. "Impressive, sir. I shall only have to avoid the bouncier reels," she teased.

He grinned. He appreciated that Elizabeth did not dwell on adversity but chose instead to concentrate on the good, no matter how small. He had observed this during her sister's illness, with her family's many transgressions, and now with him. Even at the height of distress, Elizabeth's good humor was never far. As one who shouldered a heavy weight of responsibility, Darcy considered her levity a breath of fresh air.

Braiding another section, he wrapped and tucked

her hair as he had done the first. The process was easier now. He could do this. Look at how much he had done already. Only one section remained, and he had not made a scene or a cake of himself.

She sighed, and he felt her shiver under his fingertips. She could not still be cold, could she? She had remarked on the warmth of his coat. His warmth. Darcy stilled. Who was he kidding? He was every bit as affected by Elizabeth as he had been at the first touch of her satin curls, and until now, Darcy thought he had done an infernally good job ignoring it.

What about *her*? If her shiver was not from the cold, could he be the cause? To suspect that Elizabeth might not be impervious to his touch lit a fire in Darcy's stomach. This was most certainly *not* the same as brushing his mother's or sister's hair.

Moving in closer, telling himself it would make the work easier and therefore quicker, he braided faster, twisting it around the last chunk of hair, stuffing it inside the pin, and jumping away from Elizabeth as though she were the hot oven Cook had warned him not to touch.

Elizabeth patted her hair tentatively. "I do not think—"

The braid immediately unraveled. So much for his haste. *Blast.*

Plucking the pin from a tangle, Darcy placed the clasp between his lips and resumed braiding the last strand of hair, both thrilled and terrified at the sensations coursing through him. Fingers entwined thus, he heard the door rattle a split second before it flung open.

He jumped away from Elizabeth, dropping her hair and removing the pin from his mouth to hide behind his back, as though he were a lad caught stealing the last of the jam in the pantry. It was a stupid reaction, made much worse when his boot caught in Elizabeth's train, bringing the lady along with it.

Her arms flailed, and she made a noise guaranteed to secure the attention of whoever it was who stood in the doorway.

There was nothing to do but hold out his arms. Elizabeth's body slammed against his chest, her hair tickling his nose. Without a thought, he scooped her up. Cradled against him, her hand clutched his cravat. Her lips parted and her gaze collided with his, her dark eyes burning the last of his rational thoughts. Hang the witnesses, he would have kissed her right there had Miss Bingley's shrill scream not broken the spell.

"Mr. Darcy!"

Elizabeth stiffened in his arms. Loath as Darcy was to let her go, he gently set her down on the ground. They stepped away from each other, looking as guilty as a man and a woman caught in a tryst.

Hurst snorted. "I did not think Darcy had it in him!" His wife and sister-in-law glared daggers, to which Hurst raised the glass in his hand and drained the contents.

Darcy did his best to control his countenance, though he blazed with mortification. How many times had he managed to avoid this very kind of entrapment only to fall headfirst into an uncontrived but wholly incontrovertible compromise. Darcy struggled to maintain an indifferent mien when the blow to his pride stole the air from his lungs.

A familiar voice echoed through his mind, making his stomach clench and his throat tighten. *"Badly done, Darcy. Badly done."* His father uttered those odious words only one time. It had been the day Wickham figuratively threw Darcy in front of the burning carriage, betraying his confidence and casting their friendship asunder to avoid falling out of Father's favor and thereby threatening his allowance. Darcy heard the same disillusionment in his father's voice in his head as clearly as he had that wretched day.

Never before this night had Darcy been grateful for his father's absence.

Standing in the doorway was a small assembly: Miss Bingley, the Hursts, Mrs. Bennet, and the two youngest Bennet sisters, whose uncontrolled giggles would draw a greater crowd if not swiftly subdued.

That was not the worst. Standing in the back with widened eyes and a paling complexion was Mr. Bennet. Elizabeth's proud confidence wilted under her father's disappointed countenance.

Badly done, Darcy. Badly done.

Darcy was grateful for the darkness. Although neither he nor Elizabeth had done anything wrong, by the time they finally departed from that blasted study, everyone in attendance at Netherfield would know how they had been found. Gossip would circulate like wildfire. Vicious rumors would spread unless he met certain expectations. He must make reparation now.

Reaching for Elizabeth's hand, he wrapped his fingers around hers, squeezing to communicate that she could depend on him and his protection. He despised disguise, but he felt in his bones that this was the right course, the *only* course. To do anything less would lead to disgrace and ostracism.

Darcy turned to face Elizabeth. His next words would indelibly change their lives, and yet he spoke deliberately, decisively. "We can keep our engagement a secret no longer."

Perhaps he imagined her fingers chilling and stiffening, or perhaps the iciness in her grip had been there all along and he had only just noticed.

Elizabeth was too intelligent to pull away or protest, and she was too honest to force an insincere smile even when the circumstance merited one. But there was lightning in her eyes, and it cracked like a whip through Darcy, leaving him bewildered.

CHAPTER 13

*O*f all the high-handed, arrogant, presumptuous, imperial... Elizabeth's head filled with unfavorable adjectives. She had thought they were partners!

Well, Mr. Darcy might think he could determine her future without so much as a grain of consideration for her opinion, but she would let him know that he was the last man in the world she could ever marry!

She maintained her composure remarkably well, given her duress, and her awareness of it made her align her shoulders ramrod straight. Her jaw did not gape open, she did not tug her hands away, and she did not cry out.

Her eyes, however, blazed. The bewilderment on Mr. Darcy's face added fuel to the fire of Elizabeth's fury. As if he expected her to simper and submit mindlessly to his hasty solution! He did not know her at all if he expected meek compliance! Elizabeth refused to marry a man with so little regard for her own sentiments.

Miss Bingley swooned; Mrs. Hurst suggested that some mistake had been made. Elizabeth would have agreed with her, but rational thought kept her silent.

"Lizzy can have the disagreeable boor!" Lydia's merriment had quickly turned to jealousy.

"Hush, Lydia! Think of the pin money Lizzy will have! A house in London! The carriages!" Mama's voice echoed through the study.

Papa stepped forward. "I shall have a word with you, sir, and you, too, Lizzy, while the others return to the ball." Turning to Mama, Kitty, and Lydia, he added, "Not a word from you about this until I say so, or I swear on my life that you will never grace another ballroom." Before they could produce pouts, he turned to their hostess. "Miss Bingley, if you would be so kind as to have a candle lit."

Elizabeth knew she had done nothing wrong, but she wilted under the severity of her father's tone. How many years she had wished he would reprimand Lydia and Kitty in such a way! It pained her to be the receiver of his correction—all the more so when she was blameless.

Frozen in her stupor, Miss Bingley did not react until Mr. Hurst moved her along with his wife tugging her sister's other arm. "Bingley keeps his best brandy in the bottom drawer of his desk." Whether to drink in celebration or drown their sorrows, Mr. Hurst's words could be understood either way. Together with his wife, they pulled Miss Bingley down the hall. The others followed behind. Elizabeth prayed her mother and sisters would heed Father's threat.

Lydia whined. "If only John Lucas were here, I could use him to make the officers jealous, and I could have my pick from proposals."

"You do not mean that, Lydia. John is a nice boy, and it would be cruel to use him to make others jealous." Kitty's voice faded as they moved away.

A maid scurried inside, her eyes down, working quickly to light the sconces and adding burning coals to stir the fire to life.

Mr. Darcy did not fetch the brandy.

Papa motioned for them to sit. "I cannot speak for you, sir, but I know my Lizzy, and she is too clever to allow herself to be ill-used by a gentleman, engaged or not."

Elizabeth's shoulders relaxed with her exhale. Her father was not disappointed in *her*. He would not make her marry a man she did not love.

Mr. Darcy bit his lips together. Was he blushing? It was difficult to see in the candlelight. "I assure you, Mr. Bennet, that nothing untoward has happened, though all appearances suggest otherwise. My offer stands. I am prepared to spare Miss Elizabeth's reputation, but first, I believe you deserve a full explanation."

Papa nodded his head and settled deeper into his chair, his fingers steepled under his chin as he listened to Mr. Darcy's detailed narration of the events leading to their discovery. Not one emotion or opinion shadowed his stoic telling, though Elizabeth noticed how he edited certain details in her favor. Every time Elizabeth wished to interject a point, Mr. Darcy addressed it without any need for her to interrupt.

Why should a man she disliked so much be so in tune with her own thoughts? It was disconcerting.

Finally, he finished, and Papa leaned forward. "You did not think to prevent Lizzy from pulling out so many pins in the first place?"

Elizabeth cringed. "He did, Papa. Only I was too intent on escaping. I did not heed his warning."

Papa's eyebrows raised, and then he shook his head with a sigh. "And his coat? How do you explain that, Lizzy?"

Elizabeth had forgotten she was wearing it. Taking it off, she shoved it at Mr. Darcy. "Mr. Darcy noticed I was cold, and he lent it to me." Turning to the gentleman, who had yet to accept his coat, she said, "Thank you, but I am quite warm now."

"You are certain?"

Take the blasted coat! "Yes, sir, I am quite sure, I thank you."

His fingertips brushed hers, sending a contradictory shiver down her back.

He pulled away, leaving her holding his coat.

"Please, take it." The bull-headed Mr. Darcy crossed his arms, lowering his chin to glare at her.

"Not until the fire warms the room or we return to the ballroom."

Papa snapped, "For heaven's sake, take the coat!"

With his usual sarcasm, he added, "You have already secured a proposal and therefore have no need to suffer from a chill."

Elizabeth did not appreciate his humor when it was directed at her.

He nodded at the offensive garment. "Is that tear from your efforts to break down the door?"

Mr. Darcy nodded.

"You did notice that the hinges face the wrong way for such an exhibition of brute force to succeed?" Papa seemed intent on picking at every weakness of their actions when none of that mattered anymore.

"Nonetheless, I had to try." Mr. Darcy's tone carried no disdain. "I beg your pardon for pressing the matter, Mr. Bennet, but time is precious. Will you accept my offer and clear your daughter's name of all reproach?"

No! Elizabeth wished to scream. She crossed her ankles and tightened her arms around her, her eyes intent on her father, who seemed to be in no hurry.

Finally, he addressed Mr. Darcy. "Am I to trust the gentleman before me or the man who insulted my daughter and the greater portion of Meryton and Longbourn with his taciturn manners and insults?"

Mr. Darcy took in a sharp breath.

Hope rose in Elizabeth's chest, and she loosened her hold around herself. Surely Papa would not make her marry the very man who had affronted her vanity.

Her father continued, "If the latter is making the request, I shall have to reply with a resounding no. Lizzy is the light of my life and the joy of my heart. I could not give her away to a man who has made plain his disdain of her, her family, her friends, and her neighbors."

Elizabeth could hardly breathe. Pride for her father's outspokenness dueled with shock at his plain speech and Mr. Darcy's reaction. She had expected an outburst.

On second thought, this was stoic Mr. Darcy. He was not one to lose his composure. However, observing him now, she saw a man who appeared thoroughly chastened.

What would it take to make him show some emotion? Elizabeth wondered. Not that she would ever have to find out, given the direction her father had taken their conversation. Thank goodness.

Mr. Darcy slowly raised his head to meet her father's stare, his shoulders straightening but not to their usual stiffness.

Before he could speak, Papa pressed on. "However, if it is the former making this request"—he glanced at Elizabeth, who now sat frozen in place—"the same man who is willing to attach himself to a family beneath him to spare my girl's reputation in a situation not of his or her own making, who saw to her comfort and did not lose his patience when her exertions undermined his better plan, who did not once cast the blame on her during his explanation, and who placed himself at my mercy when he implied a secret engagement…"

Elizabeth held her breath. Mr. Darcy had done all

that, but could she give up her freedom to him? Papa looked at her then, tenderness in his eyes. Her throat tightened and her eyes burned.

"... then I give my consent along with my whole-hearted desire that you seek each other's happiness."

Mr. Darcy's exhale was audible. "Thank you, sir. I shall prove myself worthy of your trust."

What?! What was this?!

Papa rose from his chair. "I believe you will, and for that reason alone, I grant my blessing."

Elizabeth leaped to her feet. "Papa!!" Her heart threatened to burst out of her chest. "We could break off the engagement!"

The askance look her father gave her was one he usually bestowed on Lydia. "After you were seen alone in a dark room with his hands in your hair and you wearing his ripped coat?"

She could not give up yet. "We could allow everyone to believe this farce, then call it off. Something about not agreeing on the settlements. It happens all the time."

Now, his eyebrows rose to his hairline. "When your mother has ensured everyone knows he has a fortune of 10,000 pounds a year?" He turned to Mr. Darcy. "I apologize for my wife's outspokenness. It cannot be pleasant for a gentleman to have his affairs pronounced so publicly."

Mr. Darcy nodded, but he said nothing.

Elizabeth was quick to fill the silence. She had more arguments, and she would voice them. Turning to Mr.

Darcy, she asked, "I do not suppose you would agree to jilt me and marry another lady post haste?"

His eyes darkened. "How would that repair your reputation? People would assume you were in the wrong."

Elizabeth felt the ground crumbling under her feet. She was running out of options. "Because people always side with the gentleman—especially if he has 10,000 a year," she grumbled. Society was unfair. Why did it allow gentlemen to do as they pleased but considered the lady ruined?

Mr. Darcy straightened to his full height. "I am no happier at the injustice females must endure at the hand of a hypocritical society than I am to have my fortune so grossly underestimated."

There was the proud Mr. Darcy she knew.

Papa chuckled. Elizabeth wanted to hit something. "Your wealth means nothing to me."

He stepped closer to her, his tone softer. "I realize that you find a union with me repulsive."

That drew her eyes to him. The look she saw in his expression was humble, pleading, concerned.

Perhaps she was being too harsh. When he spoke again, she listened with a more open mind. "The damage has been done, and I shall spend my remaining days making what reparation I can. However, it is in your hand to save the reputations of your sisters."

The truth hit Elizabeth with the force of a battering ram. She would do anything to spare her sisters from ruin. If she did not act quickly, her sisters' prospects would be vanquished before they even departed from Netherfield. Given the scandal he would have to endure, it was not likely that Mr. Bingley would propose to Jane—especially with his sisters, who would do nothing to strain their friendship with Mr. Darcy. Elizabeth's refusal would mean the end for Jane, for her sisters, for herself. Not even Mr. Collins would have them. The fact that she would even think of him right then was proof of the desperation of her position.

There was no other option. Elizabeth would have to marry Mr. Darcy.

He extended his hand, and she numbly accepted it.

Dropping to one knee, he asked, "Miss Elizabeth, will you do me the honor of accepting my hand in marriage?"

He was sincere. Had the circumstances been any different, she would have found his gesture charming. At least, he offered the pretense of a choice. It made what could have been a heartless transaction—his name for her respectability—more palatable. More hopeful.

Taking a deep breath, Elizabeth swallowed hard and said, "I will."

CHAPTER 14

*D*arcy's face flooded with heat with all he had endured over the past few minutes. First, a father whose negligence exposed his family to shame had questioned Darcy's honor and called him to account for his ungentlemanly behavior. That the accusations were not unfounded struck Darcy to the core.

However, it was Elizabeth's reaction which crushed him. Was marriage to him so unpalatable that she would rather face absolute ruin? If not for her loyalty to her sisters, Darcy was convinced Elizabeth would have stood by her decision to refuse him. Him! A Darcy!

On one hand, he grumbled at her displeasure. He was hardly an ogre! On the other hand, he admired her. Elizabeth was a lady of high principles. She did not pretend an emotion she did not possess, nor was she swayed by fortune. Her respect and affection would be honestly granted… if he could earn them.

He rose to his feet, releasing her hand as he did, and the irony of their position nearly moved him to laugh. Of all the women he could be stuck with, it had to be the one who had posed the greatest threat to his plans.

Now she had ruined his escape to London. Throughout the recent events, Darcy had spared nary a thought for Bingley, Miss Bennet, or even Georgiana. He would have to be cautious lest Elizabeth distract him altogether from his purpose: to get Bingley away from the Bennets.

That was a problem he would wrestle with later.

First, he must convince a skeptical crowd of a secret engagement. Growing up with Wickham had taught Darcy that facts were useless unless people believed them. Appearance was everything. If he and Elizabeth won over the good opinion of the majority, nobody would doubt the veracity of their tale.

Mr. Bennet took his daughter's hands in his, pressing them against his chest. "It is a better beginning than most have, my dear girl. I will own that I am encouraged toward optimism. Both of you are of strong mind and character, and I have no doubt that if you direct your energies to work together, you will find a way to be content enough. Perhaps you will be happy, and you will think upon this moment with humor some day."

Darcy did not feel like laughing, but he appreciated

the attempt at lightheartedness. He could see where Elizabeth had learned it.

Moving away from his daughter toward the door, Mr. Bennet said, "I shall tell Mrs. Bennet the good news. She will be delighted."

It pained Darcy to be the object of that vulgar woman's delight. He dreaded the day Mrs. Bennet crossed paths with his aunt Catherine.

There was another detail he must share before Mr. Bennet departed and the curtains opened to Act One of his new life. "About that… there is something you must know which will undoubtedly add credibility to our sudden announcement."

Two sets of curious eyes regarded him.

Mr. Bennet said, "You have an evil twin who called my Lizzy 'barely tolerable' at first sight?"

Wishing he could turn back time and keep his surly thoughts to himself, Darcy replied, "No, but if part of a later conversation becomes as well-known as that ungracious comment, our sudden engagement will not be looked upon with so much suspicion."

Mr. Bennet cackled. "Good play, Mr. Darcy. I accept your chastisement and take your assessment as guarantee from your own mouth that henceforth no further ungracious comments will proceed from said aperture."

Poker references. How appropriate. Darcy felt the stakes rise. Once they left the study and returned to the party, he was all in. There was no going back.

Clearing his throat, he summoned every ounce of

bravado in his possession, and continued, "The night of Sir William's dinner, I made a favorable comment about Elizabeth—"

Did his voice have to sound so gruff? Darcy had been thinking of Elizabeth by her given name since Mr. Bennet gave his consent, but to hear himself say it aloud felt like a privilege he must earn. He cleared his throat again and pulled at his cravat. He could do this.

"—I praised Elizabeth to Miss Bingley."

He could practically see the wheels turning in Elizabeth's mind. She would assume this had happened *before* she had refused to dance with him, and given the humbling Darcy had received that night, he took greater pleasure in disquieting her than in preserving his own pride. "It was immediately *after* you refused to dance with me."

Elizabeth gasped. "What did you say?"

His assumption had been correct. With greater boldness, he continued, delighting in her shock. "I remarked that you have fine eyes and a pretty face."

"You said that to Miss Bingley?"

Darcy felt smug, and he did not bother to suppress it. "She presumed to know my thoughts. I merely informed her of her error."

"She must hate me." Elizabeth did not sound troubled. Her eyes gleamed, and her lips curled upward.

"She wished us joy."

"She was teasing, no doubt!"

"It is of no import. She knew I was not indifferent to you, and she jumped to the very conclusion we now need your friends and neighbors to accept. She cannot deny the exchange. She referred to it again only this afternoon."

Mr. Bennet clapped his hands in applause. "If people are going to talk, we might as well encourage them to speak in your favor. All it will take is a little nudge for someone present at the dinner to recall over-hearing your comment."

"My own mother will profess that she knew since that evening that a match was inevitable. But it is not true!" Elizabeth pressed her hands against her cheeks.

Darcy stiffened. If their story was to be believed, they must eliminate all doubt among themselves now. "Be that as may be, I assure you that it *is* the truth and that I spoke in earnest."

"You must convince everyone that this is a love match." Mr. Bennet rubbed his chin.

"Mr. Darcy is to play the love-struck suitor to me, the starry-eyed maiden?"

She did not believe he could do it. A sensation Darcy had not experienced since his rowing days at Cambridge surged through him. Elizabeth had thrown down a challenge, and he would meet it. He would win her over. He had to.

Darcy had never been bested when challenged—and winning Elizabeth's favor would be the greatest prize he could imagine.

CHAPTER 15

*B*ingley's newfound decisiveness bore remarkable fruit. Not only was his ball a smashing success, but he had also managed to dance once again with Miss Bennet. She was so lovely, so gentle and kind—a sharp contrast to his own sisters who treated him like an incapable little boy. Well, who was capable now?

He sipped from his champagne flute and reveled in his achievements as he took a turn about the room. Was this how Darcy felt all the time? Bingley could get used to it. He felt powerful, in charge, like a captain in command of his ship.

Speaking of Darcy, he had been gone for some time. Long enough for Bingley to dance with Miss Catherine, Miss King, Miss Lucas, and Mrs. Philips. He had not thought Darcy would endure Mr. Collins' for over a quarter of an hour, much less a whole one.

Guilt threatened to dampen Bingley's triumph, but

then he remembered himself. Darcy would not need anyone's assistance to escape unwanted company. Most likely, he had tired of the crush and was presently reading a book in the library, writing a letter in his room, or smacking the ivories in the billiard room.

As Bingley neared the refreshment table loaded with buckets of iced champagne, he realized he had not seen Mrs. Bennet for some time either. She was a lady whose absence could not but be felt, especially after a few flutes of the bubbly liquid.

Come to think of it, he had not seen Mr. Bennet either. Perhaps the gentleman had found a comfortable chair in the quieter library. He seemed more suited to books than to conversation and dancing.

Then Bingley saw his angel conversing with Sir William, Lady Lucas, and Miss Lucas. All further observations of the other Bennets present—or not—fled his mind. Like a moth to the flame, he drew nearer.

"I hope you are enjoying yourselves?" He took in Miss Bennet's pink cheeks, her soft eyes regarding him as though he were a gallant prince.

"I have never attended a ball its equal," she replied with a pretty smile.

Bingley sensed his chest inflate and determined to host many more balls.

He saw the tips of Caro and Louisa's feathered turbans across the room. His heart filled with gratitude for all their exertions planning and orchestrating the event—so much so that he forgave them the extra expenses of having so much of it brought in from

London. He waved, eager for them to join their party so he might share the credit where it was due.

The crowd parted and he saw Caro's face. Her eyes narrowed when she spotted him. She shot him a venomous look, and he regretted having made himself an open target.

Behind her, Mrs. Bennet waved a handkerchief. "Lady Lucas, I have such news for you!" She darted around Caro, looking as though she might burst with joy if she did not share her news quickly. She blurted loudly for half the room to hear, "Mr. Darcy and my Lizzy are to marry!"

Bingley felt his eyes widen and his jaw go slack. Opposite him, he saw Miss Bennet and Miss Lucas exchange a confused look. Caro looked like a tea kettle about to scream and blow steam. She glared at *him* as though he were to blame. What had *he* done? Darcy would never attach himself to a young lady unless he wanted to.

Granted, it was strange that he would propose so suddenly. Perhaps he had enjoyed Miss Elizabeth's debates more than Bingley had supposed? He pondered the matter for a considerable time, long enough for a crowd to press around their group and prevent Caroline and Louisa from leaving.

Bingley was about to go in search of his friend when Mr. Bennet joined them. Mutterings of, "Is it true? How can it be?" echoed in the gentleman's wake. Placing a hand on Mrs. Bennet's shoulder, a twinkle in his eye, he addressed Caro. "Evidently, the way to Mr.

Darcy's heart is through a pair of fine eyes, is that not so, Miss Bingley?"

Caro huffed.

Mrs. Bennet pounced at the compliment. "Did Mr. Darcy call my Lizzy's eyes fine?" She clasped onto Caroline's arm, making what would have been a difficult escape impossible without dragging the matron along.

Caro attempted to ignore her, but Mrs. Bennet was persistent. "I daresay there are no finer eyes to be seen in all of Hertfordshire, London even! My girls are always praised for—"

Caro interjected, "It is not uncommon for a gentleman to compliment a lady."

Mrs. Bennet clapped. "But to be complimented by a gentleman such as Mr. Darcy, who must be acquainted with a great deal of handsome women! For him to praise my Lizzy above them all is a compliment indeed! Such superior taste!"

Caroline twisted her face as she always had when the nurse forced them to take their cod liver oil.

Mr. Bennet nodded at her. "Your insight is to be praised, Miss Bingley. I have it on excellent authority that you were the first to suspect an attachment was forming in that quarter and had the sagacity to wish the couple well."

The high color in Caro's face drained to white. She mumbled, "I cannot seem to recall."

"It was at Sir William's dinner party the better part of a month ago," Mr. Bennet said with a smile.

Sir William, upon learning his role in his neighbor's daughter's successful match, added with an enthusiastic nod, "I suspected as much."

"As did I!" Mrs. Bennet added, not to be outdone.

Lady Lucas, not to be bested by her rival, said, "I overheard the conversation myself. Do you not remember me telling you about it, my love?"

"Well, that is old news, Lady Lucas," Mrs. Bennet interrupted. "You ought to have seen how my Lizzy despaired over leaving Netherfield Park once Jane recovered from her illness. I knew then that she must be in love, and with whom else but Mr. Darcy!?"

Bingley did not remember that, but he had been wrong many times before.

Once again, Mrs. Bennet clasped onto Caro's arm. "Miss Bingley, I surely have you to thank for bringing their engagement to light! Who knows how long they might have kept their engagement a secret had you not convinced Mr. Darcy to talk to Mr. Bennet!"

"But I—" Caroline's mouth closed and opened several times, but she seemed at a loss for words.

Bingley helped her. "She has been teasing Darcy about a lady's fine eyes incessantly. I did not know she referred to Miss Elizabeth, but it all makes sense now."

And indeed, it did. How had Bingley not noticed before? Caroline's jealous comments, Darcy's somberness every time the Bennets were mentioned... He had been quiet to conceal his secret!

It was then that Darcy walked into the ballroom with Miss Elizabeth on his arm. *Hm, was that a different coat?* They looked happy. To be sure, they made a handsome couple. They were similar in intellect. While he had witnessed their temperaments in frequent opposition, they did complement each other. Miss Elizabeth would lighten Darcy's sterner moods. Darcy would give her the security any young lady craved. Really, Bingley concluded, they were indeed an excellent match.

Furthermore, there could be no objections about Bingley courting Miss Bennet openly if Darcy considered her sister worthy of an offer of marriage. Yes, that suited Bingley rather well!

The crowd parted to welcome the happy couple.

Caro and Louisa decided that they required some punch and hastened away. Caroline's feathers seemed a little droopier but, given the warmth of the room and the lateness of the hour, saggy feathers and wilted blooms were to be expected.

Sir William elbowed Darcy in the arm, and he muttered something that made Darcy's cheeks turn crimson. He turned to Miss Elizabeth and smiled. She laughed, and soon Darcy did too, his smile wider than Bingley had seen since... since he could remember!

Good Lord, the man must be smitten! How had Bingley not noticed the depth of his friend's attraction before? All the conversations, debates, exchanges of opinions...

Of course! It was just like Cambridge. Darcy had always delighted in an intellectual conversation. Bingley had never understood his need to seek out such complicated discussions, but Darcy must have found his counterpart in Miss Elizabeth.

Bingley grinned at Darcy. Knowing his best friend would be happy increased his own happiness tenfold.

Smile wide, Darcy caught Bingley's eye and signaled for him to join him off to the side. As it always did, the crowd parted to allow Darcy passage. Once they reached the edge of curious onlookers offering their congratulations, Bingley clapped Darcy on the back. "Well done, old man! I wish you and Miss Elizabeth every happiness."

Darcy met his felicitations with a dangerous glint that made Bingley squirm. Why was he looking at him like that?

"Wickham was not in the study."

Oh, that man. Just the mention of Wickham was enough to put Darcy in a dudgeon. "I beg your pardon, but I never directly said he was. However, I must apologize for seizing an opportunity presented to me. You charged off so quickly, and I was desirous of dancing again with Miss Bennet, so I did not correct you. I considered the consequences as you had advised me and thought that the worst that would come of it was you being forced into conversation with Mr. Collins. You did not see him, did you?"

Come to think of it, the clergyman had been missing for some time. He was not still in the study, was he?

Darcy clenched his jaw shut, his muscles twitching.

Bingley understood that as a *no*. Still, this was a

night to celebrate, and he could not allow his friend's happiness to be marred by an unpleasant man who was not even present. "Pray, think no more of Wickham. I assure you, he is not here, at least, not that I am aware of. Tonight is an evening for rejoicing. You are to marry a remarkably clever young woman, and I have never seen you smile with so much feeling. So much for finding her intolerable, eh?" He laughed and elbowed Darcy in the side.

Another jaw twitch and a tense, "I am determined to be happy."

That was an improvement. "Then happy you will be. Anything you determine to do is as good as done."

If only Bingley could be so resolved. Seeing Darcy merry made Bingley wish for the same. He had made progress that night, but he still had a way to go.

If Darcy gave his blessing to pursue Miss Bennet, then Bingley could be completely certain. Taking advantage of their tête-à-tête, Bingley continued, "I say, there is a matter I should like your opinion on, now that you are engaged to Miss Elizabeth."

Darcy shot him a look. "You are the man of the house. Take charge. Think through the consequences of each action, decide on the path of most benefit to those dearest to you, and act without hesitation. It is not difficult. Now, if you will excuse me, I must return to my betrothed."

Bingley sighed in frustration, but he would not insist. Clearly, Darcy wished to be at Miss Elizabeth's side, and Bingley would not deprive him of that. He turned to the orchestra to ensure they played a lively tune.

That was when he saw Mrs. Nichols approach, wringing her apron. "Mr. Bingley, there is a matter—I believe I have succeeded in keeping it quiet—but you would do well to come with me and see for yourself."

Intrigued, Bingley followed her up the stairs to the resident's wing, doing his best to assuage her distress and placate her apologies.

When they reached Caro's door, Mrs. Nichols took a deep breath, pushed it open, and stepped aside.

Bingley poked his head through the opening, half suspecting to find a tiger or some other fearsome creature prowling in the shadows. He held his breath and stepped inside. It was too dark to see anything.

And then he heard it. It was not a tiger. "Dear Lord!" he mumbled.

The next few minutes was a hushed blur Bingley would rather not recall, but he muddled his way through creditably, or so he hoped. He simply followed Darcy's steps: take charge, think through the consequences, decide, and act.

Except thinking through things was not Bingley's strength, and he worried for a solid five minutes whether he had been as thorough as he needed to be.

CHAPTER 16

*D*arcy stood between Lady Lucas and Mrs. Bennet, in agony, his thoughts far from cordial. Not only had Bingley danced again with Miss Bennet, thus furthering expectations that a proposal was imminent, but Bingley had been the one to send Darcy to his blasted study and create this whole mess!

And did the man for a moment suspect his involvement? Not at all! His smiles were genuine, his felicitations sincere. Darcy had been perilously close to thrashing his friend and found it imperative to take his leave before he said or did something a lovelorn gentleman pleased with his fate would not do. How was he supposed to pretend to be enamored of a female who only married him because she had no other option?

Had Darcy been in possession of his full wits, he would have extracted himself from Mrs. Bennet's company. But Darcy was not, and so he endured her boasts until he could conjure a means to dismiss himself politely, which, given his present mood, was easier said than done.

"We shall celebrate two weddings at Longbourn before the end of the year! What a blessing Mr. Bingley's arrival has been for my girls!" Mrs. Bennet blinked up at Darcy. "I do not suppose he intends to invite any more of his gentlemen friends?"

Darcy was still reeling over her assumption that there would be two weddings. He shook his head and looked longingly at Elizabeth, who seemed to be enjoying a rational conversation with her father and her uncle Philips. Their eyes met, she shook her head with a smile, and with a nod in his direction, said something to her father. She probably took diabolical delight seeing Darcy stuck beside her mother. This could be a test.

Taking a deep breath, Darcy steeled his resolve and smiled at Mrs. Bennet. "If Bingley intends to invite more guests to Netherfield, I am unaware of it."

"No matter," Mrs. Bennet tittered, smacking her fan against his arm, the champagne she held in her other hand sloshing over the brim of her glass. "I daresay two weddings are more than enough for one year."

Miss Lydia and Miss Kitty ran in a circle around a group of officers, squealing and making a spectacle of themselves.

"Jane and Lizzy will do their duty by their sisters and put my youngest in the way of other rich gentlemen." Mrs. Bennet accented her lofty claim with a hiccup.

Not if Darcy had anything to do with it. He was more determined than ever to prevent Bingley from attaching himself to such a family before he had gained more command over himself and his household.

"Mrs. Bennet," Mr. Bennet took his wife's glass. "Shall I fetch you a glass of punch? It is rather hot in here."

"Thank you, my dear, but if there is more champagne, I would much rather have that."

"I believe punch is in order, and perhaps a plate of sandwiches."

"Oh, I do love a cucumber sandwich!"

"Then it is settled. Lady Lucas, may I fetch anything for you?"

The lady declined, using the opportunity to take her leave. While she had attempted to brag about her eldest son at university—the handsomest young man in all of Hertfordshire, according to Mrs. Bennet—Lady Lucas' daughters were unattached and therefore of no consequence to Mrs. Bennet.

Turning to Darcy, Mr. Bennet added with a twinkle in his eye, "Perhaps you would be so good as to accompany me. Lizzy said she was rather parched, and I have not hands enough to fetch refreshments for both ladies."

Darcy bowed his head. This was Elizabeth's doing. He did not consider himself deserving of her assistance when, only seconds ago, he had credited her with a vengeful motive. She was more forgiving than he was, a trait he was grateful for, given his previous behavior toward her.

He accompanied Mr. Bennet to the refreshment table, gladly dismissing himself from Mrs. Bennet, who had no trouble attaching herself to a new cluster of females over which she could preside. All the while, Darcy pondered how much he had yet to learn about the lady he was to marry.

APPEARING to be the enchanted maiden hurt Elizabeth's cheeks, but she kept smiling. She peeked over at Mr. Darcy, watching him struggle to maintain his stoic expression and dignified posture. He had lasted much longer in her mother's company than Elizabeth had expected. Then again, if his mind was as muddled as hers was, he was not fully aware of the conversation surrounding him. Still, she was not indifferent to his plight.

If Mr. Darcy could act like the attentive soon-to-be son-in-law of a woman he surely considered ridiculous, then Elizabeth would continue to smile. She would act like the understanding betrothed and spare him.

She whispered to her father, "I am certain Mr. Darcy would appreciate a reprieve. Perhaps you could offer to fetch Mama some refreshment and request his assistance?"

Papa complied, leaving her alone with Sir William, who was adept at carrying on a conversation with little help from her. Free to muse, Elizabeth reflected on what she had learned about Mr. Darcy.

She still could not believe he had bent down on one knee to propose. A real, proper proposal. Then, he had revealed his prior admission to Miss Bingley! Not only had he saved Elizabeth's reputation and that of her family, but he had done so in such a way as to grant her a greater degree of dignity. First he knew how to be charming, and now he could be gallant?

Mr. Darcy had everything to offer a lady seeking security, comfort, and position, and he selflessly bestowed it upon Elizabeth when she had nothing to offer him. Was he truly so selfless? So heroic?

She would not have believed it, given Mr. Wickham's tale of woe, but Mr. Darcy had poked gaping holes in the soldier's claims. Elizabeth could no longer give the story much credence.

She clearly understood much less of Mr. Darcy's character than she had thought. The gentleman she was engaged to was a stranger—a stranger with the surprising ability to make her stomach flutter.

Elizabeth had always dreamed of a deep and lasting love. She knew that, of all her sisters, she was the most difficult to please and would therefore be the least likely to marry. Her father might be proud of her strong mind, but it would not be praised by society. She was more likely to disagree with Mr. Darcy than not.

But she would make the best of their situation, as she always did. It gave Elizabeth hope to see that Mr. Darcy, at least for now, was trying to do the same.

Jane and Charlotte appeared at her side. "You will have a fine home, Lizzy," said Charlotte.

Jane scooped Elizabeth's hands into hers, her eyes searching. "But do you love him?" she asked softly. "I thought you did not even like him."

While Elizabeth could not truthfully reply to Jane's first question, she could address the second implication with confidence. "There is much more to Mr. Darcy than I previously gave him credit for." She glanced at him. His tall frame made him easy to locate in a crowded room. Papa and Mr. King flanked his sides, perfectly content to philosophize without requiring his participation. When Mr. Darcy's eyes met hers, she returned his smile. He looked down at the full glass in his hand, and she shook her head. Her thirst could wait to be quenched.

The exchange did not escape Charlotte, who looped her arm through Jane's. "You have always professed you would marry for love, and I have always wished you success in your endeavor. It pleases me to see evidence that you have found what you sought. Mr. Darcy is an exceptional gentleman."

Jane squeezed Elizabeth's hands. "And he has exceptional taste to fall in love with Lizzy above all others. Oh, my dearest, I am so happy for you!"

Elizabeth felt her cheeks warm. If convincing her sister and closest friend was this easy, nobody else would dare doubt the truth of her and Mr. Darcy's sudden engagement. His plan had worked. They would have to marry. There truly was no way out of it now.

Quick to consider the more pleasant consequences, Elizabeth focused on Jane. According to her mother, Mr. Bingley had danced with her again. If Elizabeth's betrothal smoothed the path for Jane and Mr. Bingley to marry, she was content. It would be a much simpler matter to create opportunities to put them in each other's company now that she was engaged to Mr. Darcy. They would still require chaperones, and who better than Mr. Bingley and Jane?

From the corner of her eye, she saw Kitty and Lydia approaching a band of officers. She did not wish to believe them so malicious that they would entrap her with Mr. Darcy. As much as she loved them, they were not clever enough to contrive a successful compromise. But she had to know.

Carefully phrasing her inquiry so as not to kindle curiosity, she asked Charlotte, "Have you made any astute observations worth sharing this evening?"

Charlotte smiled. "Your engagement eclipses all my observations. Although I cannot help but observe how dissatisfied Miss Bingley and her sister look. Also, Mr. Collins seems to have disappeared. I have not seen the gentleman in at least an hour."

"Much to the relief of every lady's toes! Is that all? You have learned nothing shocking to share with your dearest friends?"

"Nothing which you do not already know."

Those scheming, lying, vengeful brats!

Another dance was beginning, and Elizabeth slipped away before she could be claimed. Cutting a direct path over to her sisters, she tugged them away from the officers with a sharp, "One moment, please."

Pulling them to the dreaded edge of the ballroom where those in want of a partner sat, Elizabeth whisper-hissed over her sisters' protests. "Charlotte never asked you to meet me."

Kitty and Lydia unanimously pinched their lips shut. Oh, they were guilty. So guilty!

Elizabeth restrained herself from shaking them. "Why did you send me to the study?"

"We only wanted to dance with the officers, and that was the farthest room I could think of. It was Lydia's idea."

Lydia stomped on Kitty's slippered foot. "Hush, you ninny!"

Elizabeth took a deep breath and forced her clenched fists to loosen. She never would have believed her youngest sisters capable of arranging a successful compromise, but she had to know for sure. "You will tell me the truth Lydia, or I will keep you from your dance partners."

Lydia's eyes widened. "You would make me sit out a dance?"

"You would be in good company." Elizabeth nodded at the older women and shelved ladies sitting along the wall.

"You would not dare!"

Crossing her arms, Elizabeth looked sternly at her sisters. "Do not provoke me."

Jutting out her chin, Lydia finally replied, "I do not know why you are so cross. Who was I to know that you and Mr. Darcy had arranged a tryst?"

Elizabeth's face flamed. She could not correct Lydia and risk casting doubt on the tale when her family's honor hung in the balance.

"A secret engagement! How romantic!" swooned Kitty.

Elizabeth deeply wished to correct her. There was nothing romantic about her engagement.

"I only wanted to dance," Lydia pouted. "Kitty was supposed to send you to the book room."

"Book room, study, what is the difference? You said to get her away, and I did that, did I not?" Kitty plopped her fists on her hips, apparently having had her fill of Lydia's criticisms.

"You forgot, and now Lizzy is engaged before me! If John Lucas were here, I could have secured an engagement before the end of the night. You ruined everything, Kitty!"

"You and your haughty designs!" Kitty flung back.

Lydia stood taller. "Two officers more, and I shall have danced with every uniformed gentleman in attendance! Who has Lizzy danced with tonight? I am far more desirable than she is!"

Kitty rolled her eyes. "A fine accomplishment!" More seriously, as though the thought had just occurred to her, she added, "Between you, Lizzy's engagement, and Jane's success with Mr. Bingley, Mama will not nag about my cough. She will be in raptures for days!"

Just like that, the two were allies again.

Lydia giggled. "The look on Miss Bingley's face when we opened the door and saw Lizzy in Mr. Darcy's embrace!" She turned from Kitty to Elizabeth. "I heard her call you a hoyden."

Kitty patted Elizabeth's arm consolingly. "Better a hoyden than a harridan."

Her sisters fell into a fit of giggles, skipping away to join their partners.

They had no idea what they had done.

Had it all been one, dreadful accident? Was this to be how all Elizabeth's efforts on behalf of her family were to be rewarded?

She shook her head. No, she would not dwell on despair. This was an opportunity to encourage Mr. Bingley's attachment to Jane. There was no doubt that a union with one so lofty as Mr. Darcy would provide many advantages which Elizabeth could use to help others. She could pay for tutors for her sisters with her pin money.

The final couples scurried to take their places for the minuet. Mr. Darcy appeared, standing in front of her with a glass of punch. She took the drink. "Thank you, Mr. Darcy."

He bowed. "May I have the honor of this dance?"

He had a deep, soothing voice, and the intensity in

his dark eyes made it difficult for Elizabeth to swallow her punch.

Leaning a touch closer to her, she saw a spark in his eye when he said, "I trust that a minuet is calm enough for your coiffure."

Elizabeth grinned at the jest, reaching up to pat her hair gently with one hand and pressing against the strange fluttering in her stomach with the other. "You think of everything, Mr. Darcy." Setting her empty glass on a tray, she took his arm, and they joined the other couples. Sighs and whispers of "fine eyes" and "So romantic!" swirled around Elizabeth with the stir of ladies' fans.

Mr. Darcy danced gracefully, albeit silently. Several times he opened his mouth, then seemed to reconsider and close it.

After witnessing yet another failed attempt, Elizabeth took pity on him. "Do you enjoy the minuet, Mr. Darcy?"

He answered when the dance required him to step closer. "Pray call me Fitzwilliam."

Fitzwilliam, she tried in her mind, but she could not yet bring herself to say it aloud. Not yet. Once they were better acquainted, perhaps.

Mr. Darcy stepped back. "This dance is a favorite of my aunt Catherine. She appreciates its rigid formality." The ice now broken, he continued, "You are an elegant dancer. Did you learn from a master?"

She laughed. "Observation and imitation have been my best teachers. If I perform well enough, nobody is the wiser." He did not seem to know how to reply to that, so Elizabeth asked a question of her own. It concerned her how easily he was able to cover over their compromise. Was he much practiced in getting himself out of troublesome situations? "What is your opinion of disguise?"

"I abhor disguise of every sort," he snapped.

His abrupt change of manner took Elizabeth aback. Did he refer to her comment about pretending to be a more knowledgeable dancer than she was?

Softer, he added, "By disguise, I refer not to a person's sincere efforts to master a skill by their own initiative but to a person's purposeful deceit with the aim of misleading others to their harm." A deep breath. "It was a value my father upheld and by which I have attempted to live." He winced, and Elizabeth imagined she knew the painful direction his thoughts had taken.

He confirmed it on the next step forward. "I fear I am failing my father miserably this evening."

His understanding of her thoughts and revelation of personal history inspired Elizabeth to lighten his burden. "That depends. Was not your offer made sincerely, out of a desire to protect many from harm? That does not sound like the 'disguise' you described to me."

"Then what is it?"

She thought. "Mm, I would call it initiative, or… dare I say, heroic."

He barked a laugh, causing several heads turn in their direction. After a few minutes of bows and curtsies in the choreography, he said, "It is not my custom to wallow in misery or live with regrets. What is done is done. I hope you will join me in making the best of our situation."

Hardly the words Elizabeth had expected Mr. Darcy to utter, but they soothed her. Making the best of her situation was what she did best. "I would like that very much."

The rest of the minuet passed in such pleasant, easy conversation, Elizabeth began to believe she just might be capable of liking this Mr. Darcy.

CHAPTER 17

*D*arcy enjoyed dancing and conversing with Elizabeth, but the remainder of the ball was insufferable. He smiled and danced, all the while planning how to inform his family of his engagement.

He would write them that same night and send his letters by messenger at first light. They would know by tomorrow afternoon—this afternoon. Would this infernal ball never end?

His uncle Hugh and aunt Helen, Lord and Lady Matlock, would want to meet Elizabeth, and Darcy foresaw no difficulties in her passing their inspection.

However, he dreaded informing Richard. Darcy would rather tell him the whole truth of the matter, but to do so in a letter which could be lost or intercepted was foolhardy. If Darcy was not careful, his cousin would hop on his fastest horse and race to Hertfordshire. He would feel no compunction imposing on Bingley's hospitality so he might tease and torment

Darcy until he confessed the whole story just to shut him up. He must keep Richard at bay.

And there was Georgiana. Darcy could think of nothing worse than his heartsore sister arriving at Netherfield Park to see Bingley drooling like a lovesick puppy over another lady or potentially seeing Wickham. How might he prevent it?

Georgie would want to meet her new sister, and rightly so. London was a convenient distance to travel to Hertfordshire. If Darcy was not careful, his entire family would materialize here, and that must be avoided. The image of either of his aunts meeting Mrs. Bennet sent a cold shiver down his spine.

It took two reels and a cotillion before he settled on a plan which was both plausible and appeasing. He would simply beg Georgiana to return to Pemberley with her companion to ready the house for his new bride. Richard would accompany them for their safekeeping. Two birds with one stone.

As for his aunts, he would have to depend on Lady Catherine's aversion to travel and Lady Matlock's attentiveness to Georgie to keep them away.

Confident in the success of this strategy, Darcy slept soundly once the letters had been written and a messenger secured.

Maddeningly, he woke only a few hours later at his usual time. He lay abed another quarter of an hour past six trying to coax himself back into slumber, but it was not to be.

He had too much to think about: how to separate

Bingley from the Bennets, how to prevent Georgiana from meeting Miss Bennet, how to behave like a besotted suitor…

To continue abed was futile, so he rose and dressed. A quarter hour later, he descended the stairs and out to the stables to his saddled gelding, his greatcoat fluttering behind him like a cape.

He soon found the heavily trodden path upon which Elizabeth had made her way to Netherfield during her sister's convalescence. The day she had arrived with wind-blown hair curling wildly around her, cheeks heightened to a becoming hue of pink, her eyes bright with exercise, and her petticoats damp with mud— hardly the six inches Bingley's sisters claimed. Elizabeth had presented an impressive figure of one who loved nature and doted on her sister.

Darcy frowned. He doted on his sister too.

While it pleased him to have something more in common with his betrothed, he also recognized the danger their conflicting ends presented.

On what errand could he send Bingley away?

A gentle slope rose before Darcy, the sun peeking over its edge piercing through the dawn.

When he reached the top of the hill, there she was, walking alone up the other side, her bonnet hanging down her back, fog swirling around her skirts. He raised his hand to wave, certain she saw him when she scrambled to don her bonnet and tie the ribbons neatly at her chin.

He wished she would not bother. He rather liked her hair.

Darcy dropped his hand and tempered his smile. He had not meant it to be so grand.

Handing his horse to the groom who followed behind, Darcy stood beside Elizabeth. He tried to say something clever, but the harder Darcy tried to focus, the more she smiled up at him, and the more scattered his thoughts became.

It was Elizabeth who finally spoke. "You are out early."

He could have said that! "I might say the same about you."

She tilted her head. "Do you often ride before the household awakens?"

"Yes. I need the quiet before the obligations of the day take my attention."

"I imagine property as grand as Pemberley must demand a great deal of your time. Miss Bingley described it as a jewel among estates. She went into raptures when she described the rose garden."

Darcy cocked an eyebrow. He had a very different memory of Miss Bingley and his rose garden.

Flippantly, she added, "Evidently, Pemberley's gardens are beyond comparison, or my humble comprehension." Elizabeth chuckled. She cared naught for Miss Bingley's good opinion, a quality which would suit her well once she entered Darcy's circle with all its pomp and presumption.

"Miss Bingley does you little justice. My mother

redesigned the gardens to her liking. While I have yet to see their equal, I would never place a limit on your ability to comprehend any subject you desired to understand."

She smiled softly, and Darcy fairly burst with pride at having said the correct thing. He offered his arm, and they walked. After several paces she asked, "Even you?"

It took him a moment to catch her meaning. "You wish to understand me?"

"I have observed how damaging a lack of respect and communication is in a marriage, and it is my intention to understand you so that we might at least become friends." She twisted her hands together.

A small voice in his rational mind had feared she might wish to live separate lives—to reside in London, with a large allowance and all the city's entertainments to spend it on, while he returned to Pemberley. It was what most ladies in society arranged.

Elizabeth was different, and his heart leapt with this confirmation of it. "What do you wish to know? You may ask me anything."

She arched her brow. "Anything?"

The impertinent minx! He met her bold look. "I am not one to retract an offer once it is made."

"Checkmate, Mr. Darcy. I cannot argue against that. Very well... anything." She tapped her fingers against her chin and glanced askance at him, increasing Darcy's suspense.

When he thought he could hold his breath no

longer, she said, "I would like to hear of your childhood at Pemberley. Did you ever get into mischief?"

Relief added volume to his laugh. If only she knew half the antics he and his cousins practiced! "Quite often."

She narrowed her eyes in disbelief, rousing Darcy's determination to prove he was more than she presumed him to be. "My father claimed he had no gray hair before I was born."

"I take it he had only a light dusting of gray, perhaps at his temples?"

She had guessed correctly, but Darcy would be the last to admit it. "He called me to his study at least once a week."

"On whose authority am I to believe such a claim?"

"Certainly not my own," Darcy teased in turn. "If Richard were here—he is my cousin, dear friend, and fellow conspirator in mayhem—he would describe some of our exploits with alacrity."

She smiled. "I think I will like this cousin of yours."

"Five minutes in your company will be enough to secure his loyal friendship."

"That is either a compliment of my character or a criticism of his."

"Oh, I never speak ill of my relations."

"No, that is a condescension best saved for strangers at an assembly." Elizabeth looked as though she regretted the jab as soon as it crossed her tongue.

Darcy would have none of it. He *had* behaved abominably, and he enjoyed her teasing too much to allow it to end. "I made you feel the brunt of my ill-temper that evening, and for that I must beg your pardon. My mother would have chastised me thoroughly, and my father would have lost no time summoning me to his study for a well-deserved lashing."

She fiddled her fingers and chewed on her lip. After several moments of hesitation, she said, "It is a rare father who holds his own son to such a high standard. Did he not require the same of all the children in his household?"

Wickham. Father had entrusted his steward to discipline and guide his own son, and Wickham was deceptively sly.

Clenching his jaw, he looked her in the eyes. "My behavior gave you an unfavorable impression, and I pray you would please forgive me. You have had little reason not to believe the worst of me, especially in contrast with one whose manners are designed to charm and flatter." He did not want to speak any more of Wickham, but he wanted—no, needed—to know if Elizabeth still believed that man's slanderous lies.

She spoke slowly. "You said that there was much more to your history with him."

Pressure built up inside Darcy. If she required the whole truth now, he would tell her.

He felt her fingers brush against the forearm of his coat. "Mr. Darcy, I am not a person for whom patience comes easily, but I shall not force your confidence. Trust takes time. I shall wait until I have earned yours."

Darcy whooshed an exhale of intense relief.

She continued walking, and Darcy kept pace, his step lighter.

"I shall accept your apology on one condition," she turned to him, her serious face contrasting with the devilish gleam in her eyes.

It took Darcy a moment to recall what he had apologized for. He tensed, dreading that she would attempt to take advantage of his generosity, as so many others had done. He so badly wished her to be different!

"All will be forgiven," she continued, "if you tell me about your sister."

His boot squished in a puddle, oozing up the side of his foot. What had Wickham told her about Georgie? Darcy would thrash him as he had wanted to do at Ramsgate!

Elizabeth added in a jovial tone, "I already have four sisters. If I am to have another one, I should like some reassurance that Miss Darcy is as serene and sweet as Jane. Truly, I cannot imagine her being any other way, but I shall attempt to be a good sister to Miss Darcy. It would help me a great deal if I knew something of her character."

Darcy weighed his words carefully, unsure what Wickham might have told her about Georgiana. "My sister was loved dearly by our father, more so because she never knew our mother. She died of a fever only a year after Georgiana was born."

Elizabeth clutched the collar of her coat closer.

"Losing her must have been devastating for you and your father."

It had been. Darcy's anger waned at the memory of his mother, but not enough to take away the bitterness in his voice. "A young lady such as Georgiana is often sought out for the advantages she can grant those she favors. My sister has suffered more than her fair share of betrayal by false friends she thought she could trust."

Elizabeth's hand tensed around his arm; her lips pinched. "A pox on the selfish louts who disappoint an innocent orphaned girl!"

Her spirited invective calmed Darcy's ire. If Wickham *had* spoken against Georgiana, Elizabeth chose not to believe him. "I shall not allow anyone or anything to hurt her again."

Elizabeth caught his gaze, boldly meeting it with her own. "Neither shall I."

She meant it, he could tell. She would protect a girl she had not yet met based solely on Darcy's word.

Would she defend her so valiantly when she realized that Georgiana was a rival with Elizabeth's own sister for Bingley's love? That was a conversation for *another* day.

Darcy craved Elizabeth's lightness and humor. Talking about himself had caused this solemn turn, so he must shift the conversation. "What of you? Were you given to mischief as a girl?"

"In a way." Her smile returned. "I was permitted to play out of doors, climb trees, stomp through puddles, and swim in the streams."

153

Darcy imagined her traipsing around with tangled hair, scraped elbows, and muddy hems.

"When it rained, my father allowed me to read anything I fancied in his book room. At first, I read for fun. By the time Lydia was born and it became apparent that no heir would appear, I turned to more practical subjects. I spent hours poring over his tomes, convinced that if I learned enough... oh, I don't know what I thought. In the end, I was only a girl, not the boy he needed to break the entail on our property and keep our home."

"But you did not stop reading?" He knew she had not; her intellect was proof of extensive study and enterprise.

"Like you, I needed solace before the needs of my family demanded my attention. Having five daughters with no prospects and an estate he would lose, my father changed. He could do anything he put his mind to, but he lost the will to try. My mother became more anxious than ever before." She shook her head and smiled. "Reading became my escape, as did my early morning walks."

No wonder Elizabeth prized her independence. It was all she had which was truly hers.

Darcy was not ready to arrive at Longbourn, but the house seemed to have dropped down from the sky right in front of them. His mud-caked boots were the perfect excuse to avoid entering lest he sully the carpets.

He was about to beg his leave when the door burst

open to reveal Mrs. Bennet. "Mr. Darcy! How good of you to see Lizzy safely home, though I am not surprised. Young people in love always find a way to be in each other's company." She waved them in enthusiastically. "You must come in! We have cake and punch."

Darcy looked down at his Hessians. They were beyond the help of the boot scraper beside the door.

Miss Kitty emerged behind her mother. "Hill will see to your boots, Mr. Darcy. We have cake! Cake and punch!"

Miss Lydia pushed her sister out of the way with an unladylike snort. "Only take care Hill does not lose them. He lost Mr. Collins' boots, as you remember." As she moved back to the house, she added, "Now, that is a reason to celebrate! Mr. Collins is gone, and we shall not have to endure his boring readings from those dreadful sermons!" She wailed with laughter.

Miss Mary looked up from her book. "It is irreverent for you to celebrate a clergyman's departure or malign Fordyce's sermons. I find them both edifying and instructive."

"You would," Miss Lydia mumbled.

Mrs. Bennet evidently deigned Mr. Collins' departure worthy of explanation. "He left before dawn saying his patroness Lady Catherine de Bourgh required his assistance, but that is hardly an explanation, is it? He was going to propose to Li—oh, to no one in particular, but I had hoped he would propose to one of my daughters. Mary would suit a clergyman quite well, do you not agree, Mr. Darcy?"

She did not pause long enough to hear Darcy's opinion, which was for the best. Mrs. Bennet would not have been happy with his view of the matter. With a shrug, she continued without taking a breath, "Tis no matter. You are here, and Mr. Bingley dotes on my Jane. You will dine with us tomorrow evening, will you not? Mr. Bingley accepted my invitation last night, but I do not suppose he has had occasion to mention it to you, the hour being so early."

Drat. While he had been busy writing letters, Mrs. Bennet had undermined Darcy's purpose before he could even create an effective plan. The longer he had to wait, the more difficult it would be to separate Bingley from Miss Bennet.

CHAPTER 18

"*T*is a pity Hill did not misplace Mr. Darcy's boots, or he would have stayed longer." Mama sighed.

Elizabeth suppressed a smile. How quickly an engagement altered her mother's opinion of a gentleman she had once deemed disagreeable!

"He is serious and dull." Lydia rolled her eyes. "I shall do much better."

"All gentlemen should be so dignified and solemn."

"Thank you, Mary." As Lydia launched into an explanation of why regimental officers were far superior companions than Mr. Darcy, Elizabeth reflected upon her own changing opinion of the gentleman.

If Mr. Darcy was given to gravity, he certainly had reason for it. He had shared his sister's sufferings, but had he not suffered too, and to a greater degree? He had been old enough to know and love his mother. He had understood his father's grief, had no doubt admired him and counted on him for guidance, only to lose him too, and so shortly after reaching his majority.

Mr. Darcy had spoken of heartbreak, disappointment, betrayal—always in reference to his sister—but Elizabeth had felt the tension in his arm, heard the strain in his tone, and seen the hurt in his eyes. Whatever Mr. Wickham had done beyond squandering his inheritance and lying about it must be truly reprehensible. All the clues led Elizabeth to guess that Mr. Wickham had somehow deceived Miss Darcy. If her intuition was correct, he was truly vile to speak against the young lady, calling her spoiled and as haughty as her brother.

Elizabeth had taken an instant and undeserved liking to Mr. Wickham. She had also judged Mr. Darcy harshly. Yes, he was proud, and his discomfort in company could easily be mistaken for arrogance. But he had proved under great duress and on more than one occasion that he was perfectly capable of gentlemanly behavior. He had been nothing but kind to her despite the adversity of their unwanted compromise. Not once had he accused her or implied she had manipulated events to her favor, although it was plain that all the advantage was hers.

He must understand her personality better than she understood his, a rankling realization for one who prided herself on her ability to judge others accurately.

She would make up for the disparity and gain the upper hand over Mr. Darcy. She would exert herself to see him without the taint of her original prejudices. He said she could ask him anything, and she would take him up on that offer. When she finally met Miss Darcy, Elizabeth would treat her as dearly as she did her own sisters. She would—

"Lizzy? Why do you smile at the wall like that when you know that paper has caused me no end of suffering? It is horrible and ugly and should not be smiled at!" Lydia turned her attention to Mama. "You cannot expect an officer to propose in a room with such old, unfashionable paper."

Elizabeth felt eyes on her and realized Jane was watching her. Had she truly been staring at the wall with a stupid grin? Jane's knowing smile confirmed it. Elizabeth reveled in plotting how to best Mr. Darcy, but she had not thought her glee so visible.

"I am so happy for you, Lizzy," Jane said.

Elizabeth bit her tongue to keep from correcting her sister. She was not in love with Mr. Darcy. He had improved from offensive to intriguing. It might be a promising start, but it was hardly love.

Now if only she could see Jane looking out windows starry-eyed for her Mr. Bingley. Mr. Darcy was distracting her attention, but she must not forget Jane!

How could Elizabeth be truly happy unless she knew her dearest sister was settled with the man she loved? Elizabeth must not lose sight of her aim, or she would risk missing the goal entirely.

THE FOLLOWING morning began on a promising note in the form of a hastily scribbled message from Richard.

Darcy sipped coffee as he read.

"CAN I not leave you unsupervised for an instant, Darcy? Certain remarks in your letters about a certain young lady had aroused my suspicions that your heart was not as untouched as you prefer everyone to believe, but it is clear that even I had underestimated the depth of your ardor.

You will be pleased to know that your joyous news was received with the appropriate jubilee from my mother and the adequate degree of skepticism from my father. He expects a visit from our aunt Catherine, which might explain his temperance.

Speaking of Her Imperial Ladyship, how wise of you to propose to a young lady unknown to Aunt Catherine and is not well known enough for her to use her connections to secure an introduction. Well done, Darcy! Should I marry below the expectations of our family, I shall trust you to advise me.

Pray take no offense at my remark, but allow me to express my heartfelt gratitude. Your willingness to bear the brunt of our family's disapproval may provide me with the possibility of marrying for more than a fortune. I am indebted to this bewitching Miss Elizabeth.

Georgiana is as hale and happy as I have ever seen her. Between Serafina's kittens and the news that she will shortly gain a sister, Georgie has emerged even more from her nervous shell. With Mother's help, she has already written a letter to Mrs. Reynolds with instructions.

We shall start our journey on the morrow. It is taking longer to depart than I had hoped, however, I believe you will find the arrangements I have made satisfactory. Georgie is eager to meet your Miss Elizabeth. As am I."

DARCY RELAXED against the cushioned chair. Good, they were already on their way to Pemberley. It was one less worry when the dinner at Longbourn that evening would require all his concentration.

DARCY'S FRUSTRATION mounted during dinner. The food was good, if not excellent. The furnishings in the dining and drawing rooms were no doubt relics of Mr. Bennet's family, well made and well maintained. Their simple elegance was spoiled—no doubt, by Mrs. Bennet—as every surface was littered with trinkets and each upholstery was covered with lace. Such a mixture of quiet refinement and gaudy extravagance reflected the personalities of the lackadaisical squire and his nervous wife. What Mr. Bennet lacked in initiative, his wife supplied with an excess of enthusiasm.

Darcy imagined what it would have been like to have been brought up in such a household of extremes. He could only think more highly of the two eldest Bennet sisters for their even tempers and good sense.

He could even sympathize with Miss Mary's pious views. It would take a saint to live amidst such clashes of character.

Of the two youngest Bennets, Darcy found little to approve, though he found it difficult to imagine how they could be any other way under such guidance. Mrs. Bennet seemed to think that marriage was the solution to every question. One plus one? Marriage. What is the purpose of man? Marriage. How to restore peaceful relations between warring countries? Marriage.

She single-mindedly arranged the table to her purposes, despite Darcy's and Miss Bingley's best efforts. Had Richard been there, Darcy had no doubt that Mrs. Bennet would have sat him in the middle of her three youngest daughters.

Had the matron's interference been the only obstacle Darcy had to deal with that evening, he could have bested her, but Elizabeth continued to be a powerful opponent. If conversation between Bingley and Miss Bennet faltered, she was quick to bring up a topic certain to guarantee several more minutes of agreeable discussion.

When the gentlemen joined the ladies in the drawing room, Darcy immediately engaged Miss Bennet in conversation. He also drew Miss Mary into their debate to occupy the seating available in that corner of the room, thus preventing Bingley from making himself too comfortable at his "angel's" side. Bingley had hovered around them like a vexed bee.

It was with some satisfaction that Darcy observed

his small victory... until Elizabeth approached him. Her smile warmed him even though the glint in her eye made him wary. "Would you be so kind as to turn the pages of the music so I might play, Mr. Darcy?" She tilted her head toward the pianoforte.

He could not refuse without appearing contrary. Returning her smile, he reluctantly complied. He followed her to the instrument, where she settled on the bench and straightened the pages in front of her. Poising her fingers over the keys, she flashed a brilliant smile that Darcy understood as an expression of her self-congratulation. It made his heart trip in his chest all the same. She was not making this easy, but her feminine wiles would not divert him from his objective.

Darcy turned his attention to the pages, following along as Elizabeth brought the notes to life. When she added her voice to the melody, he sucked in a breath. Her song was velvety rich. Any want in her technique was overshadowed by the passion with which she threw herself into the music and the delight she stirred within her audience. He flipped a page and risked a glance at Elizabeth.

Her eyes were closed. They stayed closed.

Every note was played from memory, and Darcy would have admired her natural skill more had it not been at the detriment of his plans. He glanced over at Bingley and Miss Bennet. They sat beside each other, Bingley leaning as close to her as he dared.

Mrs. Hurst and Miss Bingley glowered from under

the pile of music sheets Mrs. Bennet had piled on top of them with insistent pleas that they play next.

All the while, the calculating minx at Darcy's side performed the piece she had selected with as much spirit as she possessed, which was a great deal. He had forgotten to turn the final page when she lifted her fingers from the keys. She raised her chin to smile at him once again with a knowing glint in her mischievous eye.

He bowed his defeat. For now.

Had they not been at such cross-purposes, Darcy would have admired Elizabeth's skill more. But she stood in the way of his sister's happiness, and for that, he must succeed. With Miss Bennet's beauty, she would attract other gentlemen, gentlemen better suited to matrimony than Bingley.

Once Darcy and Elizabeth were wed, he would encourage her to invite Miss Bennet to London. She would not remain single through an entire season, Darcy would wager. If she lured the heart of a titled gentleman, she would be better off than with Bingley, anyway. Surely Elizabeth would prefer her sister to be accepted in the first circles to which she herself would belong. Darcy was doing her and her family a favor— or so he told himself.

Thus the evening proceeded, a dance of victory and defeat in which Darcy and Elizabeth took turns advancing and turning about like fencers at a competition.

Bingley's obligation to entertain the Bennets ought

to have ended. However, Mrs. Bennet hinted so pointedly at how lovely Netherfield Park's drawing room must be and how favorable it was for hosting a party that he had seen fit to ignore his sisters' discouraging comments and warning looks. He invited the Bennets for tea the following afternoon.

To her credit, Miss Bennet seemed troubled at the ease with which Bingley imposed upon his sisters. After all, it did not befall *him* to plan the afternoon's menu and entertainments.

The pinched look Bingley's sisters had focused on Mrs. Bennet for the greater part of the evening now turned in unison against their brother. Miss Bennet insisted that she would not dream of inconveniencing them so soon after they had hosted a ball, ignoring her mother and younger sisters, who made it plain that they held no such reservations.

Miss Bennet's consideration and appreciative praise for hosting the most majestic ball of her lifetime put Mrs. Hurst and Miss Bingley in a difficult position. They gobbled up her praise like hungry hounds while keeping their noses raised at the appropriate level of condescension.

Bingley, however, could see nothing beyond his desire to spend more time in Miss Bennet's company. His interest was selfish. For that reason, Darcy took solace in his justification to keep them apart.

CHAPTER 19

*D*arcy paced. He and Bingley were to depart for London to meet with Darcy's secretary that day. A draft of the marriage contract had already been drawn to Darcy's specifications. Though Darcy trusted his attorney to adhere faithfully to the sums and terms detailed to him, the contract presented an opportunity to roust Bingley from Netherfield.

One hour remained before the time agreed upon to leave, and Darcy had nothing to do but wait.

He settled into the library with two books which had arrived in the morning post. One look was enough for Darcy to recognize his sister's selections. He probably would hear about her missing books in her next letter; she could not have meant for them to be sent to him in Hertfordshire when she ought to have received them at Matlock House. Had she and Richard departed for Pemberley yet? Surely, they would not delay over the trifling matter of two misplaced novels.

Darcy held one up. *Self Control* by Mary Brunton. Darcy flipped open the cover, seeing that the tome he held was a second reprint. He was not surprised. Before leaving London, he had heard talk of this tale: a devout heroine who escapes from the clutches of a morally inept rake bent on spoiling her innocence and virtue. Why Georgiana would choose to read a tale uncomfortably similar to her own was beyond Darcy's comprehension. He only hoped the vile devil had a satisfying end while the heroine went on to live a happy and fulfilling life.

The other novel was written by A Lady. It was not as wildly popular as the other, but the description the bookseller included promised a story of two sisters who overcome opposition from greedy relations and nefarious rakes to marry for love. Such heroines were bound to be handsome and marry above their station and into a fortune. Darcy held out the hope that at least one of the Dashwood sisters might be clever.

The latter being more suited to his tastes, he turned open the first page, ready to switch books at the first hint of foolishness.

He took an instant dislike to Mr. John Dashwood and his greedy, odious wife. He sympathized with Miss Elinor Dashwood when she masked her depth of feeling for Mr. Edward Ferrars to her mother and sisters in a sensible attempt to protect her own grieving heart after the recent loss of her father. He rolled his eyes at Marianne's youthful romantic notions and applauded her mother when she said,

"Remember, my love, that you are not seventeen. It is yet too early in life to despair of such a happiness." And he cursed the injustice when the Dashwood women forever lost their home. He could not imagine having to leave Pemberley with no hope of ever returning.

The Dashwoods had just arrived at their new home at Barton Cottage where they were certain to meet a cast of new, intriguing characters when Miss Bingley entered the library. She sashayed over to her brother's scantily stocked shelves, pretending to search for a book. In reality, she just trailed her fingers over the leather spines and watched Darcy like a hawk circling in the sky looking for an advantage.

Darcy raised the book in front of his face, resenting her interruption. A Lady was an accomplished writer and engaging storyteller.

"*Sense and Sensibility*," Miss Bingley read aloud, now standing close enough to reach for the second book on the table. "*Self Control*." She swatted at his shoulder. "Fine traits, to be sure. Are you seeking to improve yourself through extensive reading, Mr. Darcy?"

He raised his eyebrows. Did she think they were books of sermons?

She continued, "I hardly think you need to improve in either sense or self-control, though I hope you recommend them to Charles. He has neither quality where Miss Bennet is concerned." She sat in the chair beside him, leaning forward and glancing at the open door. "What are we to do?"

Darcy wished he knew. But he was not desperate

enough to enlist Miss Bingley's assistance when he had already succeeded in convincing Bingley to accompany him to London. "You forget I am to marry the second Miss Bennet."

She huffed. "But you can escape to Pemberley. You shall only have to endure one yearly visit from her dreadful relatives, and your property is large enough to avoid their company."

He rose to leave the room, undesirous of occupying the same space as a bitter lady with disappointed ambitions disparaging the family into which he would marry.

She did not take his hint. "If Charles marries Miss Bennet, I shall have to endure daily visits from her horrible family. Oh, if only we could stay in London for longer than a day! I know Charles. He would forget Miss Bennet within a fortnight."

A fortnight. The banns would be read on Sunday, and the countdown to his wedding day would officially begin. He had fifteen days. Fifteen days to separate Bingley from the source of his current infatuation. Fifteen days to secure Georgiana's future without threatening the potential in Darcy's. It was a monumental task to undertake. Should he enlist help?

Before Darcy could contemplate the advantages of including Miss Bingley in his plan—the disadvantages being immediate and obvious—there was a muffled tap at the door. Bingley's butler stood in the open doorway. "Guests have arrived, Miss Bingley."

She sighed, her cheeks puffing out in exasperation.

"I suppose we cannot avoid the locals entirely. How tiresome." She made no attempt to rise but instead took another bolstering breath.

The butler added, "I took the liberty of showing Colonel Fitzwilliam and Miss Darcy into the parlor for tea. Mr. Bingley and the Hursts are already with them."

Miss Bingley jumped to her feet with an unbecoming squeal. "Why did you not say so immediately?!"

While she chastised the butler, Darcy stood in stunned, frozen silence, his plans for London vanishing. Why were they here? Had some disaster befallen Georgiana?

Awakening from his momentary reverie, he brushed past Miss Bingley, who would rather criticize her butler than welcome her unexpected visitors, no matter how delighted she claimed to be to receive them. Darcy only just kept himself from breaking into the parlor at a run.

Remembering himself, he composed his face into one he hoped conveyed happy surprise rather than the panicked concern rushing his steps.

CHAPTER 20

*G*eorgiana cradled Serafina in her arms.

Bingley stood beside her, leaning as close as a friend ignorant of his effect on the young lady would, talking gibberish to the cat and stroking her fur. Georgiana looked up at him adoringly. Darcy's panic turned to dread. Her infatuation had not weakened.

Richard stepped forward. His lips curved upward, but there was no smile in his eyes.

Darcy shot him a glare, which Richard acknowledged with a grave nod. He would explain later.

Satisfied on that point, Darcy opened his arms and called to his sister, who had yet to notice that he had entered the room, so fixed was she on Bingley. "Georgiana! You have taken us quite by surprise!"

She set Serafina down by a basket at her feet—a basket which rocked and squirmed like a living thing—and bounced into his arms. "You are not vexed, are you,

William? Mr. Bingley assured us that we are most welcome."

Darcy refrained from objecting to her unfavorable comparison of himself to Bingley. If he understood why they were here instead of on their way to Pemberley, then he would know better how to proceed. Perhaps he could get some of the story now, enough to satisfy him until Richard explained further. "I am trying to puzzle how you escaped from Aunt Helen."

"Oh, but she was the one who insisted that I accompany Richard!" Georgiana stepped away from Darcy—closer to Bingley—and smiled sweetly.

Darcy caught Richard's expression, the bunched mouth and furrowed brows. Had caring for a sixteen-year-old girl not yet out in society been too much for his aunt? Aunt Helen had been blessed with three boys, all now grown adults. Her only daughter was her eldest son's wife.

"Too much youth in the house," mumbled Richard, the corner of his lips flinching.

Darcy still did not understand. Aunt loved children. She had made it a point to impress upon her sons, and by extension Darcy, their obligation to produce offspring. She had a chest full of embroidered christening gowns waiting to be opened. Her oldest, Frederick, had only recently wed. The youngest, Edmond, had taken over the parish church at Kympton two years ago. It was Aunt Helen's greatest grievance that despite her best efforts, both Edmond and Richard remained single.

Bingley bounced on his toes, his grin too wide by half. "I can think of no better way to improve the day than for my dearest friends to meet the new friends we have made in Hertfordshire."

Darcy could imagine nothing worse.

Even Mrs. Hurst looked dubiously at her brother. Miss Bingley's sneer was marred by a violent sneeze. Serafina rubbed against her skirts, wrapping her tail around Miss Bingley's leg and purring up at her for attention.

Georgiana clasped her hands under her chin. "Serafina has singled you out as her special friend."

Miss Bingley sneezed again, her voice nasal when she spoke. "I am honored, to be sure."

"Then you will love her kittens. They are nearly six weeks old!" She bent down to the basket and tipped it over to reveal three balls of fur.

Georgiana frowned, her gaze darting about the room, searching. "There ought to be four. Oh, goodness, there you are!" She crossed the room to the silk curtains adorning the bay window overlooking the garden. A mottled tabby hung there partway up the fabric. When it saw Georgiana approaching, it yowled either to plead for help or to boast about how far it had climbed.

"Are you stuck, you naughty boy?" Georgiana carefully pulled the drapery off his claws and settled him on the floor, where he immediately darted to the opposite corner. "That one is quite the explorer. Aunt had to instruct the servants to keep all the doors closed after we found him coated in coal dust napping on Uncle's pillow. I do not know which was worse—that, or when Aunt found him climbing up the delicate overlay of her new gown to reach the top of her dressing screen."

Darcy now understood why Aunt Helen had sent Georgiana and her kittens away. Too much youth, indeed!

A fine black kitten with white paws and collar sat in front of the basket, its chin held up at a dignified angle. It coolly considered its surroundings.

Bingley motioned at the feline with a chuckle. "With these markings, this one looks like a butler. What is its name?"

The kitten glowered at Bingley with large, green eyes.

Georgiana smiled down at the kitten. "I was rather hoping you might help me name him... and the other kittens. He is not as friendly as his brothers and sister."

Bingley knelt to the floor. "Nonsense. I have yet to meet an animal I do not get on with." He reached out to pet the animal making kissy noises which earned him another green glare that would have discouraged a lesser man. Bingley chuckled once again, but he retracted his hand. "I shall win you over, you will see."

Richard grinned and jabbed Darcy in the ribs. "We ought to name that one Darcy."

Bingley laughed too heartily at Richard's joke. Georgiana, sweet girl she was, rose in her brother's defense. "Oh, no, Richard! William is not half as cantankerous as this little gentleman, though I admit that he does have a certain something in his air and way of walking."

As though to prove her point, the black kitten considered each of them with a look between disdain and indifference on his haughty little face, flicked his tail at Bingley, and sauntered across the room, where he found a sunny spot on the floor to lounge in.

Richard and Bingley roared in laughter. Darcy was not amused. He was tempted to leave his company and join the cat in his peaceful spot.

Georgiana pointed to another kitten sitting in front of the bay window. He was white except for a tuft of black hair sitting at a rakish angle on his head, like a top hat. He faced the window, his tail twitching from side-to-side, watching the birds fluttering by. Had they any idea how keenly they were being watched through the thick glass, they might not have lingered. "He is very playful. Uncle made a stick with feathers for him, and he loves to play with it. He likes to hide under the furniture and pounce on feet like a little tiger. Unfortunately, he startled the scullery maid—" Georgiana cut herself short, the reddening of her face displaying her embarrassment and revealing what she would never say aloud.

Richard shook his head and chuckled. He was not as delicate. "Chamber pots everywhere."

"Aunt Helen was rather cross." Georgiana wrinkled her nose.

With a glare at Richard, Darcy took Georgiana's hand and looped her arm through his. "It is not a subject talked about, but I can now appreciate the difficulties your pets put Aunt and Uncle's household through."

Richard cleared his throat. "Yes, Mother and Father have always favored hounds over felines." He looked at Darcy, then at Bingley, a grin spreading over his features as his gaze bounced back and forth between them. "I think kindly of both."

Darcy did not know what he was talking about, nor did he care to decipher Richard's meaning. He tipped his forehead at the last kitten—white with cinnamon brown ears and tail. She was clearly the lady of the litter. She sat beneath the tea table licking her paws and admiring them as she groomed. "What is that young lady like?" Darcy asked.

Georgiana gushed. "She is a lady through and through, much like her mother. She is the perfect sister, playing with and grooming her brothers. Of course, except for the black one, they do not like her attentions very much."

The little lady sashayed over to Georgiana, bumping her head against her leg and rubbing against her skirts while Georgie praised her.

"Achoo!" Miss Bingley's loud expulsion sent the female kitten scurrying back to her basket. The tip of Miss Bingley's nose was robin breast red.

Georgiana's face twisted in pity. "Oh dear, are my cats making you sneeze, Miss Bingley? I ought to have asked before bringing them, but there was simply no time."

Miss Bingley sniffed as delicately as one could do with a swollen, drippy nose. "Of course not! I am as hale as always. It must be dust. I shall take it up with the maids."

Pleased with her reply, Georgiana regaled them with more tales of the kitten's antics. After a good five minutes of uninterrupted, excited chatter, she pressed her hands against her cheeks. "I do apologize for talking so much, but are they not the sweetest little dears?"

Darcy loved seeing her so cheerful. Had he known how she would dote on another pet—or four—he would have given her a box of kittens last summer instead of surrounding her with their old friends. Then she would not have fallen in love with Bingley. Pemberley would have been overrun with felines, but he would not be in his current predicament... and there would be no mice hiding in the pantry.

Georgiana tapped Darcy's arm gently, looking up at him through her thick, golden eyelashes. "I do hope that your betrothed loves cats." Her voice was shy.

Darcy did not know how to reply. He must not have grimaced, for Georgiana continued, "I am eager to meet Miss Elizabeth. She must be lovely."

"You poor dear, how uncomfortable it must be to only now meet the woman who will be your sister. It would have been better had she been a friend of long-standing to take on such a role, but it all happened so unexpectedly." Miss Bingley *would* have her say.

Georgiana shook her head. "Oh, but I was not surprised at all!"

Darcy felt his jaw loosen, but he held it shut. What was this?

"You look shocked, William," Georgiana continued, "but you need not be. You are so careful not to show any particular attention to any young lady. When you mentioned Miss Elizabeth by name on three different occasions in your letters to me, I knew she must hold a special place in your affections. I am so happy for you! There is nothing more romantic than to marry for true love."

Darcy was too stunned to speak. Richard smirked at him with one brow arched.

Miss Bingley sputtered and then fell silent, her face as crimson as her nose.

CHAPTER 21

*M*ortification burned Elizabeth's cheeks. It all started with Kitty and Lydia's hasty return from Meryton bursting with complaints about Mr. Wickham's inexplicable absence and announcing they had seen a stately carriage with windows on all sides, a coat of arms on the doors, pulled by four matching bays, and a footman almost as tall as Mr. Darcy perched on the back with the finest silk-encased calves they had ever seen.

"A coat of arms, you say?" Mama forgot about the bout of nerves which had afflicted her all morning. "Did you notice in which direction it traveled?"

Kitty replied, "It continued up the road toward Netherfield."

"Netherfield! It must be Mr. Darcy's relatives come to meet Lizzy! His mother comes from aristocracy, and his grandfather was an earl."

"I would make an enchanting countess! What a

laugh! I would lord it over all my sisters," boasted Lydia.

Mama tapped her chin. "If they have come to meet us, then the least we can do is present ourselves."

"Mama!" Elizabeth exclaimed. "We cannot call without an invitation."

Her mother waved her objection away. "We are free to call on Mr. Bingley and Mr. Darcy whenever we wish. If their noble relatives are there, who are we to know it?" She rubbed her hands together. "A coach full of unmarried noblemen!"

"We do not know that, Mama." Jane tried to dissuade her, but their mother's head was too full of possibilities to be reasonable.

Launching herself from her chair, Mama readied her daughters with remarkable speed and attention to detail. Mrs. Hill and Sarah hastened from one room to another, ruddy-cheeked and damp with exertion. After one hour, not one hair was out of place, nor could a wrinkle be found in a skirt.

Papa tried to escape into his book room, but Mama was insistent. His argument that they would not all fit in the carriage was no obstacle to Mama.

And so, Elizabeth found herself sitting beside her father in the cart ahead of the carriage, doused in perfume, braids pinching her scalp, whalebones from the old stays Mama insisted she wear jabbing her in the ribs. It was the worst of humiliations to be a party to her mother's plan to thrust themselves on Mr. Darcy's family.

What pained Elizabeth even more was the knowledge that her first impression was bound to be a poor one. She had imagined meeting them; she had practiced conversations; she knew which gown she would have preferred to wear. But this? There was nothing she could say or do to undo the damage certain to occur.

Papa leaned down and sniffed her hair. "Much better after a good airing." He laughed.

Elizabeth pressed her cold hands against her cheeks and prayed fervently that the butler refuse them entry... or even better, that the household not be in.

But they *were* in. Before the twists in Elizabeth's stomach made her ill, the butler showed them into the parlor.

A young lady with alabaster skin, golden hair, and a stylish gown draped becomingly over her figure clung to Mr. Darcy's arm.

Elizabeth went numb... and then she felt Mr. Darcy's bold, proud gaze on her. Elizabeth stewed, an unfamiliar sensation gnawing at her gut and hardening her face. Perhaps Mr. Darcy thought it was acceptable to flaunt his friendship with beautiful ladies in town where such things were expected of gentlemen of his sort, but he had led her to believe that he was different. She lifted her chin, her eyes meeting his defiantly, demanding an explanation.

Only now that she saw his expression clearly, she noticed the sheer misery in it. His chest and shoulders rose and his cheeks puffed out like hers had moments ago when she felt nauseated, and she realized her mistake. The way he placed his hand over the young lady's was not possessive, it was protective.

Elizabeth's relief was too great to remember her embarrassment. She had been mistaken to jump to conclusions so quickly—an error she had made too frequently with Mr. Darcy. The girl at his side could be none other than his sister.

Miss Darcy tugged her brother closer and whispered into his ear. After he smiled and nodded, she released her hold on him and stepped tentatively toward their callers, her large, brown eyes looking anywhere but directly at Elizabeth. "I have been eager to meet you." Her soft voice warbled, and it was impossible for Elizabeth not to feel compassion for the girl. This was hardly the haughty heiress Mr. Wickham had described. Far from it!

Mr. Darcy introduced them to his sister and cousin Richard, and Elizabeth relaxed. They would offend no earls or countesses today. To the contrary, Elizabeth hoped to make two allies.

Mama's eyes widened when the colonel was introduced. Without looking behind her, she caught Kitty and Lydia's hands to propel them closer to the gentleman. Mary was intelligent enough to stay out of their mother's immediate reach and therefore avoided being pushed at the poor man.

There was nothing remarkable in his features, and while he cut a fine figure in his tailored coat, he was not particularly tall. For Kitty and Lydia, the final nail in his coffin was his lack of a uniform. Had he been wearing his military coat, they might have shown greater interest.

This was lost on Mama, who would not fault the gentleman for wearing civilian attire when he was a colonel in the regulars and the second son of an earl.

The charming ease with which the colonel received Mama's string of compliments and replied to her intrusive questions won Elizabeth over. He was quick to laugh without taking offense. Elizabeth could easily imagine him and Mr. Darcy getting into scrapes. Masters in mischief, the two of them.

Mr. Bingley beamed at his surplus of guests. "Now that you are all here, I insist you stay for tea. A merry party we shall make!"

Jane directed her sweet smile at Miss Bingley and Miss Darcy. "We do not wish to inconvenience you at the last minute. Your guests have only just arrived and must wish to rest. Perhaps a later date would suit better?"

Miss Bingley was quick to agree.

However, Mr. Bingley was not dissuaded. "They have had over an hour to rest, and Miss Darcy is strong. You do not mind, do you?"

Fluttering her eyelashes, her cheeks rosy pink, Miss Darcy said, "I would never take away from your pleasure." The tenderness in her tone... the way her gaze lingered on Mr. Bingley... her eyebrows furrowing into a confused frown when he went to stand beside Jane rather than her—Elizabeth had too many sisters to not recognize the signs. Miss Darcy was smitten with Mr. Bingley!

And now, she was jealous of Jane.

"Then it is settled!" proclaimed Mr. Bingley, entrusting his sisters to see to the arrangements while Jane apologized yet again to their hostess.

Mr. Darcy considered the whole scene with a disapproving frown, but Elizabeth did not know whether his scowl was directed at Mr. Bingley's attentions toward Jane or his own sister's infatuation with his dear friend.

Returning to them, Miss Bingley moved to Miss Darcy's side and took her arm as though they were the dearest friends. "Miss Darcy is accustomed to the first circles. While she shall miss the quality, her presence here is a breath of fresh air for those of us with higher tastes."

Elizabeth bit her lips. It would not do to meet such a comment with a sarcastic retort. She shot her father a warning look, but he was deep in conversation with Mr. Hurst and Colonel Fitzwilliam. Mama flitted about, still trying to get Mary, Kitty, or Lydia to take an interest in the unattached gentleman.

Miss Bingley seemed to sense her overstep. She tittered, adding, "I daresay the ladies here shall benefit from Miss Darcy's exemplary example of a truly accomplished lady."

Elizabeth arched her eyebrows and pinched her lips tighter. Poor Miss Darcy! She did not look like the paradigm Miss Bingley had described. The girl stood looking uncomfortable with her hands clasped in front of her and her gaze fixed to the floor.

It was plain Miss Darcy's accomplishments might be abundant but redirecting a conversation disagreeable to her was not one of them. Her brother's clipped replies were lost on Miss Bingley, who continued pressing the matter, assuming an intimacy that the young lady clearly did not share. "You must play for us, Miss Darcy!"

Mrs. Hurst clapped her hands, enraptured with the idea and encouraging Miss Bingley to continue in her torment. "I am certain your equal has not been heard in all of Hertfordshire. You could show the ladies how it is properly done." Her eyes flickered over to Mary and back to Miss Darcy.

Mr. Darcy looked about to say something everyone —his sister included—would regret.

Elizabeth smiled at Miss Bingley, directing her words at the lady. "We should be delighted to hear Miss Darcy play once she has rested from her travels, should she wish to exhibit her talent. But you forget, Miss Bingley, we have had the pleasure of listening to your superior skill as well as that of Mrs. Hurst over these past two months. You do not give yourself enough credit. I would be delighted and edified to hear either of you play for us again."

Once again, Elizabeth sensed Mr. Darcy's penetrating look on her. When she turned to him, she saw unmistakable, glittering gratitude.

Elizabeth felt light, happy. Indeed, who would not

feel a respectable degree of pride at having so pleased a gentleman difficult to please?

Miss Bingley forced a pinched smile, caught between pleasure at hearing herself praised before the people she most wished to impress and aggravation at the source of the compliment. She was right to doubt Elizabeth's motive, given their brief history, but Elizabeth knew when to control her tongue. She would not risk shocking an impressionable young lady merely to make a witty retort.

Mr. Bingley chose that moment to whisper to Jane. He was all smiles, and Elizabeth would have rejoiced in his warm attention to her sister had she not seen Miss Darcy's confused dismay.

Elizabeth noticed. Mr. Darcy certainly noticed. And Jane, bless her gracious, kind heart, noticed. She met Mr. Bingley's enthusiasm with a more subdued interest.

Fortunately for everyone, a woman Elizabeth supposed must be Miss Darcy's governess entered the room carrying a basket. "If Miss Bingley does not object, perhaps her guests would like to see the kittens?"

Lydia and Kitty squealed. "Kittens!" They darted across the room and reached into the basket. A black kitten gave a loud hiss and squirmed out of Lydia's hands to drop to the floor, his back arched and his fangs displayed. With his snow-white collars and gloves, he looked like a vexed butler stirred too early from a well-deserved nap.

The girls laughed and left him to lay on a warm spot on the carpet while they searched for more agreeable playmates.

Achoo! Miss Bingley sneezed and attempted to sniff delicately. "Delightful creatures, are they not?" she observed in a nasal voice.

Two maids entered to set the round table, placing the tea service in the center and surrounding it with platters of sandwiches, slices of meat and cheese, sweetmeats, and a tray of apple tarts and currant cake.

Colonel Fitzwilliam patted his stomach. "My compliments to your cook! You set a fine table, Miss Bingley. Your brother is fortunate to have you as his hostess."

The colonel's praise was joined by Mr. Bingley's, whose approbation was received by his sister with a scowl. She attempted to arrange her guests around the table while Mama followed behind, disassembling her plans.

Kitty pressed Miss Darcy to tell them more stories about her kittens, a subject upon which the young lady spoke with greater freedom and joy the longer her audience encouraged her to continue.

Not one to allow all the attention to go to another, Lydia shared a few stories of her own, to which Miss Darcy seemed grateful.

Ever eager to promote her daughters' matches, Mama said, "Lizzy especially loves cats, but Jane prefers dogs."

Colonel Fitzwilliam coughed. Reaching for his tea,

he pounded on his chest with his other hand and cleared his throat. After a sip, he asked, "Is that so? Why the distinction?"

Miss Bingley snorted. "What a question! Miss Darcy is fortunate with Serafina and her offspring. In my experience, most felines are snarly creatures who thank you for your attentions with bites and scratches."

The colonel raised his eyebrows. "You must have a great deal of experience with the species."

Mr. Bingley chuckled. "Our aunt in Scarborough keeps at least a dozen cats as pets."

Miss Bingley's teacup was not large enough to hide the disgust on her face.

Jane said, "Dogs are always so happy to see their master—even if he or she is only away for a few minutes, they make you feel as though you are their favorite person in the world."

Colonel Fitzwilliam looked levelly at Jane. "Would that people were as loyal."

Jane replied, "I have often wished the same."

If Mr. Bingley had a tail, he would be wagging it. "That is precisely my thought."

The colonel did not look away from Jane. "And can you explain Miss Elizabeth's preference for obstinate felines?"

Jane shifted her weight in her seat. "I cannot speak for Lizzy, but I have always suspected she is drawn to the independence cats are known to display."

The colonel turned to Elizabeth. "Is that so?"

Elizabeth knew better than to take this sort of

conversation—or the gentleman making the inquiry—too seriously. She promptly replied, "They do not suffer from want of personality. I love dogs too, but they tend to be more consistently loyal and agreeable. There are exceptions, of course, but to win the affection of an independently-minded cat, that is an honor worthy of some pride, for their approval is so rarely bestowed."

"Well said." The colonel clapped.

Mrs. Hurst was not as impressed. "Lovely as they are, cats are so much more work. I would rather not put forth the effort when my exertions are more easily rewarded elsewhere."

Mr. Darcy spoke. "That is precisely the point. Some enjoy the challenge."

Elizabeth felt her smile in her bones. He understood her.

"Have you picked names for the kittens?" Kitty asked.

Miss Darcy shook her head. "I have not."

That provoked several gasps around the table.

"What do you call them? Kitty One? Kitty Two?" Lydia giggled at her own joke.

Miss Darcy picked at her fingers, her voice barely above a whisper, "They have such distinct personalities. I have not been able to settle on the perfect names." She looked up and just as quickly back down at her hands. "Besides, I shall not be able to keep all of them, and I fear growing too attached if I give them names."

"Very sensible."

In response to Mary's commendation, Miss Darcy looked up at her with a small smile.

Miss Bingley suggested she name them after French authors. When Miss Darcy tentatively supplied several options. Molière, Comtesse (de Ségur), Corneille, Sevigné... every name was met with a blank look Miss Bingley attempted to disguise by proclaiming herself enraptured with their work.

Colonel Fitzwilliam could not countenance a name originating from the country with which England was at war. "Colonel or Commander would make a fine, strong name for the tomcats."

Papa suggested a Greek God theme. "Artemis is often associated with cats in Greek mythology. Her Roman goddess equivalent, Diana, was known for transforming into a cat."

Mr. Darcy suggested music-inspired names: Nonet, Cadenza, Iphigenie, Almavia, Allegra... Miss Darcy appeared pleased at his knowledge of musical vocabulary. To take such an interest in something his sister loved, he was obviously an attentive brother.

Kitty proposed names of flowers and gemstones.

Mr. Hurst shouted out names between bites of cake: Bob, Mr. Whiskers, Daphne, Clarissa. His wife even forgot herself and added a few suggestions of her own.

In the end, there were so many choices that Miss Darcy declared it impossible to select only four. It was unanimously decided that the individual who successfully named any of the kittens would have the privilege of taking that kitten home once they all were weaned in two weeks.

"Just in time for the wedding!" Mama's mind never strayed far from the subject. "Two weeks from Sunday. Of course, you will stay to attend?"

The colonel answered with a devilish gleam. "We would not miss it for the world."

CHAPTER 22

$\mathcal{C}$olonel Richard Fitzwilliam had known this was a terrible idea. Lord, how he hated being right all the time! And still, nobody listened to him. Darcy never did. Richard's own mother certainly did not, though he could excuse her more easily than he could his cousin.

How on earth were he and Darcy—two bachelors for Heaven's sake!—supposed to guide a prized heiress through the battlefield of courtship and matrimony while avoiding any mortal injury? So far, they had not fared well.

From the moment the Bennets had set foot in Bingley's parlor, charging the air with their arrival, Richard had known the concerns he had expressed five months ago in Darcy's study at Pemberley had been well-founded. He would never forget the hurt in Georgie's eyes with every display of Bingley's preference for the eldest Miss Bennet. Richard praised the heavens above that the lady's insight and sensibility had prevented the matter from worsening—not that her mother had not done her level best to try!

Miss Bennet had impressed Richard. She valued the same qualities he did—loyalty and steadiness. Twas a pity Bingley had seen her first.

Darcy's predicament unraveled in a comical display during the tea, but Richard was convinced the universe had given his reticent cousin a nudge in the right direction with Miss Elizabeth.

As for her family, it was plain that Mrs. Bennet had married up. Her manners lacked the refinement of the upper circles... or even the middling ones if Richard were being completely honest. The matron had made her hope of connecting one of her daughters to him cringingly clear. She seemed to believe she might prod him to propose to one of her daughters by the end of tea.

Mr. Bennet, quick as a whip, snapped several clever quips. He was clearly an intelligent man with a wry sense of humor. Unfortunately, where his family was concerned, the gentleman was woefully negligent. He could not be more different from Darcy.

However, the many flaws of the Bennet family proved to display the finer qualities of the two eldest Bennet daughters to greater advantage. With some sorrow, Richard watched them depart for their residence.

Miss Bingley brushed off her hands. "I thought they would never leave. I absolutely adore Miss Eliza"—she looked disingenuously at Darcy—"but her family is truly dreadful."

Mrs. Hurst rubbed her temples. "Five minutes in their presence gives me a headache."

"Shall we call Miss Bennet back? Five minutes in her presence will put you to sleep!" Miss Bingley tittered along with her sister.

Darcy, who still looked at the door through which his betrothed had departed, snapped to attention. "Criticism without understanding is the height of ignorance."

Whether Miss Bingley heard his rebuke or not, Richard could not say, for the lady erupted with a series of sneezes. Once she was capable of hearing, he clapped his hands together to make certain. "I, for one, congratulate you, Darcy. Miss Elizabeth is as charming as she is clever." Richard did not allow himself the pleasure of checking Miss Bingley's reaction, but he knew he had hit his mark. "Now, perhaps Mrs. Annesley would help Georgie collect her kittens and remove them from Miss Bingley's proximity. I have several messages to relay to Darcy from my mother. Might we occupy your study for a few minutes, Bingley?"

"Of course! Consider this house your own during your stay."

"That is very generous of you."

"No more so than you and Darcy have been to me. The good brandy is in the bottom drawer of the desk."

Richard inclined his head in thanks. Everyone occupied, he spirited Darcy to the study, closing the door behind him and pouring two glasses of Bingley's finest brandy. Raising one glass, he offered the other to Darcy. "I suspected there was a great deal you left out in your letter, and now I am convinced of it. You are too big of a fish to be easily caught."

Darcy frowned. "She did not catch me. She did not even set her cap for me."

Richard grinned, pleased at how quickly Darcy rose in his lady's defense at the expense of his own pride—proof that love worked miracles. "I did not claim that she had. Not all cleverness tends to the scheming machinations so common among the *ton*." He rubbed his hands together, liking this humbler cousin and indulging in his whim to tease. "Tell me, has she bested you in a debate?"

"More than once." Darcy sipped from his glass. "You have had enough diversion at my expense. Why are you here?"

"Now that is a fine welcome."

"You wrote that you were on your way to Pemberley. My instructions were clear. You could not have misunderstood them."

"Did you not read my reply? I clearly said that Georgiana, with the help of my mother, wrote to Mrs. Reynolds with all their suggestions to ready Pemberley for your new bride. Georgie was too anxious to meet Miss Elizabeth to travel anywhere but here."

Darcy did not look convinced.

Richard added, "Mother expects a full report."

"You were sent to spy on me?"

Richard tsked. "If you do not want them to suspect that your sudden engagement is anything less than a love match, you had better play the part of a lovesick man better."

Darcy groaned. "You know what my father said about disguise."

"Yes, I remember well that he despised it. However, I also recall that he directed those words more often to Wickham than to you."

"That is another reason you should not be here. You know he is stationed in Meryton."

"Was. I called in a favor. He was reassigned to Ramsgate, effective immediately."

"Ramsgate?" Darcy swirled the liquid in his glass, his expression pensive, lighter.

"Brilliant, is it not? Wickham will not be able to ask for credit there, as the shopkeepers are on to him."

"Yes, yes, you did well. You are very clever, but did you not think of how disastrous it is for Georgiana to see Bingley smitten with another?"

So much for a proud moment. Richard's success deflated before Georgiana's disappointment. Darcy was not yet so humble to realize that he ought not attempt to govern the hearts of others, especially not his little sister's.

Treading cautiously, Richard replied, "I am impressed with Miss Bennet's gracious comportment. She will not stir up contentions or rivalries when her disposition is to make peace. No, Darce, I realize you are unhappy that Georgie and I are here, but I think you are precisely where *you* need to be."

"What does that signify?"

Darcy, Darcy... Richard shook his head. "Georgiana still has at least two years before she will come out in society, four if we have our way. Were it up to you, you would forgo love until you saw Georgiana settled when what she needs most is to see you happy. I suspect that this interruption to your plans... that Miss Elizabeth is the best accident to befall you."

"A happy accident? You would reduce the consequences of a scandalous compromise to a foolish oxymoron?"

"Never foolish. She is a charming young lady, witty, easy to converse with. I would go so far as to say it was rather astute of you to take a fancy to her. Now, tell me the rest of the story before Bingley tires of his sisters' company and joins us. I take it he does not know."

Darcy scoffed. "He was the first to wish me joy. He is convinced it is a love match."

As Darcy relayed the rest of the deliciously scandalous story, Richard's suspicions were confirmed. Darcy did not realize it, but he was helplessly in love with his betrothed. Richard would be able to give a truthful and convincing report to his mother and father, after all.

Once Darcy was done, Richard raised his glass. "You like her already. Now, go, fall in love with her properly. Court her honestly, unreservedly."

"What about Georgie? And Bingley?"

"You leave them to me."

Richard knew Darcy preferred that another not take on what he felt was his own responsibility, but he did not object. That was progress enough.

CHAPTER 23

*J*ane had waited until she thought
Elizabeth slumbered and cried herself to
sleep again.

Although Elizabeth had gently prodded her sister to
confide her woes, Jane remained frustratingly silent.
Likely she did not want to burden Elizabeth, who was
supposed to be happy and in love. It was like Jane to
hide her troubles, and Elizabeth was worried.

She must speak with Mr. Darcy. She had hoped
their path would cross after services the day before, but
it had rained too hard to consider walking. There were
whispers and smiles as Mr. Brown read the banns. Her
friends and neighbors were delighted for her, and Elizabeth felt it even more necessary than before to appear
the blushing bride-to-be. To be truthful, it was getting
easier.

Walking up the rise where she had last encountered
Mr. Darcy, she paused and looked as far as the fog

permitted. Wrapping her arms around herself, she spun in a circle. She would freeze if she stayed here. Quickly deciding on her next step, she increased her pace down the path leading her to Netherfield Park.

She pressed on, cold, doubtful, and feeling a little foolish for persisting. Who was to say her path would cross with Mr. Darcy's? He was a sensible man and was, no doubt, at this moment sipping chocolate or coffee by a warm fire with his sister. It was what Elizabeth ought to be doing.

But the sound of Jane's tears echoed in her ears, propelling Elizabeth forward. She must learn why Miss Darcy believed she had a claim on Mr. Bingley's affections when she was far too young and insecure to consider marriage to one so far beneath her station.

A sharp gust slapped Elizabeth's wrap against her face and plastered her skirts against her legs. Her bonnet strained against the ribbons tied under her chin. A violent shiver shook through her. Maybe this was not the best idea.

Jane's tears… steaming hot chocolate…

Elizabeth gritted her teeth for one last look about her. She needed to have a private conversation with Mr. Darcy, but that would not be possible if she caught her death and had to take to bed.

Reluctantly, she turned around toward Longbourn. When she heard hoof-beats behind her, she believed her mind only played tricks on her.

DARCY REFUSED to return to Netherfield Park until he gained control of his ill humor. He was expected to call at Longbourn, but he would make miserable company.

His horse flicked his ears and tugged at the reins as though to suggest that he was not too happy in Darcy's company either.

"Grumpy brute," Darcy hissed under his breath. Another tug and nod.

"I meant the remark for you, ungrateful beast." Preferring his own thoughts to this useless exchange with his horse, Darcy considered his next step.

As yet, Bingley displayed the fickleness of an unsteady character. Darcy held every hope of his youthful friend growing into a steadier version of himself—Bingley was only twenty-two—but maturity was not gained overnight. Not in most cases.

Darcy remembered himself at twenty-two. He was hardly the master of himself. Those were carefree, pleasurable times until loss and grief cast their dark shadow over Pemberley. His father had died unexpectedly, thrusting upon Darcy the responsibilities he had been brought up to shoulder. He had not been prepared to undertake so much while he was yet in shock.

The weight of responsibility would have crushed Bingley... changed him. It had changed Darcy. Peers—people he had thought he could trust—had attempted to profit from his inexperience. Overnight, Darcy had lost his youth to emerge a serious, suspecting, resentful master and guardian. Darcy could not wish that experience on any man.

If not for his family's loyal servants, the damage would have been far greater. From the least scullery maid to his father's own secretary, they would retire in Darcy's service. He would lay down a fortune in pensions, but that kind of loyalty could not be bought, and Darcy considered it his duty and privilege to reward them. They had acted not just as servants, but as friends.

What kind of friend would allow Bingley, a man he claimed was his close friend, to treat his future lightly? The man did not approach decisions with the care necessary contemplation required to avoid unfavorable consequences for himself and his eventual bride. Bingley would be safe with Georgiana—with Darcy's guidance.

While Darcy had observed nothing in Miss Bennet's character to make him doubt her sincerity, he could not be so certain about her family. Mrs. Bennet made no effort to disguise her wishes. She would make Bingley miserable. Mr. Bennet would not take any request for advice seriously. This was a disastrous pairing when Bingley was not yet knowledgeable enough or decisive enough in his own right. Furthermore, the Bennets would limit his society in London.

On the other hand, Bingley was ill-prepared to mingle with the upper circles to which Georgiana was born.

Darcy shook his head. He valued Georgiana's future

and Bingley's friendship too highly to be governed by doubts. His original plan had a solid foundation. They both required more time.

Urging his horse into a trot, Darcy cleared the top of the hill.

There stood the one person he most desired to see. Was she real? He blinked several times to make certain the lady walking in the fog was not an apparition. "Elizabeth?"

She spun around, hands at her throat. "Mr. Darcy?"

That she addressed him so formally still irked Darcy. Confidence could not be forced, but they were now past the first reading of the banns. She might at least use his Christian name.

His groom appeared behind him, and Darcy dismounted to walk with Elizabeth. She must be chilled to the bone. The least he could do was to walk her home.

She wrapped her fingers around the crook of his arm. He pressed them more tightly against his side. For warmth.

"I was hoping our paths would cross," she said.

"Really?" He had hoped the same, or he would have chosen a different path.

"I wished to inquire about your sister. Is she… timid by nature?" The way she hesitated made Darcy think that was not the question she had wished to ask.

"Georgiana has always been shy, though until this last summer, she never had reason to doubt the affection of those closest to her." He sighed. It was difficult to utter a compliment to the same lady with the power to inflict the greatest hurt to his sister, but fair was fair. "I thank you, and Miss Bennet, for attempting to put her at ease."

Elizabeth leaned against his arm, her closeness more effective than a blazing fire. "It is no wonder she clings to you as she does. You are all she has, and she must fear that I aim to take you away from her."

Her insight was a revelation to Darcy. Was that how Georgiana felt? It explained her possessive behavior.

She peeked up at Darcy from under the rim of her bonnet. "I saw how Miss Darcy looked at Mr. Bingley."

His jaw clenched of its own volition.

She chuckled. "If I had a protective older brother, I imagine he would react as you do. Instead, I am blessed with younger sisters who suffer a new girlish infatuation every week at least."

Thank goodness Georgiana was nothing like the youngest Bennets.

Darcy must have concealed his distaste, for she continued. "I know you would never approve of a match between your sister and Mr. Bingley. For one, the difference in station alone would be a formidable obstacle for any family in the first circles. Furthermore, I hardly think you so unjust as to wish Miss Bingley and Mrs. Hurst as sisters for her. They would eat Miss Darcy alive, using her connections to their own advantage while making her life a misery."

They were the same objections he and Richard had discussed at length. Darcy remembered he had shot down each one. Yet hearing the arguments coming from Elizabeth unsettled him. How would she fare if the same objections were applied to her sister?

"You believe Miss Bennet would fare better?" Darcy asked.

"Undoubtedly!"

Darcy was taken aback. "I understand her manners to be shy, much like Georgiana."

"Jane is modest, but she is unwavering in her values and affection."

Just as Darcy hoped Georgiana would be someday.

Elizabeth continued, "She has had a lifetime of managing difficult females and keeping peace in our household. She is so gentle about it, nobody even suspects her strength."

Darcy frowned. He had not considered that. But Elizabeth had yet to address the disparity in rank. "What of his family's connections to trade? Your mother's connections aside, you were born into the gentry. To marry less than a landed gentleman would be considered marrying down."

Elizabeth sucked in a breath. "There is something I wish you to understand. It might help explain why Mama is so... insistent. Why station is not as important to us as it is to others."

Darcy looked down at her. This ought to be interesting.

"When Jane was but fifteen, she went to stay with our aunt and uncle in London."

"The Gardiners?"

Her gaze jerked up to meet his, her eyebrow arched.

If she assumed he would take exception to her relatives in trade, he would prove her wrong. He kept his expression indifferent. "I look forward to meeting them when we are in London."

Her eyebrows pinched together in a moment of visible confusion, and it was all Darcy could do not to exclaim in triumph. He had surprised her. His chest might have puffed out a bit.

"Aunt thought to treat Jane to new gowns and some of the entertainments in town before her coming out. You see, our mother insisted she come out at sixteen, and Jane did not feel ready."

A kind, thoughtful offer. "I do hope they treated you to a time in London as well?" He caught the surprise in her expressive eyes, and his coat buttons strained. *There is more where that comes from, Elizabeth.*

"I think they will be pleased to make your acquaintance." She did not answer his question. However, it satisfied him to know her family would be pleased to meet him. Most people were, but Elizabeth was not just anyone, and she obviously held her Gardiner relatives in special regard.

She wrapped the ribbon from her bonnet around her finger. "During that visit, a gentleman in town, a young man from a fine family, fell in love with Jane. His father had been an associate of Uncle's before he made his fortune and severed all connections with trade so that his children might be accepted in more gentle circles."

"Like Bingley."

"Yes, just like Mr. Bingley. He called every day, his attention to Jane growing and giving her hope. She was young and gave her heart fully. A proposal seemed imminent. Even our aunt thought so." She stopped and sighed.

Darcy saw where this story ended and wished to spare her the hurt from the memory. "He did not propose."

"Uncle wrote to Papa, explaining the advantages of such a connection and adding his own recommendation of the gentleman's character. Unfortunately, Mama learned of it, and she insisted that they join Jane in London to meet the young man."

Which put paid to the gentleman's affections, Darcy surmised. Elizabeth angled her bonnet so he could not see her face, but he still caught a glimpse of her red cheeks.

He placed his free hand over hers, turning to face her. "Then I am glad for your sister's sake that the young man revealed his weakness of character when he did. If a man is truly in love, nothing would cause his affection to waver."

Her eyelashes fluttered, but her gaze eventually met his. Softly, she said, "Not even the lady's objectionable family?"

The instinct to wrap her in his arms made Darcy cautious. They were talking about Miss Bennet's weak suitor, not his own feelings.

Resuming their slow pace down the path, Darcy

said, ""Especially not that. What mother would not desire to meet the young man who might become her son-in-law rather than trusting her young daughter's inexperienced heart with the advice of others?" Darcy had gone against his instincts, trusting his aunt's recommendation of Mrs. Younge as a companion for Georgiana. He could not think of it without a twist of regret in his stomach. Never again.

"Do you mean that?"

Darcy had the distinct impression that Elizabeth was not merely referring to her sister. Whatever he said right then was important to her. His inclination was to take his time replying in order to weigh his words adequately. But he sensed her impatience. Her sigh alerted him that unless he spoke quickly, she would look away and the moment would be lost.

"Marriage is a scary prospect for a young lady. She leaves the security of her family, who know her more intimately than anyone else, for a gentleman full of promises and good intentions." Darcy's breath was quick, his speech quicker. "If his love is based on super-ficial matters such as her beauty or her fortune, his affection cannot be expected to stand through the trials they will have to face together."

"You speak very confidently on the subject."

He had spoken rather passionately and at greater length than was his custom. But he did feel certain. It was the example he had been taught. "My mother and father loved each other."

"It must have been wonderful to be raised in such a

household." The wistfulness in Elizabeth's tone pinched his heart.

"It made the loss of them harder. I wish Georgie had known them together." She never would have fallen for Wickham's smooth trickery had she known what true, inseparable love looked like.

"I think I understand her infatuation with Mr. Bingley. It makes perfect sense."

Darcy jerked his head to face her. "You do?"

"Of course. She lost her mother, then her father, and now her only brother is engaged to marry."

"I would never leave her," Darcy recoiled.

"I would never expect you to. However, as you and I both know all too well, circumstances can change in the blink of an eye. Your mother and father could not have wished to leave either, but they could not prevent it." She chewed on her bottom lip. "I see that I shall have to do my best to reassure her that I do not intend to replace her in your affections."

Before Elizabeth mentioned it, Darcy had not considered the possibility of Georgiana being anything but happy at the idea of gaining a sister at Pemberley. Elizabeth had, and solely for the benefit of his sister. The realization stunned him.

Resting his hand on top of hers again, feeling his skin tingle and burn at the contact, he said a heartfelt, "Thank you."

He had thought the favor he was doing in raising the Bennets' social standing and the stability he offered to them enough, but Elizabeth's kindness toward his little sister far surpassed the connections and security he would give her. He would simply have to try harder to be kinder to her family in turn. Perhaps she would value his exertion as much as he cherished hers.

She smiled at him. "Good, then may I ask you a favor?"

"Anything."

"Do not let Mr. Bingley break Jane's heart."

Her request punched the air out of Darcy's lungs.

CHAPTER 24

he question that had seemed reasonable before she heard herself say it aloud now sounded petty and meddlesome, and Elizabeth was neither of those. Nor was Mr. Darcy. No wonder he gaped at her.

"Pray do not take my request seriously, Mr. Darcy. As commanding of a gentleman as you are, I doubt you have authority enough over Mr. Bingley's heart to make him do anything he is not pleased to do."

Mr. Darcy looked struck. She smiled, trying to lighten the air and figuratively kicking herself for her foolish request.

Finally, he spoke. "It is perfectly natural for you to wish your sister advantageously settled."

Elizabeth lifted a finger. "And happy in love."

"And h-happy… in l-love." The way he tripped over his words, the pinch in his eyes, the unsteadiness of his breath made Elizabeth wonder if he was thinking about their own impending marriage.

Her uncle liked to say that the truest test of a person's character was to observe them in hot water. Mr. Darcy had proved himself honorable, understanding, and loyal. She liked him more each day. She could see herself in love with him...eventually. She prayed so.

"Do you believe we shall be happy?" she whispered, the noise of her heartbeat in her ears deafening.

His dark gaze slammed into Elizabeth, vibrating through her limbs and making her stance unsteady. She clutched onto his arm, too shaken to trust her own body to support her or to look away. He moved in front of her, so close the lapels of his coat brushed against the folds of her wrap. She did not mean to, but her hands rested against his chest, not to push him away or to create a barrier, but just to feel the rise and fall of his breath under the wool of his greatcoat. Warmth radiated off him in waves like rays from the sun, pulling her up to her toes, to get closer to its source. His breath tickled against her cheek, her lips.

He smelled of bergamot and spice, hot tea on a cold day. Elizabeth parted her lips, a thirst she had never known overwhelming her.

Splat! A fat, frigid raindrop plunked onto the end of her nose and dribbled down her chin. *Splat! Splat!* More thunked onto the brim of her bonnet. She held her hand out, disbelieving and resenting the interruption. When had it started to rain?

A blast of cold air smacked against her where Mr.

Darcy had been standing. He held his hat in one hand and tugged through his hair with the other, looking supremely apologetic.

Elizabeth was not sorry. Not in the least. She was giddy with hope and the stirrings of budding love. She was falling in love with Mr. Darcy! And he was not indifferent to her.

Playfully, she raised her skirts to the top of her half boots to better run and set off down the path. "Race you to Longbourn!" she tossed over her shoulder.

He caught up with her, his long strides easily keeping pace.

Leaping over a particularly muddy patch, Elizabeth slipped on the landing. Before she could squeal properly, Darcy's arms were around her, steadying her, holding her up, and pushing her forward with his momentum toward the warmth and safety of Longbourn.

"Thank you," she gasped, marveling at how expertly coordinated their movement had been and wondering how suspicious it would be if she were to slip again so she could feel his strong arms around her once more.

He could have won the race, but he stayed at her side, his hand close to her arm should she slip again.

Together they reached the gravel, and that was where Elizabeth's competitive spirit rose. Lungs screaming, legs burning, she dashed down the drive to Longbourn's door, laughing as she heard Darcy behind her.

Mrs. Hill opened the front door just as they reached

it. She pointed to the boot scraper with a stern look and a dry shawl in her hands, which she wrapped around Elizabeth's shoulders.

"Your mother is receiving callers in the drawing room." With a smile and a glint in her eye, she added, "You will find the fire warm and the tea plentiful."

Darcy returned her smile. "Thank you, Mrs. Hill."

The woman grinned wide enough to show the gap where she had a tooth pulled the year before. Elizabeth beamed up at Darcy. When had he learned the house-keeper's name? He might be above his company, but he was courteous to the servants.

A welcome sight greeted them in the drawing room. Miss Darcy sipped tea along with her companion and took a delicate bite of cake while the colonel regaled his captivated audience with a lively tale, a kitten perched on his shoulder.

Kitty and Lydia played with the fluffy white and cinnamon kitten on the settee.

"There you are!" Mama jumped up from her chair, ushering Elizabeth and Darcy closer to the fire. "Do not stand too near, Lizzy! You remember the time you singed your bottom. I told Mr. Bennet that you would get caught in the rain, but I did not worry. I knew Mr. Darcy was with you to keep you warm."

Elizabeth held her breath, trying in vain to control her blush. She glanced up at Darcy, needing to make sure he was not offended by her mother.

"I assure you, madam, your daughter is too quick on her feet for any such attempts to succeed."

Papa chuckled, and Elizabeth once again had to wonder. Who was this tall, handsome man standing beside her at the fire and teasing her mother good-naturedly?

Mama continued prattling as she rearranged the seating so that the two chairs nearest the fireplace were free for Elizabeth and Darcy. Elizabeth hoped that he would notice her mother's thoughtfulness more than her empty conversation... especially when the topic turned to Mr. Bingley.

"I had hoped Mr. Bingley would call today, but the colonel assures us that only the most urgent business would keep him away from Jane."

The color drained from Miss Darcy's face despite the warmth in the room.

Colonel Fitzwilliam cleared his throat. "A meeting with his bailiff, if I recall." Had Elizabeth not been watching the colonel, she might have missed the look he exchanged with Darcy and the nod he received in reply.

She, too, approved Mr. Bingley's discretion. His consideration did him credit.

The colonel raised his plate, plucking a crumb to feed the kitten on his shoulder. "My compliments to your cook, Mrs. Bennet. This is the finest gingerbread I have enjoyed in a long time. Is that not so, Georgiana?" He nudged her gently.

The dear girl looked up at Mama with a timorous smile. "Oh, yes... it is delicious. I-I wonder if your... cook might be willing to... share her receipt?" Her cheeks flushed and she clutched her hands in her lap. "That is, if she does not mind... if it is not a family secret." She picked at her fingers.

Elizabeth's heart went out to her. While it was strange that Mr. Bingley did not accompany the rest of his party to call, Elizabeth suspected that Miss Darcy's brother and cousin were doing their best to encourage a distance until her heart was strong enough to stand on its own. It was what she would do for her sisters.

Mama was delighted. "Imagine that! Our cook's cake served to the finest families in London!"

Jane said, "Colonel Fitzwilliam was entertaining us with stories of his time in Portugal."

Kitty asked, "Did you ever find your boots?"

"That I did, although the state in which I found them rather made me wish I had not."

Everyone leaned forward except Darcy, who must already know this story. "They were beyond repair, much to my chagrin and that of my batman. What was not chewed up was covered in drool." He slapped his hand against his leg and guffawed. "They are still buried in Vimeiro! I learned a valuable lesson that day: The latest fashion is never worth a month's wages. I had to hobble around in the old, patched pair for months."

Lydia furrowed her brow. "Why did you not borrow the sum to have another pair made?"

The colonel shook his head. "I have known too many men who live on credit. They are wretched creatures always looking for relief and the next handout."

Lydia giggled, "But they look so handsome in their new boots and waistcoats. Surely, we are meant to live with pleasure. I would rather die than show up at an assembly in a gown that was horribly out of style."

Jane spoke softly. "Men who face death every day would be more concerned about remaining alive than looking handsome in their boots."

The colonel smiled at her, ignoring Lydia's protests to the contrary. Mama filled everyone's empty plates with more cake, handing an especially generous portion to the colonel.

"Ah, the way to a man's heart," he said graciously, accepting his plate and feeding the kitten another crumb.

Elizabeth took advantage of the pause in conversation to ask about the kitten. "Is that the one that likes to climb the curtains?"

"The very one! Poor lad kept getting stuck partway up the silks, so I decided to give him a better view from my shoulder." He rubbed under the kitten's chin. "He yowls every time I try to put him down, so we decided to bring him along."

"I am glad you did! We are fond of cats at Longbourn," Mama cooed.

"Why did you not bring them all?" Kitty asked.

"We did not wish to impose," Miss Darcy replied. Her confidence increased as she spoke about the cats she adored. "That adventuresome one is too mischievous to leave behind with my maid, so we had to bring him. Then I could not leave his sister behind. We probably should have brought the white one that likes to hunt feathers."

"He is my favorite! The black fur on his head looks just like a top hat set at a rakish angle! So charming! Pray bring them all the next time you call. They are no trouble at all." Kitty ran her hand down the length of the female feline.

Miss Darcy looked about the room, looking less uncertain with every encouraging smile. "I would love that."

Papa moved farther away from the fire. "Since that is now settled, I shall take my leave. I fear I am occupying too much room and shall therefore remove myself to my book room."

Mama rolled her eyes.

"How thoughtful of you," Elizabeth commented dryly.

He tipped his head toward her. "Anything for the comfort of our guests."

Darcy leaned toward Elizabeth. "I shall have to have a bed and wash basin installed in Pemberley's library."

Papa stopped mid-step. "Is that a promise, young man?"

The colonel interjected, "There are far worse places to encamp."

"Is your library as grand as Miss Bingley claims?" Elizabeth was enjoying how well Darcy teased.

His eyes twinkled. "Grander."

She arched her brow. "Maybe I shall insist on having a cot installed there for me!"

The gleam in his eye said *Not if I can help it.*

A tap at the door interrupted their flirtation, perhaps for the best. Her face was hot enough.

If Papa had heard it, he pretended not to, and he calmly proceeded to his book room.

"Who would be out in this weather?" Mama frowned at the fogged window glass.

"Someone in need of a warm fire, a dry room, and hot tea." Kitty dangled a ribbon for the kitten in her lap. "Is that not so, you little angel?" She gasped. "That is the perfect name! Angel!"

Lydia shook her head. "Angel is too common. I shall call her Angelina."

Miss Darcy smiled. "Angelina is a perfect name. Serafina would approve." With her younger sisters, Miss Darcy seemed relaxed, like a girl without a worry or insecurity. "When Angelina is fully weaned, she is yours."

Their unexpected callers entered the drawing room. Elizabeth's two youngest sisters beamed, but Miss Darcy's smile faded.

Lydia leaped to her feet. "Mr. Denny and Mr. Wickham!"

Elizabeth saw Mr. Wickham blanch and swallow hard while sensing Darcy tense and grow larger beside her.

CHAPTER 25

*W*ickham flipped his trepidation into a smile in the blink of an eye. He stepped in front of Mr. Denny to swoop an exaggerated bow. Hand over his heart, he addressed Mrs. Bennet. "We apologize for our sorry state, but we knew we could count on you to provide refuge from this dreadful rain."

The skin over Darcy's knuckles tightened. Wickham never had been one to learn from his mistakes.

Mrs. Bennet divided the last of the cake, poured tea, and fussed over the arranging of the chairs around the fire. She was an attentive hostess, even if one of her guests was a slippery viper.

Darcy was loath to leave Elizabeth's side, but he moved to the other end of the room to stand behind his sister, his hands wringing the back of her chair. Richard, too, moved closer to Georgiana, closing ranks.

"I thought you were reassigned," said Richard.

Mrs. Annesley looped her arm through Georgiana's, lending support.

Wickham smirked belligerently. "To Ramsgate. I had thought you had a hand in the recommendation, Colonel." His gaze flickered to Georgiana. "How can I thank you for returning me to a place with so many pleasant memories?"

The chair creaked under Darcy's grip. Elizabeth crossed the room to stand beside him, behind Georgiana. Elizabeth might not yet know the whole of it, but she was perceptive. She glared daggers at Wickham.

"Shall we roll back the rugs and dance?" Mrs. Bennet noticed none of the tension growing in the room.

"No!" Darcy shot her suggestion down immediately.

Richard placed his empty plate on the nearest table. "We have trespassed on your hospitality long enough, madam."

"You mean to leave? In this downpour?" She could not countenance their departure. "You cannot leave when you arrived on horseback! Miss Darcy would catch a terrible chill."

Of all people, how ironic that Mrs. Bennet should say such a thing. Darcy could not help but glance at Miss Bennet, whose lips were pinched together in the most marked sign of disapproval Darcy had yet to witness on the lady. He further saw her shoulders heave up and down in a large sigh, and Darcy nearly laughed at her marked display of restraint. The lady must have nerves of steel and the forbearance of a saint. She would fare well with his own aunts.

And then there was Elizabeth. She observed, "It would not do for anyone to depart in this downpour. If the storm passes as suddenly as it arrived, then it shall not last much longer." She watched Georgiana and deftly influenced the conversation, all the while with a smile on her face and her usual light touch. It made Wickham's presence at the opposite end of the room almost bearable. Would that the flames at the fireplace rise to scorch his coattails!

"Perhaps some music will help us pass the time," Elizabeth suggested. "Would you agree to a little duet at the pianoforte, Miss Darcy? Something to lighten the mood and help us pass the time?"

Georgiana—play music in front of that lout? She was too shy. She would falter. Darcy opened his mouth to oppose the idea but Richard jabbed him in the ribs, preventing him from speaking.

Rubbing his side and glaring at his cousin, Darcy missed whatever it was that propelled Georgiana to stand. He rushed to her side to escort her to the instrument. The distance was not great, but he would block her and Elizabeth from that devilish rake flirting shamelessly with the younger Bennets.

Darcy shot Richard a look and nodded over to them. Wickham had come so near to ruining Georgie, who now had two protectors to look out for her. Miss Kitty and Miss Lydia had no such advantage. Mr.

Bennet had disappeared into his book room, and Mrs. Bennet seemed to think that every man donning a uniform must be an honorable gentleman seeking a wife.

Georgiana sat beside Elizabeth on the bench just as Richard joined Wickham and Mr. Denny. The panic on Wickham's semblance was most satisfying. Richard would tease and torment him at his leisure, like a cat playing with a mouse. Even with a kitten crawling over his shoulders, he looked intimidating.

Darcy's sister played beautifully, as she always did. Elizabeth lacked her perfected technique, the work of hours of practice under the tutelage of the most proficient masters, and she played with gusto and charm. Darcy could not help but admire her performance.

Their audience clapped. Elizabeth leaned into Georgiana, "You play splendidly! The praise I have heard for your accomplishment on the instrument pales in comparison to the reality."

Miss Mary offered to play, and Darcy tried to conceal his cringe. Mrs. Bennet would have none of it, though, insisting instead that Georgiana play for them again.

Georgiana bowed her head at the enthusiastic praise. "Oh, I could not."

Darcy had hoped she might agree. One act of boldness might lead to another. Unfortunately, the Bennets' encouragement only wilted her courage. He spoke over the melee of persuaders. "My sister is not accustomed to exhibiting. Perhaps she might play for you when we are not such a sizable crowd."

Wickham snorted, the ugly sneer on his face seeming to say *Have you ever seen a young lady weaker than Miss Darcy?*

Elizabeth pushed her shoulders back, her jaw jutted forward in the same manner he had noted the two times she refused to dance with him. Leaning over on the pretense of searching through the pages of music, she whispered to Georgiana, "You have nothing to prove to anyone, and especially not to that man. Play no more."

Georgiana was shy and diffident in many ways, but she did not like to be told what to do. Her expression tightened, and she lifted her chin defiantly—the same tenacious look their father had in his most stubborn moments. Turning to face her audience, she looked pointedly at Elizabeth. "I would be delighted to play another."

Elizabeth slipped off the bench and stood on Georgiana's other side, the mischievous quirk in her lips revealing that she had maneuvered his sister to do exactly as the situation required. Darcy shook his head in appreciative awe, his gaze lingering on the curl of Elizabeth's lips. He ought to have kissed her when he had the chance. Lord knew he still wanted to.

Georgiana launched into a piece which startled him to his senses. Wrenching his attention away from Elizabeth, Darcy attempted to focus on the performance. It was difficult with Elizabeth only an arm's length away.

When he peeked at her, the smile greeting him made his clothing feel too tight.

He looked away before he made a spectacle of himself. He imagined himself in the coldest, dullest place imaginable: his aunt Catherine's drawing room where a beautiful piano nobody in her household played sat neglected in a corner.

Georgiana displayed the infallibility of her fingering and added her soprano voice to the greatest advantage. She was radiant. The longer she played, the stronger her voice became. Even Mr. Bennet appeared in the doorway, his eyes closed, his head bobbing and swaying along with the ebb and flow of the music.

Everyone clapped enthusiastically except Wickham. He looked as though he had swallowed sour wine.

Georgiana swiveled to face her audience, her head high. Wickham was nobody to her—had been nobody for a while—and now it was plain that any influence he held over her had disappeared with the high notes of her aria.

Darcy's chest swelled with pride. After fifteen minutes in Elizabeth's company, look how Georgiana's courage rose. Elizabeth had done that.

As if to crown Georgiana's triumph, a ray of sun peeked through the clouds and shone through the window across the worn carpet.

"It stopped raining!" she exclaimed.

Richard stepped forward. "We ought to return to Netherfield while we can."

Bowing to Mr. and Mrs. Bennet, Darcy added, "Thank you for your hospitality."

"You are always welcome, Mr. Darcy, Colonel Fitzwilliam. Such pleasant company is always welcome in our home. Perhaps we shall see you on the morrow?" Mrs. Bennet's eyebrows raised in twin question marks.

"Of course." To his amazement, Darcy realized that he looked forward to returning.

He took Elizabeth's hand, her fingers small and strong against his. Slowly, his eyes never leaving hers, he bent closer and brushed his lips over her knuckles. Her lips parted, and she sucked in a breath. Her cheeks pinked a bright hue—Darcy's new favorite color. His lips tingled for more, but he suddenly realized a resonant silence had fallen over the room.

He looked up to see the ladies of the house clutching one hand over their hearts, their heads tilted, smiling eyes watching him and Elizabeth. Mrs. Bennet fanned her face vigorously.

It was the disbelief on Wickham's face that filled Darcy with the most satisfaction. His foe's smooth manners and slick speech no longer had any effect on Elizabeth. She had made her choice—and she had chosen Darcy. It was the sweetest, most perfect revenge.

Wickham shuffled his feet, his smile forced. "We would hate to get caught in the rain again. We had better depart as well. Ladies." He bowed gallantly, albeit a touch stiffer than before.

The youngest Bennets pleaded for him and Mr.

Denny to stay longer, but he ignored every objection. "I am expected at my regiment in Ramsgate. I fear I shall not be able to return for some time"—he looked at Darcy—"if ever."

Darcy nodded. Miss Kitty and Miss Lydia would be safer without that wolf slinking around. Now that he knew they were not unprotected, Wickham had to abandon any ruinous ideas he may have plotted against them.

With one last smile at Elizabeth, Darcy finally released his hold on her hand to step into the hall.

Miss Bennet ushered Wickham and Mr. Denny out of the drawing room to stand in the hall with Darcy. She returned to console her bereaved youngest sister, who was lamenting both the wallpaper in the room and her lack of proposals.

Mrs. Hill came bustling out of the kitchen, Darcy's coat draped over her arms. "Pardon me, sir, but I took the liberty of drying your coat in the kitchen where the stove is warmest. It is mostly dry." She handed it to her husband, who held it up for Darcy to shrug into.

"Thank you, Mrs. Hill, Mr. Hill" he was rewarded with matching gappy smiles.

Wickham shot him a confounded look. His coat dripped from the coat rack by the door. The tables had turned. "I do not know how you did it, Darcy, but you won."

Darcy had never seen Wickham so discontented. Maybe now that Wickham had failed to take Darcy's fortune, his sister, his good name, the woman he loved… he might direct his energies to his own improvement. Darcy hoped so.

With a nod, he and Wickham parted ways. Gone was the resentment Darcy had held against that man for years. In its place, he found peace.

He had been a fool to spurn Elizabeth as he had done, to avoid her and insult her family when a more intelligent man would have begged her for a dance, her friendship, her heart, her hand.

Darcy hastened across the yard, happy to spend the three miles to Netherfield contemplating the appeal of a pair of fine eyes.

CHAPTER 26

*E*lizabeth watched Darcy cross the yard, his stride purposeful. Everything he did was deliberate. When he chose to pursue an objective, he did so without wavering. When he spoke, he meant every word—a quality she had misunderstood as unsocial and taciturn before but which she now appreciated for its honesty and certainty. Darcy was not a man to raise her expectations and then shatter them with disappointment. He would not lie to her.

What a contrast to Mr. Wickham. He slinked away, his hat low over his eyes, his shoulders rounded. There was more to his history with Darcy than he had implied—none of it favorable, given Darcy and Colonel Fitzwilliam's restrained hostility and Miss Darcy's obvious unease. Something significant had happened there. Remembering Mr. Wickham's panic and false bravado, Elizabeth could no longer excuse him from blame. He would lie if it served his purposes.

Lydia still lamented and whined over the absence of the officers while Kitty consoled her. *Good riddance of bad rubbish.* Elizabeth dusted off her hands and left the window.

Mary was nowhere in sight.

Jane sat serenely humming over her embroidery, and Elizabeth joined her. "I am sorry Mr. Bingley was unable to call with his party. He is certain to make an appearance once his business is done."

"He shall call if he is able." Jane did not look up from her stitches.

"It is good he takes the management of his estate so seriously." Elizabeth did not wish for her sister to think any less of Mr. Bingley.

Jane continued stitching. "As a gentleman should do."

Elizabeth's forehead tightened. It was not like Jane to put her off like this. "It was gracious of Colonel Fitzwilliam to call."

Jane's needle hovered over her whitework, and she pressed her lips together. "Pray do not distract me with conversation, Lizzy. I promised Mrs. Lamb I would finish this gift for her niece, and I really must finish today."

Was Jane irritated at her? Stranger and stranger.

As her sister was not inclined for conversation and Elizabeth could not very well press her with Kitty and Lydia there to observe it, Elizabeth went upstairs, grateful to abandon the gloom downstairs for the peace and quiet of her room. She trailed her fingers over her lips, remembering how they had tingled and burned. The thrill of an almost kiss.

Sobs echoed down the hall, and she raised her hands heavenward. What was going on in their household?

Following the cries into Mary's room, Elizabeth sat beside her and wrapped her arm around her sister's stiff shoulders. "What is wrong, dearest?"

Mary's voice came out in a squeak. "I have sinned. I am an envious wretch." She buried her face in her hands, her sobs violent.

Elizabeth rubbed her back and handed her a clean handkerchief. "Of everyone I know, you are the last person I would ever suspect of envy."

Mary dropped her hands and sniffed. "When I heard Miss Darcy play, I wished I possessed such talent. If that is not envy, what is?"

Prying the unused handkerchief out of Mary's grip, Elizabeth dabbed her sister's eyes. "It is not wrong to wish to improve oneself."

"I wish to be applauded and praised as she was." Mary seemed determined to convince Elizabeth of her sin.

Pressing the handkerchief into Mary's hand again, Elizabeth said saucily, "And why should she not play beautifully when she has had the advantage of music tutors and grand masters?"

Mary bowed her head. "I suppose so."

"It is a fact! Mary, you should be proud of what you have accomplished through your own initiative and exertions." Elizabeth's chest tightened as she spoke. How many times had she felt her inferiority whenever she was exposed to gentry outside her comfortable circle? It pained her enough, but she had learned to make light of her faults. Mary took herself and everyone else too seriously. Instead of being received kindly, she was too often mocked. Elizabeth was ashamed she had not recognized this before. Was Mary not as deserving of happiness as Jane and Elizabeth? Did not all her sisters deserve at least a chance at something better?

A fire flamed inside Elizabeth, bright and hot. She had thought that she was helping her sisters by attempting to cover their weaknesses and indiscretions, but she had been engaged to Darcy for a week and had yet to use her influence to improve her family. No more.

Elizabeth stayed with Mary until the tears had dried, and then she marched into her father's book room. If she was going to marry in two weeks, she would do well to take advantage of her new station. Elizabeth would use it to benefit her sisters.

By the time she reached the door, her arguments were in place. Mary wished to learn. Kitty and Lydia would benefit from an occupation other than chasing after soldiers in Meryton. And the clincher: if Papa ever wanted her to invite her sisters to London or Pemberley, they must learn to behave appropriately in higher society.

Half an hour later, Elizabeth emerged, having secured Papa's permission to hire a music teacher.

She returned to her room with her step firmer, her head higher. So this was what it felt like to take command. It was exhilarating, empowering, delicious! No wonder Darcy looked proud all the time.

Now that Elizabeth had tasted success, she wanted more. Having nothing else on which to expend her energies, Elizabeth sat at her writing table, brushing the tip of her quill over her lips, remembering the kiss that almost was—and soon would be if she had anything to do with it.

Inspired, she dipped the tip in ink and listed all the ways she could fan the flames of friendship, respect, and attraction into an ardent, lasting love.

CHAPTER 27

*R*ichard removed the kitten from inside his coat before its sharp claws ruined his shirt. Plopping the intrepid feline on his shoulder and receiving a nuzzle of thanks for it, Richard guided his horse to fall in beside Darcy. Georgiana and the lady kitten rode ahead with Mrs. Annesley, providing the perfect opportunity for frank conversation. He hated to interrupt his cousin's reverie, but questions must be asked. "What do you think Wickham was up to?"

"Hm? Wickham?"

Richard rolled his eyes. "You remember the man? Reprobate. Lecher. Parasite. Thorn in your side."

"Of course, I do," Darcy snapped.

Ah, there was his taciturn relative. "I like you better when you are with Miss Elizabeth."

"I like you better when you are silent."

Richard ignored the hint. "You have not told her about Wickham and—" He nodded toward Georgiana.

234

"No."

That was it? Richard was not satisfied with the clipped reply. Judging by Darcy's silence, his cousin knew he ought to have confided in her too. "You marry in ten days. Do you not trust her?"

"I trust Elizabeth."

"Then why have you not told her?"

"I have told her most of his history with me. She knows there is more I shall tell her when the time is right."

"Darcy, the time is right. It could not be more right."

"An observation easily made from one not deprived of a normal courtship. What most gentlemen need months or years to accomplish, I have been forced to do in three weeks and with an excessive number of chaperones."

While Richard commiserated with Darcy—it had been Georgiana's idea to call at Longbourn to find her brother—he held strong objections to Darcy's other point. "Years? How would that progress? You stare at her at dinner parties for a month before you work up the gumption to ask her to dance? Then you applaud yourself over the next few months for your attentions while the lady remains oblivious to them?"

"She would know if I was courting her."

Richard jerked his head so quickly, his collar protested with a high-pitched *Mew!* "I doubt that. Courting is too akin to small talk, and you were never any good at it. No, Darcy, you were wise to skip the courtship entirely and just marry the lady. Three weeks is ample time if one is quick about it."

"The power of doing anything with quickness is always prized much by the possessor and often without any attention to the imperfection of the performance."

"Good advice to remember on your wedding night."

Darcy turned a brilliant shade of red. "Will you shut up if I agree that you are right and have every intention of telling her?"

It pleased Richard immensely to see how thoughts of Darcy's bride-to-be discomposed the groom, even more satisfying than getting his cousin to admit he was right. "Good. There is no reason for Wickham to sniff around Longbourn unless he means to benefit from your marriage into that family. He could ruin the youngest easily enough and then demand regular payments for his silence."

"A possibility I had also considered."

"Excellent! Then I shall say no more on the subject."

How satisfying it had been to see Wickham dumbfounded. The look on his face when he had seen Darcy hold Miss Elizabeth's hand, his heart in his eyes, the likeness of a lovelorn buck...

For months, Richard had dreamed of exacting justice from Wickham, of calling in his debts, or sending him to debtor's prison, of disfiguring his pretty nose... but this was infinitely better! Who knew that the ultimate dagger to Wickham's heart was for him to see Darcy sublimely happy? Ah, it did a man good to see justice served on a silver platter filled with Wickham's own envy.

Richard could have basked in his cousin's triumph the rest of the way, but he had granted Darcy enough contented silence. There was another question burning in his mind. "What about Bingley?"

Darcy made a noise between a growl and a sigh.

"I take that to mean you have said nothing to her about your little scheme? What *do* you talk about?"

Darcy spoke through clenched teeth. "It was not an issue until *you* showed up."

"Is that what you think? I had hoped you would abandon the foolish plan entirely."

"And watch Bingley make a muddle of his life?"

It pained Richard to think of Bingley with Miss Bennet, but he would not hear her maligned. "Miss Bennet would be the making of him." She was the kind of woman to make any man better himself.

"My misgiving has nothing to do with her."

"Then what?"

"What would Bingley do for *her*? Thrust her into the company of his pernicious sisters, who would never forgive him for marrying below their outrageous expectations? He has learned a great deal over the past months, but he has no permanent home to offer and still relies too heavily on the opinions of others."

"Except when it comes to choosing a wife. He seems firmly settled on Miss Bennet despite his sisters' advice and your influence to the contrary. Had I not bribed his bailiff to create a crisis requiring his immediate attention, Bingley would have accompanied me and Georgiana to Longbourn today."

Darcy frowned. "I had not thought his bailiff the type of man to accept bribes."

Richard grumbled. "I am out five pounds."

"Methods aside, I am grateful to you for detaining him. I cannot stand by and watch Bingley ruin his life and Miss Bennet's or hurt Georgiana. I swore I would protect her, and I shall live up to my promise."

Sucking in a lungful of air, Richard released his breath slowly. Darcy genuinely believed he was shielding the ones he loved, but instead he denied them a choice in the matter. Even worse, he could lose Elizabeth over this. "An admirable goal, but who are you to make these decisions for everyone?"

Silence.

Richard tried another angle. "You cannot always protect Georgie."

"I have to try."

"Then you will do so at too great a cost."

"She trusts me like a father. To withdraw my protection would be a betrayal."

"But you can betray your betrothed? All Elizabeth will see, all that matters, is that you chose your sister over hers. You are choosing for everyone, and the choice is not yours to make."

"You would have me stand by and do nothing?"

"Have you discussed your concerns with Bingley? He trusts you; he would listen."

"But what if he does not?"

"Then he will make bad choices. That is what people do. They make poor decisions and suffer the consequences, but they learn from their mistakes and do better next time."

Darcy's shoulders tensed to his ears. "This *is* Georgiana's next time. She chose Bingley."

"And he chooses Miss Bennet," Richard said with a deep sigh. There was no point in arguing with Darcy when he believed himself to be right. If only he would be as stubborn for his own happiness as he was for his sister's and his friends'.

They reached the stables. After helping the ladies down, Richard plucked the kitten off the brim of his hat and carried him into the parlor, where the rest of the household was gathered.

"How are the Bennets today?" Miss Bingley asked with a sly smile. "I do not know why you must call so often at Longbourn when your charming mother-in-law will make sure she and her lively daughters are frequent guests at Pemberley." She giggled behind her hand, the bird of paradise feathers in her bandeau quivering. There was a meanness in her laugh that Richard could not ignore.

He turned to Darcy. "Mrs. Bennet is not in the habit of assaulting rose bushes, I hope?"

"She holds a certain hostility toward hedgerows, but I have never heard her speak against any other flora." Darcy maintained a neutral expression, a true testament to his deeply ingrained manners.

Georgiana buried her face behind the cinnamon-spotted kitten.

Miss Bingley turned her nose up and huffed.

Her brother pouted by the window. "I wish I could have gone with you instead of being stuck here. It is impossible to get anything done in this weather."

Wickham aside, the company was far superior at Longbourn than here, but Richard had teased Miss Bingley enough. He could not in good form insult his hostess by agreeing with her brother.

Tickling his furry friend under the chin, Richard set the kitten down on the floor. "Go explore, Little Crusoe," Richard said under his breath.

Too curious to waste time lamenting the loss of its elevated seat, the little explorer set his sights on the large Palladian windows Miss Bingley had decorated in garish extravagance. Blue and lilac taffeta curtains trimmed liberally with gold-colored trimmings, tassels, and fringes—the perfect playground for a climber to test his claws and reach glorious new heights.

Serafina sauntered into the room, followed by the rest of her litter. Georgiana scooped her up in her arms. "May they stay for a few minutes, Miss Bingley?"

"Of course, my dear! I have always said there is no finer pet than a cat, have I not, Louisa?"

Mrs. Hurst dutifully agreed.

"How much sooner one tires of a dog than a feline," Miss Bingley continued. "When I have a house of my own, I shall be miserable if I do not have the companionship of a cat like Serafina and her adorable kittens."

Georgiana's face lit up with pleasure. "It would please me more than anything to gift you one of them. You may have your pick of the litter."

Except for Angelina, Richard thought, hoping Georgiana remembered that she was already promised to Miss Lydia.

"You are too generous! I could not possibly presume to accept when I know how precious they are to you."

"Oh, but you are one of my dearest friends!" Georgiana insisted.

Richard grimaced. He had feared this outcome.

Puffing up like a peacock at the compliment, Miss Bingley fluttered her fingers over her heart. "I am flattered, but pray address me as Caro as all my intimate friends do."

Of course, Georgiana insisted that Miss Bingley use her Christian name.

All the avowed friendship in the room threatened to sour Richard's mood.

A flicker of movement behind Miss Bingley caught his eye. The next moment, before he or anyone else could intervene, two paws batted at her bandeau in a fight worthy of the boxer's ring. The prize: two long, colorful feathers. The contender: one white kitten with a hat-shaped splotch on his head.

Miss Bingley waved her hands and screeched. Had she held still, she might have fared better.

Bingley pulled the Mighty Hunter off his sister's head, the kitten taking one feather with him and leaving the other dangling broken from Miss Bingley's mangled headpiece.

Wrapping his arms around the cat, Bingley hid behind the creature, disguising his laughter behind poorly disguised coughs and an occasional half-hearted reprimand. "That was awfully rude of you. Your mother looks distressed."

Serafina did not, in fact, look distressed. Richard could not claim the ability to read an animal's mind, but he would bet that she was rather proud of her son's improving hunting skills.

A cry from the decorated window pulled Richard away from the diverting scene and spotted Crusoe stuck on top of a gilt-carved rosette. The little bugger had climbed higher than Richard could reach.

Darcy, quick to react, pulled a chair closer to the window sash, but it was Richard who climbed atop it to rescue his pal. Stretching to the tips of his toes, he coaxed the kitten onto his arm. With all the practice it had balancing on Richard's shoulders of late, this was no trouble for the daring puss.

Heart calming to a normal rhythm, Richard stepped onto the floor, the precious cargo safe in his arms.

"Grandmama's vase!" cried Mrs. Hurst.

Darcy leaped back across the room in four long strides, just in time to catch the vase the feline butler had pushed off the ledge. Lifting the black kitten by its scruff, Darcy removed the perpetrator from the table before it could attempt to break any more heirlooms.

"That was close," Bingley observed.

A collective sigh of relief pervaded the room. Who knew how disruptive the tiny creatures could be?

Richard stroked Crusoe's fur, watching as Bingley attempted to soothe his sisters as well as the kitten who was fascinated with feathers. Darcy, too, cradled the cantankerous black and white cat against his coat, letting the kitten settle on his lap when he took a seat.

What a laughable picture they made! Three gentlemen indulging the whims of three pocket-sized troublemakers.

CHAPTER 28

*D*arcy had more reason than ever to seek Elizabeth's company, but he found himself in the frustrating position of being often in her presence but never in a circumstance allowing private conversation.

It was true that her friends and family—with the expected exception of Miss Mary—were happy to turn the other eye and allow a pair of young lovers to steal a few moments together.

Not so his own sister.

Not only did Georgiana stick like a bur to his side, but she had also adopted the custom of riding early with him, thus preventing his morning encounters with Elizabeth.

All obstacles aside, Darcy did manage to relate the story of Wickham's nearly successful seduction of Georgiana during a soiree at Lucas Lodge. Thankfully, Elizabeth was insightful and had drawn the correct conclusion that the betrayal Georgiana had suffered had been at Wickham's hand. She would tell her father what was necessary, and Wickham would never again be permitted to cross Longbourn's threshold.

But Georgiana's attachment to Bingley and Darcy's reasons for approving of the eventual match required absolute privacy and more time to fully explain. Darcy resented the necessity of telling Elizabeth at all when the precious exchanges they shared were too few and far between. He craved her clever conversation. They were in each other's company every day, and yet he missed her.

With only one more week until their wedding day, Darcy despaired of ever having a private word with Elizabeth before they were wed. If only Georgiana were stronger. If only she did not rely so much on him. If only he were a better brother... These guilty thoughts gnawed at his bones.

Already that day, Georgiana had frustrated his plan to speak with Elizabeth during his morning ride even though he had departed a good quarter of an hour earlier than normal. She did so again at the Philipses, who had kindly invited them for tea.

Now Darcy paced Netherfield's music room while Georgiana practiced and Miss Bingley turned the pages, planning how he could escape to Longbourn unnoticed and without being followed.

There was a knock at the door, and the butler cleared his throat. "Miss Elizabeth Bennet and Miss Catherine Bennet," he announced.

Elizabeth breezed inside the room like a breath of fresh air to a suffocating Darcy. Her complexion was bright from exercise, her skirts damp from the fields and paths.

Darcy's favorite kitten followed her, bumping his head against her leg and rubbing against her skirts until Elizabeth leaned down to rub her hand along his shiny black back. He arched to match the movement, wrapping his tail around her hand and meowing up at her while all the usual pleasantries were exchanged.

Bingley exclaimed, "He likes you! I did not think he liked anyone except his own mother and Darcy."

Richard added, "He is a gentleman selective in his friendships." Jerking his head toward Darcy, he added with a wink, "Reminds me of someone else I know."

Elizabeth laughed, and Darcy's mood lightened. "Then I am doubly honored." She stroked down the cat's back one more time. If Darcy could reverse time, he would not have been in such a hurry to escape from Bingley's study. What he would give for just five minutes alone with Elizabeth.

"Darcy would make an excellent name for a cat," Richard mumbled, rubbing his chin.

Teasingly, Elizabeth called "Darcy" to the kitten. He yawned and blinked his eyes slowly at Richard as though to convey the ridiculousness of his suggestion. A finer feline Darcy had never met.

Elizabeth chuckled. "He does not agree with you, Colonel."

Miss Kitty joined the other ladies by the instrument

after snatching up another kitten, who had been flicking his tail and staring at the fringe dangling from Miss Bingley's sleeves. She planted a kiss on top of his head. "Is this the rudy—"

Miss Bingley pounced on the mistake. "Rudy? What is a rudy?"

Miss Kitty giggled, too accustomed to her sister's teasing to be bothered by Miss Bingley's mean-spirited question. "Rude, rowdy. I could not decide which one, so they must have decided to tumble off my tongue together."

Bingley observed, "The same happens to me all the time. There are simply too many words to describe one thing."

"Precisely! How am I to choose only one when there are so many choices?"

"My thoughts exactly!" Bingley looked about the room for support and then back to Miss Kitty when he got none. He reached out and scratched the top of the kitten's head. "Rudy. That would make a fine name for this cat."

Miss Kitty beamed. "Rudy. Sounds like the name of a mischievous little boy with muddy boots, torn trousers, and jam smeared on his cheek."

"And a frog in his pocket!" added Bingley.

"Or it could be short for Rudolph! A fine, dignified name!"

They laughed until Miss Bingley spoke. "It is a pity Mr. Collins left Longbourn so soon after his arrival."

The mention of Mr. Collins had the same effect on

their party as a wet blanket over a fire. Bingley, who had been so talkative moments before, went noticeably silent.

With a shrug, Miss Bingley added cheerily, "I had thought he hoped to marry one of your sisters."

Miss Kitty blushed. "Yes, well, he had his eye on Lizzy… but…"

"Then you might be the fortunate one," Miss Bingley said, clapping her hands together in spurious glee.

"Me?" Miss Kitty choked. "Dear me, no, no, no. I could never agree to marry such a ridiculous man."

"Oh, but your mother made it very clear that he meant to take one of you as his bride. I do not suspect he will be away for long."

What did Miss Bingley mean by this questioning?

Elizabeth replied, "Just because a gentleman proposes does not signify that the lady is obliged to accept his offer. The decisions we are allowed to make are few and precious, and I hope my sisters would choose happiness and love over security and expectations."

Darcy frowned. Elizabeth's argument was sound, but was that how she still felt about their match? She had not wanted to accept the arrangement, but Darcy had thought they understood each other better now.

Bingley broke his uncharacteristic silence. "Let us enjoy our present company without lamenting Mr. Collins. I am sure he had his reasons for departing when he did. Let us speak of something else." His words and accompanying facial expression directed to his sister brooked no argument.

Miss Kitty asked Georgiana, "Will you spend the rest of winter in London or at Pemberley?"

Georgiana's eyes shifted between Miss Kitty and Darcy. "I do not know. I have always spent the winter at Pemberley with my brother."

Elizabeth jumped in. "Then you must come with us." She turned to Darcy, "That is, if we are to return to Pemberley. Your family might wish us to stay longer in town."

An image of Elizabeth sliding down the snow-covered hills, peals of laughter trailing in her wake, flitted through Darcy's mind. Skating on the lake and warming their fingers with cups of hot cider, throwing snowballs, reading by the fire... Elizabeth had not yet been to Pemberley, but Darcy already saw her there as clearly as though the images in his mind were memories—as though she had always been a part of his life. That she might feel trapped in their arrangement gutted Darcy.

Richard clapped him on the back. "You must bring your bride to the hot springs at Matlock. Mother will insist on packing a picnic and making a day of it."

Miss Kitty swayed on her feet. "How romantic! Imagine sipping chocolate and eating cake in the pools while the snow fluttered down around you?"

The thought of Elizabeth surrounded by steam, snowflakes drifting onto her hair and glistening off the tips of her eyelashes stirred Darcy's blood and conjured all sorts of images which were entirely inappropriate to contemplate.

He had to talk to her. He had to tell her his plan for Bingley. She would not be happy, but he would plead his case and be honest with her.

"It is settled. If Pemberley is where everyone wishes to go, then we shall travel there directly after the wedding. Now, if you will excuse me for a few minutes, I promised to lend Mr. Bennet a book from the library."

Darcy saw Richard's smirk. If Elizabeth did not take his hint, his cousin would make certain she did.

He left the room and turned down the hall, wishing he had thought of a better excuse when the stark shelves offered few books to lend to a well-read gentleman like Mr. Bennet.

Picking up *Sense and Sensibility,* Darcy found his place and attempted to resume reading, but the words on the page failed to capture his attention when his thoughts were full of Elizabeth. Would she ever have chosen him?

The white-collared kitten trotted into the library and hopped onto the window seat, pretending to ignore Darcy while never letting him out of his sight.

Darcy sat, trying to take no notice of the cat and purposely sitting with his back to the door so he would not obsess over how long it would be before Elizabeth walked through it.

How should he begin? Darcy fretted.

The kitten hopped down from the window seat to

sit at Darcy's feet. Stretching in place, he looked up expectantly.

Setting aside his book, Darcy scooped him up, resting the fluff ball against his chest. "You have excellent taste in friends, if I do say so. What think you of the name Darcy?"

The kitten bumped his head against Darcy's chin and purred.

"It is a grand name, but something tells me you already know that."

Another head bump.

Darcy chuckled. "So long as you do not befriend Miss Bingley. No end of rumors would be started should someone say, 'Darcy, climb down from Miss Bingley's lap. You will ruin her gown.'"

The kitten yawned, showing his pointy teeth.

Darcy remembered the stories his father had read to him of brave knights and their leader, King Arthur. Darcy had dreamed of going on daring adventures with his band of closest friends, freeing their domain of monsters and uniting the kingdom. One of the knights had also served as King Arthur's butler. Not only was he a warrior, but he was one of King Arthur's most trusted men.

"Lucas." Darcy spoke in a low tone appropriate for a library. "Do you like that? Sir Lucas Darcy, unless you prefer a different title. His Lordship the Right Honorable Lucas is a mouthful." The kitten yawned.

With a chuckle, Darcy said, "Of course. Why named after the brave butler when you could be named after the king? Does Arthur suit you better?" The kitten purred contentedly, and Darcy told him the stories he remembered from his youth as he waited for Elizabeth.

ELIZABETH WAITED until Kitty engaged Miss Darcy in conversation to slip away. How strange that Jane had claimed other obligations and could not accompany her to Netherfield Park. Mary had a lesson with her music tutor, and while Lydia was eager to walk as far as Meryton, she had no interest in any gentleman not wearing a red coat. Fortunately, Kitty had offered to walk with Elizabeth, and now she was grateful for the distraction Kitty provided. Elizabeth had understood Darcy's look and had waited on pins and needles until she could escape.

She paused at the open library door, stopping when she heard Darcy's soothing voice talking softly. He sat facing away from her toward the gardens, but she saw his reflection in the glass.

He cuddled the black kitten with the white paws and collar, talking to it gently while it paid rapt attention. It was a tender moment. Elizabeth's reaction to it was so intense, it stole her breath. She imagined Darcy holding their first child. He would make a wonderful father. He would be an excellent husband. Elizabeth could hardly believe her good fortune—she who had been intent on refusing his offer! What a mistake that would have been.

Stepping inside the library, Elizabeth tiptoed to the chair. The cat saw her and instantly lost interest in the story he was being told. After an impressive yawn, he hopped down to the floor. "Sir Arthur has a nice sound to it."

Darcy rose, his smile quickly fading. "Thank you for coming." He stepped forward, careful to avoid Arthur's tail flicking back and forth on the carpet. "There is something I must—" Like a flash, Arthur darted between Darcy's feet, bumping against him with a vociferous meow and pushing him off balance.

Elizabeth reached for him, doing her best to avoid trampling the kitten.

They weaved and wobbled until, with a firm tug, Darcy pulled her into his arms. Equilibrium, which neither of them had managed on their own, was secured once they were supporting each other. He held her, his breath as ragged as her own. His fingers touched her jaw, his thumb trailed over her lips. "Elizabeth?"

"Fitzwilliam," she whispered huskily.

The next moment, his lips brushed against hers, featherlight. Grasping his coat lapels, she pulled herself up, higher, closer. A delicious hum spread over her, tingling from the top of her head to the tips of her toes.

"Miss Elizabeth?" a voice in the hall called.

Fitzwilliam groaned, and Elizabeth audibly sighed.

Miss Darcy had been like a thistle stuck in Fitzwilliam's coat since her arrival. Elizabeth did her best to be patient with the girl, but with only a week until the wedding, Elizabeth wanted every moment she could steal with Fitzwilliam—more stolen kisses.

With profound regret, she whispered, "I should go to her."

He twisted his lips and nodded, his discontent plainly writ on his face.

She pulled against his arms half-heartedly, and it was only with a groan that he finally released his hold.

Would it really be so bad if we were caught in an embrace? Elizabeth wondered. They were engaged; the wedding would be in a week.

"Miss Elizabeth?" Miss Darcy called.

Elizabeth sighed again. She must be patient. Turning to leave, she glanced over her shoulder. The yearning she saw in Fitzwilliam's eyes nearly drew her back to him. She knew he would not object and would risk his little sister seeing them embrace.

At his feet sat a self-satisfied kitten, who licked his paw and watched her with one eye. Content with his ministrations, he set his paw on the ground and very notably winked at Elizabeth.

She gasped. "We are keeping him, are we not?"

Voice still gruff, Fitzwilliam replied, "I would not dream of Arthur living with anyone else."

If the kitten continued to throw Fitzwilliam and Elizabeth into each other's arms, he would be a most welcome addition to their family.

CHAPTER 29

*M*ama and Lydia were away when Elizabeth and Kitty returned to Longbourn.

Jane looked remarkably composed—contented even. Elizabeth knew her sister's graciousness kept her from seeking out Mr. Bingley's company while Miss Darcy continued as his guest, but surely Jane would appreciate some reassurance.

Sitting closer to her, Elizabeth spoke loudly enough for Jane to hear her over Mary's playing but not so loud to interrupt her playing or encourage Kitty to join them. "Mr. Bingley asked about you."

She would have said much more, but the family carriage clambered to a stop in the drive. Through the window, Elizabeth saw the door fling open and Lydia spill out of the conveyance before the footman could even lower the step.

Elizabeth sighed. There would be no talk of Mr.

Bingley until their mother was out of hearing. Poor Jane had enough to manage suppressing her own ardor until Miss Darcy departed for Pemberley to worry about the added burden of their mother's expectations.

Mother handed Kitty a fist-sized package of twisted brown paper. "I stopped by Mr. Jones' shop for more nerve tonic, and he gave me these lozenges for your cough." She caught Kitty before her daughter could wrinkle her nose and stick out her tongue, adding, "He says they are made of honey and taste quite nice."

Jane set aside her embroidery. "Are you feeling unwell, Mama?"

"To the contrary, my dear. I am in excellent health and spirits. With the final reading of the banns for Lizzy and Mr. Darcy this Sunday and their wedding the following day, and you and Mr. Bingley shortly thereafter—"

"Mama, he has not—" Jane attempted to correct her.

Their mother continued, congratulating her daughters' good fortune and praising her own effectiveness as a parent. With a contented sigh, she lowered herself into the chair nearest the fire. "I anticipate many more good days."

Mary, ever practical, asked, "Then why did you get more nerve tonic?"

Mama shrugged. "No day is perfect. An ounce of prevention is worth a pound of cure."

Elizabeth wished her father had been present to hear his wife quote Benjamin Franklin so perfectly.

Lydia pouted. "Meryton is dull without Wickie."

Mama fanned her face. "He is a handsome man, so dashing in his regimentals, but with your sisters marrying men of fortune, you will be in a position to marry a gentleman of greater fortune and consequence, dear."

"What do I care so long as he has a handsome face and a cutting figure? What a perfect pair we make!"

"You will care very much when your sisters can afford new gowns and you are stuck wearing second-year gowns and cast-offs."

Clearly, Lydia had not considered that likelihood. Turning to Elizabeth, she asked, "Will you invite me to London during the season?"

Kitty scowled at her. "And what of me and Mary? We are both older than you."

Lydia rolled her eyes. "And Kitty and Mary too, of course?" She returned Kitty's cross look, as though to say, *Are you happy now?*

Mama clapped her hands. "What a marvelous idea! Of course Lizzy will invite you!"

So that they might scandalously flirt and expose themselves to Fitzwilliam's family and peers? Elizabeth thought not. "Miss Darcy is not yet out in society."

"That is easy to fix. Have her come out into society, and then she can have fun with us!" Lydia shrugged, the matter resolved in her own mind.

"But Miss Darcy is sixteen!" Mama exclaimed.

Elizabeth smiled softly. If she were to have any positive influence at all on her sister's futures, now was the time. "All the same, her guardians consider that she is yet too young. How would it look if I encourage my sisters in society while Miss Darcy remains behind?"

Mama frowned.

Elizabeth continued, "Miss Darcy assured me that her mother, Lady Anne—"

"A viscountess!" Mama swooned.

"Lady Anne did not come out until she was eighteen years of age. Many families of the first circles consider it best to give their young ladies more time to see to their education and accomplishments."

Mary opined, "Mr. Darcy will not wish for us to reflect poorly on his family. He is a gentleman with elevated standards, and it befits us to live up to them." As though to prove her point and her diligence in attending to the matter, she spun around on her bench and resumed playing the scales softly.

Mama sat pensively for a long time, longer than Elizabeth could ever recall her doing. She prayed her mother would draw the right conclusions. How many times had Elizabeth pleaded with her directly—to no avail. Perhaps she ought to have resorted to subtler means sooner.

Mary played a simple, pleasant piece, and still Mama contemplated. Under the tutelage of the master, Mary's technique had improved noticeably in only a few lessons. As diligent as she was in her practice, her progress was bound to be rapid. She seemed to know it, and her increased confidence improved her performance. She turned to face them, a smile gracing her features and making her quite lovely.

Papa clapped as he turned the corner to enter the room. "That was very good, Mary."

Mama brightened. "Mary, you must teach Kitty and Lydia! If they cannot go to London for the season until they are eighteen, then they might as well play as well as you do."

Elizabeth attempted not to look too relieved. Much good could be done in one year for Kitty and three for Lydia.

Lydia, of course, balked. But Kitty rose to join Mary at the instrument, and the two huddled over the ivory keys while Lydia angrily tore the trim off a bonnet that had the misfortune to be resting on a nearby table.

Papa returned to his library.

Mama watched Kitty and Mary with a calculating gleam in her eye while the two played. Lydia continued complaining, but she was ignored. Pinching her lips together, Jane returned her attention to her embroidery.

CHAPTER 30

*D*arcy attempted to commit his hopes for Georgiana to paper without success. He imagined Elizabeth's face as she read, heard the comments she would mutter under her breath, felt the paper crinkle under her tightening grip. Richard's words echoed in his mind. *Who are you to make these decisions for everyone?*

Who was he? His plan had been made with the best intentions for his sister's happiness and his friend's advantage, but Elizabeth would see it as high-handed. Precisely as Richard had said.

While Darcy stood by his original reasoning, circumstances had changed. He now saw that to persist without alteration to his scheme would be unwise. However, he was responsible for Georgiana, and from the moment he had convinced Bingley to let Netherfield Park, Darcy had become responsible for him too.

Anticipating the clarity a good gallop over Nether-field Park would render, Darcy stopped two steps short of the landing when he saw his sister in her riding habit.

"Where shall we ride today?" she asked with a bright smile.

Vexation calmed to disappointment before guilt swallowed Darcy in its clutches. In a blink, he felt her tiny, infant fingers clasping his, saw her wide eyes look up adoringly at their father, heard her laughter as he twirled and danced with her. All the promises Darcy had made within himself to protect her flooded his mind. How could he be vexed at his own dear sister?

Holding out his arm, he smiled. "Where would you like to go?"

"We so often ride toward Oakham Mount, I would like to see the other side of the property for a change."

Darcy suppressed his scowl. There would be no conversation with Elizabeth that morning.

They mounted their horses and set off in the oppo-site direction than the way they usually went. Darcy, intent on some exercise if he was to be deprived of Elizabeth, suggested a race.

"Actually," Georgiana began, chewing on her lip. "There is an important matter I wish to discuss with you." She sucked in a breath, her cheeks puffing as she exhaled.

Darcy walked his horse closer, worried that she might swoon. "What is it, Georgie? Are you ill?"

"No, only nervous."

Panic and concern rose in Darcy's chest. Did she still fear he blamed her over Wickham? He thought he had convinced Georgiana that he held Wickham accountable and that her innocence was no match for Wickham's perfidy. "Nothing you can tell me will lessen your place in my regard. You are as dear to me now as you have ever been or will be."

"I know that, William, I do. It is only that I know you will not be pleased with what I wish to request, and I cannot disappoint you." She shook her head. "No, I cannot. Pray forget I said anything at all."

Now Darcy *had* to know what she thought would displease him so much. "Georgie, speak. Please."

She straightened her shoulders. "If you insist."

He nodded, urging her on, his heart knocking against his ribs and his stomach tying in knots.

"You have been so considerate to include me in appropriate outings and gatherings while I am not yet out in society. It has come to my attention that you have refused more than one invitation because I could not attend."

"Elizabeth agreed. Neither of us wish to exclude you."

Her gaze shot up to his, and she looked away just as rapidly. "Oh. I... I suppose I must thank her." Her reluctance confounded Darcy. Elizabeth had been everything kind and considerate to Georgiana. Instead of befriending her as Darcy had hoped, Georgiana had become closer to Miss Bingley recently.

Blinking repeatedly, Georgiana continued nervously, "Would it not be easier for everyone if I were allowed to come out in society?"

Darcy hardly knew what he had thought Georgiana would request, but that was not it. "Are you certain that is what you wish? I had assumed you wanted more time." A minimum of two more years—that had been the time they had agreed on. No less than two years to mature into a confident young lady bold enough to repel unworthy suitors and, in time, attract a responsible gentleman who would treat her with devotion.

A sickening thought sent a wave of nausea through him. Was this Georgiana's way of trying to secure Bingley, by announcing to all and sundry that she was ready for marriage? Whatever the motive, this conversation did not sit well with Darcy.

"Miss Lydia is out already, and she is younger than me."

"By three months!" Mentioning Lydia Bennet hardly improved Georgiana's argument. "And I am sure her neighbors agree that she is not ready to be out."

"Are not the invitations we receive proof enough that they do consider me mature enough to make my coming out?"

Darcy could not believe his ears. The invitations were meant to celebrate his and Elizabeth's upcoming marriage, not for Georgiana. His disappointment that she would use such fickle arguments to prove her point rendered him speechless.

She added, "Miss Bingley agrees that I would do

well to come out quietly in the country. When we return to London, I might receive callers and accompany both her and Aunt Helen on their calls."

As if Aunt Helen would ever choose to exchange more than a polite greeting with Miss Bingley!

"You cannot imagine how mortifying it is to hear how Lydia and Kitty Bennet go everywhere with their sisters while I must stay in my rooms with Mrs. Annesley. Do you not see how much I have matured? I played the pianoforte before an audience, and I gave Wickham the cut direct."

Darcy's recollection of that rainy day was vastly different from his sister's. Had it not been for Elizabeth, Georgiana would have cowered on the settee while Wickham sneered at them.

"Thanks to Miss Bingley's direction, I have become more confident. If I were called upon to entertain an audience, I should gladly do so."

Darcy could take no more of this nonsense. "You do realize that coming out implies more than playing an instrument when called upon. It signals that you are ready to marry—that you are prepared to run a household of your own and care for the needs of the children certain to come from that union. It means you are prepared to live no longer for yourself but for others. Why not enjoy the freedom you have now?"

Georgiana's jaw set at an unbecoming angle. "I thought you wanted me to be happy."

"I do! But if you cannot be happy in your own company, then I cannot fathom how you think you will be happy when others are allowed to impose on you."

"Is that what I am to you? An imposition?" Her chin quivered, and a tear slid down her cheek.

How had the conversation had deteriorated so quickly? Baffled and clueless, Darcy did his best to console her. "I did not say that. I would *never*, not even in my heart, consider you an imposition."

"Then you will allow me to come out?"

"Of course not. You are too young." He handed her his handkerchief. "Come now, Georgie, dry your tears. Let us race back to the stables."

"I do not wish to race," she sputtered between sobs.

She cried more, but Darcy would not budge. What she asked was unreasonable and went against the decision she had agreed upon months ago with him and Richard.

What was more, her arguments and mawkish behavior troubled him. Darcy had never understood how other men were so easily manipulated by tears. It pained him to see his own sister use that tactic against him. In his experience and observation, the use of such feminine arts rarely proceeded from an honest, unselfish motive.

He did his best to cheer her. The patch of azure sky promising a fine day, the flock of pheasants streaking the green and brown fields with their colorful plumage, the way the dew clung to the grass and sparkled in the morning sun—he pointed out all the things Elizabeth would have delighted to see.

Georgiana had composed herself before they reached the stables. By the time they entered the breakfast parlor, she was able to greet Bingley and the Hursts convincingly.

"Where is Miss Bingley?" she asked.

"Still keeping fashionable hours," Richard replied, piling sausages onto his plate with one hand and patting the empty chair beside him for Georgiana.

Bingley shrugged. "I do not suppose I could convince you to accompany me to the lower field, Darcy? The bailiff says the lack of drainage will be a problem if left unattended before winter."

They buttered toast and sipped coffee while they made plans for the day, their conversation dwindling as they ate.

An ear-splitting scream jolted them from their seats. Bingley, Richard, and Darcy ran upstairs, following the continuing sound. Once they reached the residence wing, it was apparent the screams came from Miss Bingley's room. "Get it out! Get it away from me! Oh, the nasty, vile thing! Out! Out! Get it away!"

Darcy waited in the hall with Richard and Mr. Hurst, who still wore his dressing gown, while Bingley and Georgiana, charged inside the bedchamber followed by a panting Mrs. Hurst.

"Rudy!" they heard Bingley exclaim. He departed from the room, holding the kitten in the crook of his arm. "That was better than the time I put a frog in Louisa's jewelry box!"

"What did he do?" Richard asked.

Bingley chuckled. "He left a dead mouse on Caroline's silk pillow."

Richard covered his mouth, his shoulders shaking with the effort to contain his mirth.

Of all the people the kitten could grace with the prize of his first kill, he had chosen Miss Bingley. Darcy looked anywhere but at his laughing companions lest he lose his composure.

Georgiana flitted out to the hall. "Mrs. Hurst will stay with Caroline until she is calm." Looking more like the girl Darcy knew, she said excitedly, "I am sorry for the shock she has suffered. I tried to tell her what a compliment it is for a cat to leave his first hunt on her pillow. He must really like her to favor her with such a gift."

Bingley's grin returned as bright as before. "Say, I already named Rudy. Does that mean I get to keep him?"

"If you really want him," Georgiana said.

"He and I get along famously. Far be it from me to separate Rudy from his particular friend," he said with a wink at Miss Bingley's doorway.

The next few minutes passed pleasantly as they returned downstairs and attended to their plates. Georgiana was her usual self, much to Darcy's relief. It was as though their unpleasant conversation had never happened.

When Miss Bingley finally joined them, she ate only dry toast with weak tea, claiming she was still too agitated for anything more.

The butler brought in the post on a silver salver, which Bingley took enthusiastically. Opening the note on the top, he said, "Jolly fun! How does a picnic at Oakham Mount sound on this fine day?"

Georgiana clapped her hands. "It is a glorious day, much too fine to waste."

"Indeed! It was good of the Bennets to suggest we join them."

Georgiana's face changed. Gone was the joyful girl, replaced a surly miss Darcy did not understand.

"Must we always be in their company?" protested Miss Bingley.

"I rather enjoy their company," defended Bingley.

"I have a terrible headache and cannot go, but I shall not spoil your fun if you wish to leave me behind." Miss Bingley pressed her fingers against her forehead and sighed too loudly for one truly suffering a headache.

Bingley, either ignorant to her hint or purposely ignoring it, dabbed his mouth with his napkin and pushed back from the table. "Then it is settled. We shall leave you here to rest while we enjoy a picnic out of doors."

Miss Bingley scowled.

In the end, the Bennets would not dream of excluding Miss Bingley, and they suggested that a picnic at Longbourn in the garden by the pond would be just the thing to suit everyone. Mrs. Bennet offered several draughts from her collection for Miss Bingley's comfort along with her favorite chair by the fire so that

Miss Bingley might observe the picnic from the window without worsening her condition.

It was not the ideal place to converse with Elizabeth, surrounded by their friends and relatives, but Darcy was determined to find a way.

CHAPTER 31

*E*lizabeth had suggested they sit under the bare arbor by the pond, but now she understood why Fitzwilliam had been too agitated to sit. Not only had his little sister settled on Mr. Bingley as the solution to her heartbreak, but she had also attempted to persuade Fitzwilliam to allow her to come out in society. Elizabeth hugged his arm closer to her, matching him step for step as they paced along the edge of the pond. "It is a difficult age. What do you mean to do?"

"I mean to uphold our unanimous decision to wait." He sighed heavily and raked his hand through his hair. "Am I doing what is right?"

Elizabeth beamed. "You are asking me?"

"Yes. It would ease my mind to have your support."

Her chest tightened and her stomach fluttered. "You bear too many burdens alone, Fitzwilliam. I shall support you"—she donned her most impertinent grin —"so long as I agree with you."

"Say that again." Fitzwilliam clasped her hands, his tone low.

"I shall support you so long as we are in agreement?"

"No," he chuckled. "My name. I heard you say it in Bingley's library, and I have longed to hear you say it again."

She looked down at their entwined hands, embarrassed, though she had no reason to be. Looking up at him boldly, she repeated, "Fitzwilliam."

"Elizabeth," he whispered throatily, pulling her closer and lowering his forehead to hers. A kiss would have been imminent had her sisters not been on the other side of the pond. Already Elizabeth could hear Lydia's giggles.

With mutual sighs, Elizabeth and Darcy stepped away from each other and resumed walking.

"Why would a young lady wish to come out before she is ready?" Fitzwilliam asked.

For the excitement, the dancing, the parties, the stolen kisses. Elizabeth would not say this aloud when they all applied to Fitzwilliam's sister. Despite Miss Darcy's secret courtship and near elopement, he still believed her an innocent child. He did her no favors treating her that way. Her petition and the reasons she gave for it proved it.

He would not like what Elizabeth must say, but if they could not speak freely with each other now, then they must practice and improve. "It seems that she is testing you. What could she possibly gain from coming out now and here, other than to steal Mr. Bingley away from Jane? Surely, you have told her how inappropriate such a match would be." She huffed. "Can you imagine what Miss Bingley would do to her?"

She felt Fitzwilliam's ribs stretch and collapse, heard his breath. "I felt so guilty entrusting Georgiana to Mrs. Younge. It was a negligence on my part which nearly led her to ruin. Georgiana was shattered. All I could think of was cheering her, and Bingley is always cheerful."

"Yes, I agree. And he would seem safe after suffering from the likes of Mr. Wickham. But a girl her age is prone to heartbreak. It would have been preferable for her to learn from the experience and grow stronger on her own rather than to rely on another gentleman for her contentment. People too often disappoint."

Fitzwilliam's eyes pinched. "I see that now." He sounded defeated. He did not think she meant that he had disappointed her, did he?

She spread her hand over his arm. "You have not disappointed me. To the contrary, you are a treasure trove of surprises."

The pinch in his eyes deepened. Pressing his lips together, Fitzwilliam dipped his chin to his chest. "Then I shall apologize in advance, for what I must tell you will surely be disappointing."

Elizabeth laughed half-heartedly. "What could you possibly tell me that weighs on you so? Tell me at once so that you may be free of the burden, and we may carry on as before." Her attempt to lighten the mood only seemed to worsen his agony. Her stomach twisted into knots. All sorts of horrible possibilities flooded her mind.

"Lizzy!" she heard a muffled call. Fitzwilliam dropped Elizabeth's hand and stepped away as she heard another cry. "Lizzy!" Lydia ran around the pond toward them.

There was no black smoke rising from Longbourn, nor was a royal carriage parked in their drive. Elizabeth was unable to account for her sister's interruption and unwilling to leave before Fitzwilliam had told her what troubled him. "Just a few minutes, Lydee."

With a ferocious glare at Fitzwilliam, Lydia grabbed Elizabeth's hand. "You must return with me *now*. Jane needs our help." Lydia tugged, mumbling something about viperish guests and forcing Elizabeth to follow or risk toppling over.

Fitzwilliam followed. "Shall I accompany you?"

The dear man would intervene with Mr. Bingley's loathsome sisters for Jane's benefit. Elizabeth might have swooned had Lydia not been dragging her down the path.

Lydia spun, swinging Elizabeth around with her and pointing her finger toward Fitzwilliam. "Is it true? Have you been discouraging Mr. Bingley to offer for Jane so that he might marry your sister?"

"Lydia!" Elizabeth gaped at her sister's rudeness. Such a wild claim should not be borne! What on earth had come over her? Lydia pulled her away, preventing any further explanation.

"Lydia, you were terribly rude to Mr. Darcy. I had not thought you capable of such behavior."

"Do not slow down, Lizzy. Jane needs you." She let go of Elizabeth's hand to help her untie her bonnet, and Elizabeth realized how quickly her sister must have dashed out of the house for her to have forgone her bonnet or a wrap. The day was fine, but it was still chilly.

"Lydee, you will catch your death. What would Mama say?"

"She will not care about me once she hears about Mr. Bingley." Lydia dashed behind Elizabeth, pulling off Elizabeth's wrap and redingote. With a shove, she pushed Elizabeth across the threshold and toward the front parlor. Elizabeth hardly had time to gather her bearings or straighten her blowsy hair.

She knew Lydia was right to fetch her as soon as she saw Jane's pale face, shiny eyes, and forced smile. It was a stark contrast to the pink complexions and haughty postures of Mr. Bingley's sisters, who sat calmly across from Jane. So much for the headache Miss Bingley claimed to have.

Mrs. Hurst set her teacup on the table and rose. "Miss Elizabeth, what a pity we must take our leave just when you have returned, but we have overstayed as it is. We would not dream of intruding on your family's hospitality a moment longer."

Miss Bingley's chin rose to a triumphant angle. "We will leave Miss Bennet to share our glad tidings with her sisters. I am certain you will share in our joy."

Elizabeth stepped out of the doorway, curtsying as they passed and widening her eyes when Lydia gave them both the cut direct.

Brushing past Elizabeth to sit beside Jane, Lydia clasped her sister's hands between her own, her lips set in a thin line like an angry sentinel determined to offer comfort. "It is a good thing you convinced Mama to sit out in the garden for a spell. We should put her smelling salts by her chair."

Jane explained, "Mama thought it best for Mary and Kitty to entertain Miss Darcy. Lydia was told to stay by the fire because Mama heard her cough—"

"One trifling cough," interjected Lydia with a pout.

"—and Mama did not wish her to catch a cold before the wedding," Jane continued. "I was enjoying a lively conversation with Mr. Bingley and Colonel Fitzwilliam when Mrs. Hurst asked me to come inside. She said that Miss Bingley had some wonderful news to share."

Jane shed no tears. The longer she spoke, the steadier her voice became.

"Jane, what happened? What did those spiteful women say? Whatever it was, you must not believe it." Elizabeth glanced at her father's book room door. It was firmly closed, and she could only suppose he had avoided all the turmoil by staying inside, ignorant of his daughter's suffering.

Pulling her hands free of Lydia's grasp, Jane clasped her fingers in her lap. "Do not call them that, Lizzy.

They only spoke the truth, and they should not be criticized for it."

Lydia huffed. "How can you say such a thing? They clearly came with the intention to crush your hopes! Did you not see how they gloated over your disappointment? I have never been more tempted to toss my tea down another lady's bodice! They sat there looking so smug and satisfied."

Jane regarded Lydia. "I am glad you restrained yourself."

Lydia grumbled. "I shall not be so restrained next time."

"You will do no such thing."

Elizabeth simmered with impatience. "What happened?!"

Jane met her gaze evenly, her voice soft, "They told us that Mr. Bingley is intended for Miss Darcy."

Elizabeth scoffed. She did not believe that lie for a second. "Surely that is what Mr. Bingley's sisters wish. An attachment to the Darcys would elevate them in society. It is wishful thinking, Jane. Nothing more."

Jane twisted her fingers. "Surely you have noticed Miss Darcy's attachment."

"A childish infatuation!"

"Mr. Bingley does not call as often as he did before she arrived."

"Neither do you encourage him to!"

"I refuse to be the means by which an impressionable young lady is disappointed. I could not be so cruel to Miss Darcy."

"Like you, Mr. Bingley is modest and does not wish to hurt his friend's little sister."

Lydia blurted, "Mr. Darcy himself encourages the match."

"Lydia!" Jane hissed.

Ignoring her, Lydia continued, "He was the one who arranged for Mr. Bingley to let Netherfield Park with the aim of advising and guiding him in order to secure a match with Miss Darcy."

Jane's lips pinched. "That was not for you to say. We do not know for a certainty that it is true."

Elizabeth laughed. "That could hardly be true! Miss Bingley is delusional in her pretensions."

Lydia lifted her chin. "I asked Mr. Darcy just now. He could have denied it, but he did not."

Elizabeth bit back her retort. He had not denied it.

Jane interrupted, "Lydia, if you cannot keep malicious gossip to yourself, then you would do best to hold your tongue."

"But it is not gossip! This was not passed on from footman to stable boy to maid. Miss Bingley heard it directly from Mr. Darcy. When I asked him directly, he did not deny it."

Elizabeth could not believe it. A union between Miss Darcy and a gentleman whose fortune came from trade? Preposterous! Of course, Mr. Darcy had been good friends with Mr. Bingley for years, but that did not signify he held such a hope.

Did it? Fitzwilliam had asked if Elizabeth thought that Mr. Bingley would make Jane happy. What had been his purpose? Was he attempting to discourage Jane from Mr. Bingley so his own sister could marry him? No, it was ridiculous! But that troubled look in his eye, his frequent attempts to speak with her privately… Could it be?

Jane reached over to set her hand on top of Elizabeth's cold fingers. "Mr. Darcy is an honorable man. If he said such a thing in Miss Bingley's hearing, I daresay there was a good reason for it. Or perhaps she misunderstood. He is an attentive brother who wants the best for his sister. You must not allow anyone to lessen your respect and regard for your betrothed."

Lydia rolled her eyes.

Elizabeth straightened her shoulders. "You are right, of course, Jane. I would do well to ask him directly before I trust a word out of that vicious termagant's mouth. He will reply honestly."

The rational solution displeased Lydia. "But Lizzy, what will you do if Miss Bingley spoke the truth? What if she did not misunderstand?"

The thought alone hurt, and Elizabeth shoved it aside. She had already fallen in love with Fitzwilliam, and such a betrayal would devastate her.

She forced a smile to bolster herself and soothe her sisters. "One cannot live their life imagining all the dreadful things that might happen. More often than not, nothing becomes of it, and all that worry was for naught. I shall afford Fitzwilliam the courtesy of belief. I am certain there is a reasonable explanation."

"What if there's not?" Lydia pressed.

"Hush, Lydia," Jane demanded. "You are bitter because Mr. Wickham is gone, and you are bored. Have you nothing better to do with yourself than make everyone as miserable as you claim to be? You ought to be ashamed of yourself."

The force of Jane's speech stunned Lydia into silence. With a confused huff, she slunk away in search of a more favorable audience.

"I am relieved Mr. Wickham is gone, or she would have ruined us all," Jane commented after her. Taking Elizabeth's hand, she asked, "It looks like Miss Bingley's early departure put an end to the picnic. When will you ask Mr. Darcy for an explanation?"

Elizabeth forced her smile wide, though the temptation to feed the flicker of anger was great. "I shall confront him in church. I cannot kill him there."

Jane's eyes widened. "Lizzy!"

"I tease, Jane." Elizabeth looked through the window to the garden. Mr. Bingley had seen his sisters home—probably Miss Darcy too. Elizabeth did not see her.

What she did see through the glass sparked flames in her blood. Never had she seen a guiltier-appearing man than Fitzwilliam looking at her from the other side of the window.

CHAPTER 32

*H*ands clenched, back stiff, shoulders tensed to her ears, Elizabeth walked toward Darcy. She looked fierce without her customary smile.

Richard elbowed him. "You are in for it now."

Darcy was powerless to move. All he could do was brace himself for the tempest to strike.

"Is it true?" she demanded.

"I believe I shall leave you two to chat." Richard bowed and retreated.

Assuming nothing, Darcy asked, "Is what true?"

Elizabeth gritted her teeth, speaking through them. "Do you plan for Mr. Bingley to marry your sister?"

Nothing could help him now, so Darcy held his head as high as he could and told the truth. "Yes, I did."

She snapped, completely overlooking his use of the past tense. "It is ridiculous! Do you really expect Mr. Bingley to wait years until Miss Darcy is ready to marry?" She flailed her arms heavenward. "How do you even know she will remain in love with him that long?"

Darcy knew the folly of rational speech to an impassioned woman, but Elizabeth was wrong about Georgiana. "She is of a steady character."

"Really? Was she not in love with Mr. Wickham only this last summer?"

She had him there. He clamped his teeth down on his tongue, thinking maybe it would be best to say as little as possible.

"What of Mr. Bingley? Surely, he does not agree with your plan or he would not have paid any particular regard to Jane."

"No, he would not have. I never openly encouraged the match."

Elizabeth gasped. "But you wanted it! You would presume to dictate his future without a word of permission? Is that what you do with your sister, too? She would have sensed your approval and understood it as encouragement! Can you not see that by indulging her every whim, you are preventing her from experiencing consequences? In so doing, you deny her the opportunity to learn and grow, to strengthen her character. No, she relies on her protective brother to swoop in and sweep the mess under the rug, swatting my sister out of the way so that yours may trample all over Jane's heart while she has her fun. It is a selfish love, and it will not last."

Darcy's blood lit afire. "Do you doubt Georgiana's loyalty?"

"To Mr. Bingley—yes."

"I thought you of all people believed in long-lasting love."

"I do! But that is not what she has toward Mr. Bingley. She is full young! She does not even know herself enough to love someone else."

"She is a Darcy." Darcy emphasized every syllable.

They stood toe-to-toe now. "You are determined to discourage Bingley away from Jane? He loves her, I am convinced of it. And she is ready to marry now."

Calmly, rationally, Darcy asked, "Are you convinced she loves him?"

Elizabeth raised her chin. "Yes."

"Do not presume to know my sister better than I do when you are blind to the indifference of your own."

"You think Jane indifferent?"

He crossed his arms over his chest. "Yes."

Her chin trembled as she spoke, and her eyes sparkled. "I can forgive a great many things, but I could never love a man responsible for the ruination of my dearest sister's happiness. How can I marry a man who held my family in such disregard, who proclaims himself an expert of my sister's heart?"

"And three weeks have made you an expert of my sister? Come, Elizabeth, this is madness!"

She blinked over and over, her voice shaking. "If you choose to insist on protecting your sister at Jane's expense, then I must insist we call off our engagement."

Darcy reached for her, but she was too swift, and he was too numb to stop her.

ELIZABETH WAS proud of herself for making it upstairs and to her room before the tears came. But once the first spilled down her cheek, they kept coming in heaves and swells.

Throwing herself on her bed, she buried her face in her pillow and wept. She would have cried longer, but she had to comfort Jane. Dear disappointed, heart-broken Jane. Oh, if only she had never met Fitzwilliam Darcy!

Tears burned her eyes anew, but Elizabeth choked them back. She washed her face and dabbed it dry, dreading the conversation she would have to have with her sister and wrapping her burgeoning anger around her like a shield.

Feeling stronger, she grabbed the door handle, took a deep breath, and yanked it open to step squarely on Jane's toes.

"Ouch!" Jane protested, grabbing her foot.

"Oh, bother! I am sorry, Jane!" Elizabeth wrapped her arm around her sister and helped her hobble over to the bed.

"'Tis no matter."

It was to Elizabeth. Aside from an injured heart, Jane now had an injured foot! "It is my fault. I should have been more cautious."

"All will be well, you will see." Jane nudged Elizabeth in the side. "A fine, steadfast love cannot be swayed by a misunderstanding."

Oh no. She and Fitzwilliam would never agree about their sisters. As far as Elizabeth was concerned, she was through with him. She swallowed the lump in her throat and blinked hard. That high-handed, arrogant, selfish man! How dare he pretend to be chivalrous and charming when all the time, he was willing to sacrifice Jane's prospects for his sister! "I do not want to speak of him, Jane. He is not the man I thought he was."

He knew Jane had been hurt before. He knew Elizabeth would not stand to see Jane hurt again. He knew that, and he still took Mr. Bingley from her. How did he justify his actions? By claiming to understand Jane's heart better than Elizabeth! Of all the arrogant, self-serving claims! A harsh laugh escaped her.

Jane looked at her questioningly.

The last person Elizabeth wanted to talk about was proud Mr. Darcy, but she had to explain. "He presumed to understand your heart better than me. He believes that you are indifferent to Mr. Bingley. Can you imagine? After all the consideration you have shown his sister, instead of recognizing your grace, your compassion, and your patient serenity, he assumes you are indifferent!" She laughed bitterly, waiting for Jane to join her.

Jane did not. She pinched her lips and calmly clasped her hands. A niggling fear choked Elizabeth's laughter dry. "You do love Mr. Bingley, do you not, dearest?"

"Ought a woman love a man too fickle to make his own decisions?"

Elizabeth steadied herself against the headboard. "Tell me you love Mr. Bingley, Jane."

"There was a time, a very brief time, when I believed myself in love. But it was a flicker of a flame, and it died when I learned more of his character."

Elizabeth clenched her stomach. "He is everything amiable and gentlemanly! You told me so yourself!"

"And I stand by what I said. But while Mr. Bingley possesses many fine traits, he is still a boy in many ways." Jane clasped her hands in her lap and smiled. "I would rather marry a man."

Elizabeth groaned. That the insufferable Mr. Darcy had been right was unbearable. Especially after what she had told him. She groaned again.

Jane looked at her in alarm. "What is it? You do not look well."

Truth be told, Elizabeth did not feel at all well. "Oh, Jane, I said some things I should not have. I spoke too plainly about his sister, and when he would not be reasonable, I called off our engagement. I told him I could never love him for disappointing my sister, and now I learn that he was right?"

She covered her face with her hands. Oh, what had she done?! Elizabeth had always prided herself on the quickness of her tongue, but not today. Today she had spoken impulsively, emotionally, irrationally.

"Oh, Lizzy!" Jane rubbed her back. "You will have to apologize for that."

Elizabeth sat up to look at her sister. How could she be so calm?

"And I must apologize to you for leading you to believe that I am still in love with Mr. Bingley. In truth…my affections belong to another." Jane caressed her cheek.

"I am going to be ill," Elizabeth grumbled.

"Nonsense. Do you not see how similar you are? It was presumptuous of him to arrange Mr. Bingley's future as well as his sister's, but did you not try to do the same with me? You were foolish to speak to him so boldly about his sister, but did he not do the same? I daresay you are right about Miss Darcy, and Mr. Darcy *was* right about me. Both of you would sacrifice your own happiness to protect others who do not need your protection! Apologize, Lizzy! Make amends!" She sounded so certain.

"I do not know if I can."

"Now is not the time to be stubborn," Jane said sternly. "Especially not on my behalf." With a sly smile, she added, "Allow Mr. Darcy to grovel sufficiently first, and then forgive him."

"I do not know if he can forgive me after what I said."

"Love is complicated enough. Do not make it harder! Love is a choice, a decision made by two imperfect people to trust each other through triumphs and tribulations, to exert themselves for each other's happiness."

"You make it sound easy."

"I do not mean to. You and I both know that nothing worth having is easily gained."

Ah, but that was the problem. Elizabeth loved Fitzwilliam, but she had given him an impossible ultimatum. If he chose his sister over her, then her love for him would die a slow death. That was not good enough.

CHAPTER 33

*I*f Richard said anything on the ride back to Netherfield, Darcy did not hear it. He did not hear Bingley ride back to join them either. What did it matter? Little by little, Elizabeth had worked her way into Darcy's heart, and now there was not a piece of him she did not possess. He wanted no future in which Elizabeth was not a prominent part.

Darcy would have to disappoint someone, and that someone could not be Elizabeth.

Not knowing how to begin or how to proceed once he started, Darcy chose to speak to the point and in as few words as possible. "Bingley, Georgiana fancies you."

The effect on Bingley was immediate. His mouth gaped open, then he chuckled awkwardly. "Merely a girlish fancy, I hope. Nothing she will not recover from in a week or two? That is how it usually works with me."

"You have been the sole recipient of her admiration since late summer."

"Two months?" Bingley's voice squeaked. "B-but we spent the summer together. You encouraged it! You told me she had suffered from a heartbreak and asked me to treat her as I would a little sister, with the utmost care and kindness. Why did you not say anything sooner? I might have—I could have—"

"Behaved differently?" Darcy supplied. "Would you have really?"

"But I was only kind! Should I have ignored her entirely?"

"If need be."

"You would have me act like... like..."

"Like Darcy would," Richard supplied, a mockingly innocent expression on his face.

Darcy was in no mood for his cousin's humor. "If I am not interested in a lady, I find it best to avoid her entirely. Too much is often read into a polite smile to indulge in social niceties at the risk of unwittingly encouraging a young lady's affections."

Richard scratched his chin. "Not a bad philosophy. Not very sociable, but nobody would dare accuse you of flirting with anyone other than your intended."

Bingley gawked at them. "I do not know how to act. If I keep from smiling or conversing with every lady I meet, I would soon gain a reputation as a taciturn brute." His eyes widened, and he covered his hand with his mouth. "My apologies, Darcy. I do not, nor have I ever, considered you a brute."

"I have at times," quipped Richard. "However, you both make good points. There must be a polite, socially acceptable balance between a flirt and—as Bingley so well coined it—a taciturn brute."

Darcy was in no mood for a philosophical discussion. He focused on Bingley. "Are you certain of your regard for Miss Bennet? Would you make her an offer?"

"Yes!" he began enthusiastically. "I think so... Well... I am almost certain."

Richard shook his head. "Miss Bennet is a diamond of the first water."

"She is an angel." Bingley sighed.

"Will you still think her an angel when the years gray her golden hair, dim her rosy complexion, and wrinkle her alabaster skin? Consider it, man!" Richard spoke quickly, without stopping for breath. "Marriage is forever; 'til death do you part. Do you love *only* Miss Bennet? Can you foresee ever loving another woman? Or is she little more than this season's distraction?" Richard's chest heaved.

"I think so. I mean, I think I love her." Bingley spoke weakly.

Hot anger stirred in Darcy's chest. "Do you not know? I suggest you refrain from giving hope where it is not warranted until you are certain beyond all doubt. Consider the lady's heart and reputation! You cannot dole out your attentions indiscriminately without consequences. It is not fair to either Georgiana or Miss Bennet."

"But surely, you would never encourage your sister t-to," Bingley circled his hand as if the air would produce the words for him. Finally, he uttered an agitated, "To… you know what I mean!"

"I was not against the match," Darcy stated plainly.

Bingley looked like he might be ill. "She is like a sister to me—a nice sister. I do not think of her…" his face twisted and a shiver shook him through. "What should I do?"

"That is not for me to decide. My hope is that you will strive to be a man your future wife, whomever she may be, will look up to. You have it in you to be a great man, Bingley, but you must begin making your own decisions."

Looking a little less ill, Bingley spouted, "Like I did with Mr. Collins!"

Richard looked at Darcy. "We have not heard about that, have we?"

"I would have remembered."

Bingley laughed. "I shall never forget it! I think I handled it rather well, but"—Bingley looked about and lowered his voice—"it is not something we should discuss openly. Join me in my study, and I shall tell you the whole tale over drinks." They approached the stables.

"I shall join you after I have a word with Georgiana." Darcy dismounted and handed his reins over to the stable boy.

They climbed the steps to the house, and Bingley stopped, one hand tapping Darcy's arm. "I am not ignorant of the honor you were willing to grant me. There is no other man on earth I would rather have for a brother, but I could never use Miss Darcy so poorly. I hope I have not offended you—or your sister. I apologize with all my being if I have."

As heartwarming as his apology was, Darcy was more impressed with what it stated about Bingley. "I am honored you still consider me your friend when I have given you every reason to take offense. It did not occur to you to use my friendship and Georgiana's favor to elevate yourself. That is proof of your honest character."

Richard dabbed at his eyes and slapped his hand over his heart dramatically. "I am honored to witness this tender moment."

Darcy rolled his eyes. "You are only jealous that Bingley would rather have me for a brother than you."

Richard crossed his arms over his chest. "Now, we both know I would make a better brother than you. Bingley is only too polite to say it."

Bingley shook his head. "Actually, I have always been a little terrified of you, Colonel. One misstep, and quicker than a snap of the fingers, you could dismember me in any one of a dozen ways."

"Tut tut," Richard waved his hand dismissively. "Two dozen, at least."

Bingley's curiosity overcame his fear. "Really? Two dozen?"

Richard clapped his hand on Bingley's back. "Come, let us inform the ladies of the house that we are in, and then we shall hear all about Mr. Collins. Darcy will need a good laugh after he has conversed with Georgiana. I do hope your tale has a strong element of comedy?"

"For a certainty. Except, of course, for Mr. Collins—and another individual who shall remain nameless until we are safe in my study."

"There is nothing safe about your study," Darcy retorted.

While his two friends chattered, Darcy tried to determine the gentlest way to approach the subject of Bingley with Georgiana. If only his conversation with her would go as well as his talk with Bingley.

The ladies were in the music room. Georgiana practiced a new piece while Miss Bingley sat beside her on the bench. Serafina, Angelina, and Arthur napped in the sunny window seat at the far end of the room while Mr. Hurst napped on the settee opposite and Mrs. Hurst attended to some needlework.

Richard burst into the room first, scooping up Crusoe when the kitten attempted to clamber up his leg. "Not that way, young man. We do not climb the master's leg like a savage, but we politely ask for a hand up to his shoulder. Like so, you see?" The kitten clambered from Richard's hand to the top of his shoulder, happily meowing.

Miss Bingley was unamused. "Will you teach it to fence with its claws next?" She barked a dry laugh at her own joke.

Georgiana smiled. "Only if Richard promises to make Crusoe a fine pair of boots."

"Like Puss in Boots." Miss Bingley tittered, finally understanding the reference she had inadvertently made. "Oh, but he will need a castle and a change of clothes if he is to charm the princess."

"Only if he means to prove that disguise is the way to the heart of a worthy lady. I always thought the real moral of the tale promoted the virtues of industry and dexterity." Richard rubbed his finger against Crusoe's cheek.

Miss Bingley tsked. "Unless the estate is entailed to the next male relative, in which case, the princess will have to marry the heir presumptive whether she likes it or not."

The room fell silent.

Richard pounced on the opportunity to goad Miss Bingley. "Like Longbourn? I did not know you thought so highly of the Bennet sisters! Which one do you consider the princess?"

Miss Bingley huffed. "Miss Jane Bennet's beauty is highly praised amongst the locals. In wider circles, I dare say she is only average."

Bingley looked struck. "I thought she was your friend."

"I have an excessive regard for Jane Bennet. She really is a very sweet girl, and I wish with all my heart that she were well settled. But with such a father and mother and such low connections, I am afraid there is no chance of her marrying better than Mr. Collins. She shall make a lovely mistress of Longbourn. Goodness knows the house could use some improvements. It is barely livable as it is. I would be ashamed to invite my friends into that garish parlor." She leaned into Georgiana and laughed behind her hand.

Georgiana tried to smile but, to her credit, she did not join Miss Bingley's spiteful laughter.

Richard's face flushed red. "If you speak so meanly about a friend, I wonder what you think of the rest of her family."

"Me? Mean? I only speak the truth as I see it. From the moment we arrived at Netherfield Park, I have heard of little else but the eldest Misses Bennets' beauty. I own that Miss Bennet deserves the reputation, but I confess that I cannot say the same about Miss Eliza."

"Really? Do tell!" prodded Richard.

Miss Bingley was happy to oblige. "Her face is too thin, her complexion has no brilliancy, and her features are not at all handsome. Her nose wants character—there is nothing marked in its lines. Her teeth are tolerable, but not out of the common way; and as for her eyes, which have sometimes been called so fine, I could never see anything extraordinary in them. They have a sharp, shrewish look."

"The only shrew I see is right in front of me." Darcy was hot with indignation. "You dare malign my betrothed, the woman I love more dearly than anyone, to my face? What is that if not mean?"

"Jealous, spiteful, peevish," Richard commented.

And this was the lady Darcy had allowed to befriend his sister.

Mrs. Hurst added her protests to her sister's, but Darcy's low tone cut through their cries. "You pretend to be my sister's friend for the advantages she gives you, and how do you return the favor? With empty, self-serving flattery. You have no eye for real beauty if you cannot see it in every inch of Elizabeth's person. Though I could describe what I love about every feature you criticize, my tongue cannot do justice to her inner beauty."

Miss Bingley's face was as red as a ripe tomato. She pointed at her brother. "Georgiana is ten times more accomplished than Jane Bennet. I would rather die an old maid in a house infested with cats than allow my stupid brother to ruin his prospects with an unrefined young woman."

"That can be arranged!" Bingley cried.

Serafina leapt into Georgiana's lap, and Georgie buried her face in the cat's fur. Angry people are rarely wise. Miss Bingley, in her ire, had unwittingly said aloud the words certain to break the heart of her so-called dearest friend.

Darcy moved closer to his sister.

"You would go against your plan and let your closest friend ruin himself by marrying into that dreadful, scandalous family?" Miss Bingley demanded of him.

Speaking slowly to ensure he was understood, Darcy said, "Miss Bennet is as gracious as my mother was. It is my dearest wish that Georgiana become close friends with her and Elizabeth." Folding his arms over his chest, he considered Miss Bingley sternly. "What I want to know is how you knew of a conversation you were not privy to."

Mr. Hurst woke up then. "What is this? What has she done now?" he asked his wife.

It was Richard who answered. "Caroline foolishly admitted to eavesdropping on a private conversation and selfishly using the information to her advantage."

Hurst nodded his head. "Sounds about right. Would anyone else like a glass of brandy?"

"Answer Darcy, Caroline." Bingley's look was as stern as his tone.

Miss Bingley glared at him, but her brother did not back down.

"Tell him, or I swear on my life, I shall send you to live with our aunt in Scarborough."

She huffed. "By chance, I overheard Mr. Darcy tell Colonel Fitzwilliam that you would make a safe match for his sister, that he would not discourage it."

"Where did you overhear this conversation?" Bingley pressed.

Miss Bingley jutted out her chin and clasped her hands together. In a small voice, she replied, "Outside his study."

"What were you doing outside Mr. Darcy's study?"

She fidgeted on the bench.

"Caroline, unless you tell me otherwise, I must

conclude that you were listening to a conversation you knew you had no right to hear."

She did not deny it.

Bingley rubbed his hand over his face. "All this going on under my nose, and I was oblivious. I have been the worst fool. That you would take this ill-gained intelligence and use it against an innocent young lady you called your friend… it is despicable."

Georgiana peeked out from behind Serafina. When she saw Darcy hold his arm open, she jumped up to bury herself and Serafina in his side. Darcy held her tighter. To have her disappointment exposed so openly was cruel.

He knew the role he played had hurt her, and Darcy had no desire to add to her distress. Kissing the top of her head, he said, "Come, Georgie. Let us away so we may speak."

He turned her away, but Bingley stopped them. "Please, one minute more. There is something I must tell you."

"We have heard quite enough from you, Charles," Miss Bingley said with a sharp sniff, her voice nasal.

Bingley's eyes gleamed like Richard's did when he was about to parry a sharp retort. "Oh, but Caroline, this involves you. I was going to tell Darcy and the colonel what happened to Mr. Collins the night of the ball. Now I believe it better for you to know too. Hurst, do I have your attention? You would do well to stay awake for this one."

Hurst raised his glass of brandy.

"Mrs. Nichols was deeply distressed that two rooms in the residential wing had been left unlocked during the ball. You already know one of them was the study. What you do not know is that someone"—he looked directly at his younger sister—"had told Mr. Collins to go to there in order to free herself from his unwanted company."

Miss Bingley clenched her jaw and sniffed again.

Bingley continued, "What you did not know is that Mr. Collins got lost in the hall. Instead of going inside my study, he stumbled into your bedchamber. He was accidentally locked inside it for well over an hour." He paused.

Richard burst, "You mean, you have had the perfect scandal to hold over your sister's head, and you have not used it?!"

"Not until now." Bingley turned to his ashen sister. "If you behave in a manner I do not consider appropriate, you will find yourself saddled to a lowly clergyman and mistress to the very estate you ridicule."

"You would not dare!" Miss Bingley jumped to her feet, positioning the bench between herself and her brother.

"Do not tempt me, Caroline. I am not in a forgiving mood. I can supply witnesses in a blink of an eye. Now you will forever have to depend on the discretion of the friends you have abused to ensure your freedom to marry someone other than Mr. Collins."

With a huff, Miss Bingley crossed the room. She was too vexed to see the kitten twitching his tail and staring at the fringe on the bodice of her gown. With a mighty leap from the couch, the cat landed on her bosom.

"Rudy!" Bingley ran to the kitten's aid.

"Get him off me!" Miss Bingley screeched and flailed, slapping at herself, her gown, and anyone else nearby.

"Stop it, Caroline! You will hurt Rudy!" Bingley pulled the little hunter away from where the pet hid in Miss Bingley's coiffure, a tassel dangling from his mouth.

"You horrid beast! I hate you! I hate cats! They are vile, wicked creatures!" Miss Bingley screamed. She stomped away, the effect of her huff ruined with a sneeze that echoed through the hall.

Bingley cuddled Rudy to his chest. "Do not listen to her. You are wonderful! I am going to keep you forever so she never overstays her welcome."

Mr. Hurst trailed behind his wife out to the hall, laughing all the way. "Good show, Bingley! Good show!"

Richard leaned against the instrument. "Hurst is right. That was better than Drury Lane." More seriously, he asked, "Are you sorely disappointed, Georgie?"

"I hardly know what to think," she replied weakly.

Bingley set Rudy on the floor and pressed his hands together in supplication. "I beg your forgiveness for being the ignorant fool I have been. It was never my intention to encourage expectation. Believe me when I tell you I am incredibly flattered—honored, really—that you would spare more than a passing glance at me. Unfortunately, I have come to realize that I am not yet qualified to take on the privilege of keeping any lady's heart, let alone one as precious as yours. The fault is mine and mine alone."

Bingley's letdown was the kindest Darcy had ever heard.

A knock at the door prevented Georgiana from replying, but her forgiveness was apparent. The butler peeked inside. "I apologize for the interruption, sir, but Mr. John Lucas is calling. Shall I show him in?"

Kindly, Bingley looked to Georgiana and waited for her consent before he told the butler to see the young man in.

"I hope we can still be frie—" Georgiana began, her eyes widening and her tongue tying when John Lucas entered the room. He was a handsome young lad. Darcy remembered Miss Lydia had praised him for his good looks. The immediate effect he had on Georgiana was baffling, but so had been her previous behavior.

Darcy supposed he must get used to deferring to Elizabeth's better judgment regarding his sister… and so many other things.

CHAPTER 34

*B*eneath Mr. Lucas' handsome features was a curious mind. As the heir who would inherit Lucas Lodge, he was eager to learn estate management. Bingley had quickly befriended the young man and agreed to share what he knew. Darcy was pleased, hoping the lessons he had taught Bingley would not be so quickly forgotten this way.

Bingley invited him and Richard to accompany them to the problematic fields in need of better drainage, but Darcy refused. Bingley could make that decision himself, and there were still things he must say to Georgiana.

She had shown no inclination to leave the room since the arrival of Mr. Lucas. Her gaze followed the young men out to the hall and out of view, where it remained fixed until Darcy stood in front of her, feeling invisible.

"I, too, owe you an apology. I had no right to interfere in affairs of the heart. You are young. While the freedoms allowed an unattached female are few, you ought to be allowed to enjoy them fully."

She looked down at her hands. "You sound like Miss Elizabeth with her talk of independence and choices. What choice do I really have but to be left behind? You have not yet married, and already I miss you. Whom shall I have when she takes you away?" A tear dripped onto the carpet.

Darcy closed the distance and wrapped his arms around her narrow shoulders, her head pressed against his heart. "I would never abandon you, Georgie. Our family is only growing. When I am occupied with estate business, you will have Elizabeth to keep you company. She will make you a wonderful sister. She has already shared her plans, and they all include you. We shall travel more. When the war is over—for it cannot last forever—we shall go to the continent. Elizabeth has never had a private tutor, and she looks forward to learning new things with you. You can invite your friends from the seminary to Pemberley."

Georgiana sniffed. "You will allow it? I have not entertained much before."

"A deficiency for which I take responsibility." Darcy pulled back to hand her his handkerchief. "Mother loved to entertain. She would be proud to know that her daughter desires to follow in her footsteps."

A brilliant smile lit Georgiana's face. "I wish I could be just like her."

"You already are in so many ways. She was kind and

gentle, but there was a firmness to her character that even Father knew not to cross."

Georgiana picked at her fingers and chewed her lip. "Was she never nervous that other people would not approve of her?"

"You cannot help what others think of you. All you can do is determine what sort of lady you would admire, and aim to become her. Your real friends will continue to seek out your company, and you will intimidate the others away when they see you are unwilling to change yourself to suit them."

"Elizabeth is not intimidated by you."

Darcy shook his head. "No, she is not, but there are times she terrifies me."

"No! Really?" Her shock made Darcy chuckle. He understood his father better now.

"Elizabeth is a self-assured lady with firm opinions. She does not hesitate to tell me when I am wrong… and I have learned that I am wrong more often than I thought." She had given him an ultimatum, and Darcy had no doubt she meant it. She would rather face ruin than be attached to a man she could not respect. Blast it all! He had bungled everything into a horrible mess.

A loud, rhythmic clap startled him. He had been so intent on Georgiana and his own thoughts, he had forgotten that Richard was still in the room.

Richard continued to clap. "Well done, both of you." He rested one hand on Darcy's shoulder. "It is about time you realized that you cannot save everyone, nor is it your business to do so." He rested his other hand on

Georgiana's shoulder. "You allowed Miss Bingley to tickle your ears with fanciful wishes and self-serving compliments. You do not want to be like her, do you?"

Georgiana grimaced. "She said some cruel things." She bowed her head. "I have not been very kind to Elizabeth or Jane."

Darcy reassured her, "You could not have chosen anyone more disposed to forgive than those two ladies."

She did not look so certain. "In time for the wedding?"

If there was going to be a wedding.

Richard supplied what Darcy could not say. "He and Elizabeth had a… misunderstanding."

"About what?" The ensuing silence grew more uncomfortable the longer Richard and Darcy stared at everything in the room except the source of the argument. Georgiana was not fooled. "Was it about me?"

"In a way. Elizabeth is convinced her sister loves Bingley."

"And you meant him for me!" Georgiana buried her face in Darcy's crumpled handkerchief. "Oh, what a disaster! But"—she peeked from behind the cloth—"if Jane truly loved him, would she not have fought harder for him?"

Darcy sighed. "That was what I argued. I called her indifferent."

"You did not!" Georgiana cried.

"Oh, yes, he did," Richard commented. "Dunderhead here claims to have more insight into Miss

Bennet's character than her own sister does. Elizabeth, with three younger sisters, is well-versed in the ways of sixteen-year-old ladies. She contended that your inclination toward Bingley was likely not of the till-death-do-us-part variety."

Georgiana grasped onto Darcy's arm with both of her hands. "You must apologize at once, or I will have ruined everything! I beg you not to allow it! Please, go to her and apologize."

"I shall try."

"Grovel is the word," contributed Richard.

"I shall do my best, but"—had Darcy's arms not been immobilized by his little sister, he would have shoved his hands into his hair and pulled—"she was severely disappointed... to the point of calling off the wedding."

Georgiana's reaction stupefied Darcy. He had expected a gasp; instead, she grinned at him and squeezed his arm. She finally let go to cross her arms and tilt her chin. "I am told that Elizabeth is disposed to forgive."

Impertinent lass! Darcy shook his head, a smile breaking through his gloom.

Richard roared.

They did not hear the ruckus out in the hall until the door burst open and Bingley's butler stepped inside. The poor man was so flustered that Darcy thought to offer him a chair.

The cause of the butler's shaken appearance

brushed past him. "Darcy, I shall have a word with you," snapped Her Ladyship, Aunt Catherine.

Uncle Hugh entered next. "Not now, Catherine."

Anne came in next, rolling her eyes, her voice dripping with exasperation. "I wanted to return to Kent, but Mama insisted we come here."

Aunt Catherine stabbed the Aubusson carpet with her cane. "You do not know what is best, Anne. Your engagement to Darcy has been a long-standing arrangement since you were infants. I shall *not* allow a country chit to make a fool out of my nephew and ruin your future."

Uncle Hugh looked heavenward. After a deep breath, he spoke with strained forbearance, "Darcy is a grown man, fully capable of making his own decisions without your interference. It is about time you got that through your thick skull." With that, his patience had reached his limit. It took Richard and Aunt Helen's intervention to separate the quarreling brother and sister.

Darcy was frozen in place. It struck him like a lightning bolt: he had very nearly done to Bingley what Aunt Catherine had been doing to him since birth. Had he really expected Bingley to wait years and then marry the lady of Darcy's choosing? How arrogant and high-handed! Granted, he had taught Bingley a great deal and had made no official claim on him for Georgiana, but Darcy had *hoped* it would happen and did everything he could to *make* it happen.

Richard had challenged him; so had Elizabeth.

Although Darcy had heard their words, had thought he understood them, it was not until this instant, seeing a glimpse of himself reflected in his most unreasonable aunt, that Darcy finally recognized how right they had been.

He had been ridiculous, arrogant, and nonsensical. That Elizabeth saw this in him and still favored him at all was a miracle that infused Darcy with hope. If Elizabeth might love him, even just a little, with these terrible faults, he could not let her go without a fight.

Taking his aunt Catherine by the shoulders and stopping her mid-rebuttal, Darcy did his best to adapt Bingley's pretty speech to his present circumstances.

Aunt Catherine slapped his hands away. "Have you gone mad?"

Clasping his hands before him, Darcy replied, "Thank you for believing me to be the best match for your only daughter and wanting to entrust Anne's happiness to me. However, she has made it plain to me that she does not wish to marry at all, and I am in love with a lady whom I do not deserve but shall marry on Monday, if she will still have me."

"Harrumph! I would sooner convince the over-reaching miss to release you from her clutches. Two thousand will do it."

Richard shook his head and clucked his tongue. "You should have gone with the mad argument, Darcy. There will be no shaking her now."

"Elizabeth cannot be bought. Nothing you can

tempt her with will persuade her to change her values to suit you," Darcy said proudly.

Aunt Catherine blustered and quibbled, but Darcy had to return to Longbourn.

Rising from the fainting couch, Anne kissed him on the cheek. "Allow me to wish you and your Elizabeth happy. You will not be received at Rosings before a twelvemonth, but I pray that does not prevent you from inviting me to visit you at Pemberley." Her gaze flickered over to her irate mother. "She will refuse to accompany me, I am sure."

"I shall disown you if you go without my blessing!" Aunt threatened.

Anne shrugged. All her mother had brought to her marriage was a title and a dowry. The fortune and estate would pass to Anne from her father whether Aunt Catherine approved or not. "I shall spend a merry time at Pemberley with Darcy and his new bride. It is your choice to persist in this stubborn manner, Mother."

"And watch you willfully cast away your birthright? Foolish child! Until you are capable of making advantageous decisions on your own, I see no alternative but to choose for you."

"I am hardly a child, Mother. I am twenty-seven and firmly shelved."

"Another imprudent choice!"

As mother and daughter flung "poor choices" back and forth at each other, it occurred to Darcy that he should give Elizabeth what she most wanted: a choice.

Caution told him the risk was too great to proceed with his idea. Despite that, he realized that caution may have served him well in his lifetime, but if he were to make amends with Elizabeth, he must accept the possibility that she could refuse him.

However, if it worked...

He would need Anne's permission. "Anne, might I have a word with you and Richard?"

Both looked at him agape, but they agreed.

After a quarter-hour discussing his plan, they parted ways from Bingley's study—Richard with Darcy, and Anne with a warning. "This had better work, Darcy. Not only will Mother make you miserable, but I shall make you pay if you fail."

Richard unlodged the ball of nerves lodged in Darcy's stomach with a firm clap on the back. "I cannot believe you are doing this. It is madness. It is perfect madness."

Darcy could hardly believe it either. Perhaps he *had* gone mad.

CHAPTER 35

*D*arcy would have preferred not to have an audience accompanying him to Longbourn, but he could not shake Richard from his side. They cut through the fields and came across Bingley and John Lucas. Bingley joined them and parted from the latter, who wished them well and agreed to return to Netherfield on the morrow.

After the trio scraped their boots to Hill's satisfaction, they were shown into Longbourn's drawing room where the entire Bennet family sat at apparent leisure. Darcy knew better. The panting breaths, flushed cheeks, bits of ribbon escaping from under cushions, and the empty teacup he saw Mrs. Bennet shove behind her back made it evident that no callers were expected that afternoon. Least of all him.

Elizabeth sat watching him like a cat feigning indifference. He should have brought Arthur. She could not stay cross with *him*.

Miss Bennet greeted them warmly, prompting her mother to ring for tea. "Mr. Bingley, I pray Miss Bingley has recovered from her headache?"

Bingley shuffled in place. "Yes, yes, thank you for inquiring."

"Of course. We could do no less for our neighbors and *friends*." Miss Bennet emphasized the last word, capturing Bingley's full attention when she continued. "It is my sincerest hope that we may continue as friends, Mr. Bingley. Nothing less and nothing more."

Darcy held his jaw up. Had she just let down Bingley?

Bingley's relief was instantaneous. Miss Bennet had spared him from disappointing any expectations. In doing so, she encouraged him to act as agreeably as he always did. Darcy checked Mrs. Bennet, but the lady contentedly fanned her face, mumbling, "An earl's son!"

So *that* was how the wind blew! Now that Darcy saw it, he wondered how he had not noticed before. Richard tried not to blush or smile too widely, but he had rarely been successful at hiding his emotions.

Seats were taken—Darcy sat as near to Elizabeth as he dared—tea was served, and polite conversation reigned. Bingley would stay at Netherfield Park for the next two years at least, after which he would decide whether or not to purchase the estate. "I already like my neighbors, and with my sisters returning to London, I daresay it will be more peaceful."

At this news, Elizabeth perked up. Her eyes

brimmed with questions, but she asked only one. "Do all of your guests plan to return to London?"

While Darcy preferred not to expose his plan before everyone, he could not request a private audience with her. He needed the assembled group to play its role in his scheme for it to succeed. "That depends on you. My family arrived today from London for the wedding."

Mrs. Bennet squirmed in her chair. "The earl and countess?"

Richard winked. "As well as the Right Honorable Lady Catherine de Bourgh."

Darcy addressed Elizabeth directly. "I believed my motives to be unselfish, but you were right about my sister."

"And you were right about mine," she confessed.

Her admission fueled Darcy's courage. "From the beginning, you have borne the circumstances forced upon you... our engagement... with grace and good humor."

"A forced marriage?" whispered Miss Bennet, lips parted, looking between her sister and Darcy.

"I hope you believe me when I say that, at the time, in Bingley's study, I did not see another alternative. Over the next weeks, I did not want one." Darcy's voice faltered, but he pressed on. "You were never given a choice, Elizabeth, but I have the means to give you one today."

Mrs. Bennet stopped fanning herself.

"Mary, the smelling salts." Mr. Bennet spoke in a low tone.

"Ha! I knew it had to be a compromise! There is no way Lizzy would marry before me otherwise," Lydia boasted.

Kitty hissed. "Oh hush, Lydia! You would sooner ruin us than see your sisters happily settled. You ought to be ashamed."

The rebuke from her erstwhile partner in crime silenced her.

Darcy waited impatiently until the room fell silent. "Here is my offer, if you wish." He swallowed hard. That was not enough, so he downed the rest of his tea. Clearing his throat and taking a deep breath, he said, "If you would rather have your freedom than marry me, I"—rubbed his hand over his face and clutched his stomach—"I will jilt you to marry my cousin Anne de Bourgh." He talked as quickly as he could, anxious to be rid of the detestable words. "I shall make myself out to be the worst sort of rascal to spare your reputation. You will have your friends' pity, but you will not have to endure their scorn."

"You would ruin your reputation, cast shade on your own honor, for Lizzy?" asked Mr. Bennet.

"Have you gone mad?!" Mrs. Bennet exclaimed. She fanned her face and called for her salts.

"If Elizabeth asks it of me, I would do it." Another hard swallow. "Furthermore, my solicitor will prepare a settlement to be paid to Elizabeth and dispensed in the manner of her choice to demonstrate legally that I was the one at fault. I also have it on good authority that Lady Catherine means to offer a bribe of two thousand pounds."

"I would settle for no less than five thousand," offered Richard.

Mr. Bennet stood. "It is a tidy sum to secure a lady's independence. What say you, Lizzy? Your freedom and a fortune—or Mr. Darcy. He places you in the enviable position of having your own choice in the matter."

Richard rose to his feet with a bow. "It would give me great pleasure to call Darcy out publicly. I can also ensure the sympathy of the earl and countess."

"Will you sit down?" Darcy snapped.

"I can be very convincing, I assure you." Richard gave another bow.

"If you refuse to sit, then is there not somewhere—anywhere—else you would rather be?"

With a roguish grin, Richard held one arm out to Mrs. Bennet and the other to her eldest daughter. "Care for a stroll in the garden, ladies?"

Mr. Bennet followed suit, gesturing with his hands for the others to join him.

"I would take the money and run!" Miss Lydia exclaimed.

"Nobody cares what you think on the subject," Miss Mary said dryly, shoving her sister out to the hall, leaving Darcy alone with Elizabeth.

They stood facing each other for an eternity. Her eyes, always so open and expressive, instead were a closed book. He would give his entire fortune, even Pemberley, to know Elizabeth's thoughts.

Finally, she spoke. "I need a few minutes to think on the matter alone."

He nodded. What else could he do? He was at her mercy.

She left the room.

Darcy sat watching the seconds tick by on the mantel clock until his limbs could be still no longer. He paced the length of the room until he had memorized how many steps it took him to get from one end to the other. Then he paced the width until he knew the dimensions of the room and the position of every piece of furniture—no small number, given Mrs. Bennet's exaggerated tastes.

Usually vulnerable to uncertainty, Darcy was tormented by anguished doubts. What if Elizabeth did not want him? What if he had to marry Anne? Dear Lord, what had he done? Another bout of nausea gripped him, and he sat in the nearest chair with his head between his knees. Of all the bad ideas he had ever avoided, this was the worst.

The floor creaked, and he looked up to see Elizabeth in the doorway. Mrs. Hill was behind her, grinning her gappy grin, though Darcy failed to see what there was to be happy about. He had never been so miserable. He stood, holding on to the back of the chair for support.

Calmly, without expression, Elizabeth entered the room. In a heartbeat, the door slammed behind her, and Darcy heard Mrs. Hill lock them inside the parlor.

In the next moment, Elizabeth's hands were spread

against the lapels of his coat, sliding up to his collars, twirling his hair around her fingers. Her breath tickled his lips as she rose to her toes. "I want you, Fitzwilliam. Not your money, not your protection. You, you mad, lovable fool!"

He was too stunned to believe his good fortune. "Pray do not trifle with me. I love you too much."

"I love you, Fitzwilliam. I choose you."

His lips crushed down on hers. There was nothing tentative about the way she responded. For a few blissful moments, they lost themselves in the comfort and promise of each other.

The sound of clapping brought them to their senses. A crowd of mostly grinning faces gathered in the now-open doorway.

"It is a good thing you marry on Monday," Richard said.

Miss Kitty slapped at Miss Mary's hands, which were blocking her view. "We should not look," Miss Mary said, although her actions attempted to protect her sister's eyes rather than her own.

Miss Bennet swayed in front of Richard, her hands over her heart. "I knew you were a love match all along."

A love match. Darcy preferred that over a compromise and forced marriage. In that moment, he made a choice of his own—nay, a vow befitting a Darcy: he would court Elizabeth every day of the rest of their lives.

EPILOGUE

*F*itzwilliam and Richard did their best to smooth Bingley's hair into submission, but their friend was too excited to stand in one place for long enough.

"Will you hold still?" Darcy demanded.

Bingley spun around, rubbing his hands together, his face too small for the grin he wore. "I apologize. I must look a fright, but I simply cannot wait. Is it time yet?"

"Very nearly. Now, let me just fix this," Richard licked his thumb and went to work. "No more tugging. Cross your arms over your chest if you must, but we cannot allow your bride to think you rode here through a windstorm."

Bingley did as he was bid, and Elizabeth exchanged

a smile with Jane and Georgiana.

The parish fell silent, the doors opened, and Papa walked the bride down the aisle.

Kitty looked resplendent in a cream gown with rose petal pink trim.

Georgiana wrapped her arm around Elizabeth's and whispered into her ear. "Is she not stunning?"

Kitty was radiant. Judging by the look Bingley gave her, he certainly thought so too. He had become everything Fitzwilliam had taught him to be as the master of Netherfield. As a gentleman, he was the perfect blend of amiability and responsibility to suit Kitty.

A glimmer of gold caught the corner of her vision, and Elizabeth looked over to see the sun shining on John Lucas' hair. She squeezed Georgiana's arm and nudged her chin in his direction.

Georgiana stifled a giggle. "No wonder Lydia is behaving so well."

Elizabeth smiled. Lydia's determination to be the first to marry had been frustrated with each one of her sisters' weddings. She would instead be the last Bennet to marry. Lydia liked to say that if she could not have the wealthiest or best connected or most amiable husband of her sisters, she was determined to marry the handsomest. Of course, that was Lydia's opinion. After three years of marriage, Fitzwilliam still sent Elizabeth's heart racing and her stomach aflutter.

"I suspected she would had she known he would be here," Georgiana continued.

A gasp escaped Elizabeth, eliciting a stern look

from Mama, who would not have Kitty's wedding interrupted for the world. Very quietly, Elizabeth said, "This must be *your* doing! He was supposed to be at a house party in Shropshire."

Georgiana shrugged, her smirk proving ownership of the change in John Lucas' plans. Gone was the uncertain, apprehensive girl from three years before, replaced by this scheming minx who would be the toast of the *ton* this season. "I was not convincing enough, or Edmond and Charlotte would have come."

"You can hardly blame Charlotte. She cannot travel in her condition." Mama had presumed for months over Lady Lucas when Jane married Colonel Fitzwilliam, but when Charlotte had traveled to Pemberley for a visit, it had not taken long for her and the last of Lord Matlock's unmarried sons to come to an agreement. They were very happily settled at Kympton parish, and Elizabeth was delighted to have another friend nearby.

Notably absent was Mr. Collins, who had not appeared at Longbourn since Mary had married her piano tutor. With Kitty soon to be wed, he would have to settle for Lydia or find a wife by other means. Mama no longer worried about being cast out into the hedgerows when she could rotate from one daughter's household to the next.

As for Miss Bingley, after two seasons with no proposal, she had worn out her welcome in the Hurst household. She now resided in Scarborough with her aunt. Surrounded by cats.

The vows were exchanged. Before her mother could whisk Elizabeth away to the wedding feast, she sneaked away. Fitzwilliam met her outside the church, breathtakingly handsome in his dark blue coat and snow-white cravat.

"I thought you might like some company," he said with a crooked grin.

Her hand disappeared inside his, and they swung their arms synchronously during the short walk to Longbourn, where a disgruntled guard paced in front of the door of Elizabeth's old bedchamber.

"He is cross with us," Fitzwilliam said.

Arthur yowled.

Mrs. Hill creaked up behind them and set a small plate with pieces of chicken on the floor. "Sir Arthur has been vigilant since you left for the wedding. I hope you do not mind me sharing a bit of sugar plum with the baby before her nap. Miss Darcy is still asleep."

Appeased with his peace offering, Arthur allowed the proud parents entry to the chamber. Dark curls and eyelashes splayed over red apple cheeks. Their daughter was not yet two years old, and she was already stunning. Their downy haired son was wrapped in a bundle of soft blankets. He had the sweetest temperament and the most adorable dimples when he laughed.

Arthur rubbed against Elizabeth's skirts, wrapping his tail around her legs as he wound around Fitzwilliam, tugging them closer.

"Oh, no, Arthur, we shall have none of that today."

Fitzwilliam twirled Elizabeth into his arms and planting a firm kiss on her lips. "I do not need help."

Elizabeth hooked her arms over his shoulders. "Arthur seems to think you are remiss in your affections to your wife."

Another kiss. "Does my wife agree?"

"I always agree with the cat. He is very wise, you know, but let us not wake the children too soon, or we shall never get them abed tonight."

The look Fitzwilliam gave her made her wish for one of her mother's fans.

Although their marriage had not been free of troubles, Elizabeth was confident in the constancy of her husband's love. He was as considerate now as he had been during their courtship. The more Elizabeth learned about Fitzwilliam, the deeper her love for him grew.

One day, her children, her nieces and nephews, would ask how she and Fitzwilliam fell in love. She would tell them. She would relate the story of Uncle Bingley and how a cleverly uncontrived compromise turned into the greatest love match. It was a beautiful story which still continued on.

If Elizabeth could go back in time, she would choose it all over again.

When love needs a helping hand—or paw—these lovable critters come to Darcy and Elizabeth's rescue.

Read all the standalone books in the L Helpers series here!

Visit jenniferjoywrites.com to see all Jennifer's books!

THANK YOU!

Thank you for reading *A Cleverly (Un)contrived Compromise*! I hope you enjoyed it, and I'd love to hear your thoughts in a review on Amazon and Goodreads!

I had a lot of cheerleaders in my corner encouraging me along, and I'm so grateful for each one of you.

First and foremost, Renan for cooking lunch so I had more time to write. You're my Mr. Darcy!

To Mom for talking me through the rough patches and plot holes.

To Debbie Brown for her meticulous editing. This book needed a little extra love, and you bravely rose to the occasion!

To Marie Hudson and Diane Chen for being my extra set of eyes when I'd read my manuscript so many times, I couldn't see any more typos!

They say it takes a village to raise a child... Well, evidently it takes a small army of fans to name four kittens! A special thanks to each one of you who commented on my Facebook page and replied to my newsletter for helping me name the fur babies in this story! I'd run out of pages if I tried to name you all. You guys rock!

Want to know when my next book is available? Join my newsletter for regular updates, sales, bonus scenes, and your free novelette!

ABOUT THE AUTHOR

When Jennifer isn't busy dreaming up new adventures for her favorite characters, she is learning Sign language, reading, baking (Cake is her one weakness!), or chasing her twins around the park (because ... cake).

She believes in happy endings, sweet romance, and plenty of mystery. She also believes there's enough angst on the news, so she keeps her stories light-hearted and full of hope.

While she claims Oregon as her home, she currently lives high in the Andes Mountains of Ecuador with her husband and two kids.

Connect with Jennifer!
jenniferjoywrites.com

Made in the USA
Coppell, TX
12 November 2022